A DARK FICTION LITERARY ANTHOLOGY

Volume 7

Guest Editor
Kristi Petersen Schoonover

Dark Alley Press

INK STAINS ANTHOLOGY
Volume 7

ISBN 13: 978-1-946050-07-6
ISBN 10: 1-946050-07-5

© 2018 by Dark Alley Press
Individual stories copyright by authors

Dark Alley Press
http://www.darkalleypress.com

An imprint of Vagabondage Press LLC
PO Box 3563
Apollo Beach, Florida 33572
http://www.vagabondagepress.com

First edition printed in the United States of America and the United Kingdom, January 2018

10 9 8 7 6 5 4 3 2 1

Front cover art by Bliznetsov. Cover designed by Maggie Ward.

INK STAINS

A DARK FICTION LITERARY ANTHOLOGY

INTRODUCTION

These are the things we lose: decay is a pervasive ghost that not only haunts the physical world; it invades our bodies, minds, relationships, and societies, and perhaps the greatest terror is watching it devour as we are helpless to stop it.

It was Miss Havisham in Dickens' *Great Expectations* that first made me fall in love with decay. This collection explores the complicated facets of it through fictions by seasoned professionals, talented first-timers, and burgeoning young adults. Each speaks powerfully to these inexorable, everyday things: the degradation of innocence, the rot of the body, the erosion of self, and the decline of sanity; the failing of ideals and crumbling of relationships, the breakdown of society, the abandonment of faith, and the corruption of morals.

We open with Taro Turner's "As We Rot," a claustrophobic portrait of a woman putrefying from the inside out as she struggles to revive a once-golden romance. Grounded in a poverty-stricken urban environment, it's an eloquent, illustrative comment on the price we pay when we cannot let go of what's toxic.

Conversely, Robert Mayette's magical "Christmas in Connecticut" maroons us in a frigid, endless wilderness alongside heartbroken elves—but the worst is yet to come. This soul-rending tale of shattered innocence and all-consuming regret chills long after the last sentence.

In a run-down, desolate beach house, an empty woman must battle the reality of her own emotional decline in Elizabeth Allen's "The Depths." Set in the 1970s, this seaside ghost story is skillfully barnacled with frightening images, each instilling that there is no use in fighting eventual demise.

It isn't only individuals who are affected by the corrosive power of nature. A family unit can be like a machine; when one part breaks down, the others, trying to compensate, wear down in turn. In honest, perceptive prose, Jackie Logsted's "Heroes" not only examines this dynamic, it lays bare the extreme emotional detachment that often occurs in the wake of sudden familial instability.

We always assume that it's unhealthy things that will spell our ends, and Dorianne Emmerton's "The Mating Habits of the Late-Adopting Smoker" questions whether our conditions truly are affected by choice—or whether they lurk in our DNA; it also addresses shifting perceptions of an unwell self. This magic realist thriller twists and turns until its unexpected dénouement.

Sometimes it's passion that onsets disintegration, and in Travis D. Roberson's gritty "Stikini," we meet a man whose dogged pursuit of evil is already monopolizing him. This gripping, gustatory yarn is inspired by a Seminole legend; I won't give any more of Roberson's story away, so, instead, here's a tasty tidbit from the original lore: it has long been held that anyone who hears the cries of the stikini will die.

Alluding to the terrors of knowledge and ignorance referenced in Carl Dennis' "Worms," there is no better follow-up to "Stikini" than the equally afferent poem "The Fate of the Worms" by Page Sullivan, which suggests that if we were aware of our innate fragility, it would sear us instantly.

Harkening to Marquez' "A Very Old Man with Enormous Wings," and Beckitt's *Waiting for Godot*, Rhonda Zimlich's "Ignorance Is" is an artful, contemporary allegory about being careful what you wish for. Zimlich's protagonist becomes an existential freak show in hope of the arrival of that which she most desires—even as her initial, horrific sacrifice eats away at her body, mind, and soul.

Like "The Mating Habits of the Late-Adopting Smoker," newcomer Pablo Patiño's "Black-Hooded Caller" focuses on the body's deterioration but deftly tackles a real-world horror: cancer. As the protagonist watches himself morph in disheartening ways, he begins to stray from his already-eroding faith—even as he is visited by the same specter which preyed upon his late father. It's a disturbing reminder that not even what we believe is guaranteed.

Meanwhile, the heroine in Mary Thorson's "The Cold Gets In"— set in the 1950s—clashes with losing faith in the boy she loves. Like "Christmas in Connecticut" and the crime that ruined the tight-knit community of Holcomb, Kansas, this moving, iconographic tale rebukes the gentle coming-of-age transformation in favor of the fracturing of innocence, and the mourning of our left-behind perceptions in its wake.

It's the spare render and lightly-sketched characters in Megan Neumann's "Do the Faceless Remember?" that telegraph its stunning criticism of the breakdown of communication under our invasive technology. These stark characters, through their obsession with a medium that allows us to archive our pasts in ways we've never before seen, speak to social media's slow erasure of our humanity.

Brilliantly penned in inverse chronological order, Bri Faythe's flash "Suicide in Reverse" unfurls the spiral of emotional ruination in raw, unsettling imagery—but it is the final line, shrewdly delivered without embellishment, which hammers home that our own finalities are part of an insidious cycle.

Heather Sullivan's haunting, poetic "The Leaf People" bemoans our evolving disconnect from reality, nature, and each other, resulting in both a dissolution of marriage and a desperate attempt to rediscover one's roots. Just as "Do the Faceless Remember?" illustrates the impact of today's technology, "The Leaf People"—which was written in the late 1990s—envisions the impact of a technological future that is now: there are whispers of Skype, instant doorstep delivery, and online doctors.

Honoring Poe's "The Black Cat" and rendered in shades of Daniel Keyes' "Flowers for Algernon," Kaitlyn Downing's "Letting in the Cat" lures us into the decline of sanity; in this nerve-shredder, we can only curl our toes and scream "Don't do it!" even as we are hyper-aware the impending tragedy is foreordained. "Letting in the Cat" first appeared in 2006's defunct, now-out-of-print magazine *Sinfully Twisted*, and I feel it deserves to be back in print.

Finally, "Overdrawn at the Time Bank" is a classic, fantastical *Argosy*-style look at the corruption of morals and politics. Inspired by John Varley's "Overdrawn at the Memory Bank," it's the final first draft of the late Daniel Pearlman. It was still in progress when he passed, but it is complete; this is a piece we could not allow to languish in a drawer. We're proud to feature it here through special arrangement with his widow and *Read Short Fiction*.

There is a strange hope in decay. Abandoned amusement parks and resorts are razed and redeveloped into housing and entertainment areas where new happy memories will be created, just as broken plastic toys are recycled into deck chairs and leaves decompose and make rich soil for new plants.

There are things we lose, but there are also things we gain.

Kristi Petersen Schoonover
Guest Editor
Ink Stains Volume 7

THE SINGER'S LAST STAND

Christopher Petersen

ABOUT THE PHOTO

On a cold February morning, my youngest brother's home burned to the ground. He told me through this photo posted on my Facebook timeline with the caption, "I just thought you'd want to know about Mom's Singer. I'm really sorry. The kids are fine."

The oddly apologetic post was a gut-punch at first—Who cares about the damn sewing machine? But emotions can transcend language. The Singer was an antique that our late mother, in her healthy days, had used to sew many things—cushions for our boat, upholstery for the camper, drapes for the lake-facing sliders. His "I'm really sorry" wasn't about the loss of an object; it was a mourning of so many intangibles: the memory of happier times, the loss of innocence, a symbol of our connection as siblings. On a converse note, "The kids are fine" was his overwhelming gratitude that everything was going to be okay, that there was hope, that life—even after something so devastating—would continue.

This powerful image serves as a poignant reminder that none of us is safe from the destructive power of nature, and of life itself—but that destructive power is also what clears the way for new growth: letting go of the past, and looking toward the future.

Kristi Petersen Schoonover

A DARK FICTION LITERARY ANTHOLOGY

TABLE OF CONTENTS

As We Rot

Taro Turner

I come home from my double shift at Pete's Diner to discover that the orchids I just bought this morning are dead, along with my boyfriend.

Though, of course, Huxley's been lifeless for months now.

Muted, he sprawls across our worn couch with the television on, watching violent movies with all the foul dialogue chopped out for daytime viewers, so it's just a fuzz of grunting and gunshots for two hours until the credits roll. He doesn't look at me when I come through the door or blink when I graze my fingertips across his pale, stubbly cheek.

"Hux." I remove the orchid remains from the vase behind him. They've managed to turn black and shriveled in only a few hours. "This is the *fourth* bouquet I've bought this week. They all keep shriveling, just like that. First the daisies, then the heathers, the sunflowers, the orchids…Strange, right?"

He groans and looks up. His eyes are bloodshot, the irises empty of anything besides a dull grey. They were blue once, a broken-in denim shade, like a nice pair of jeans you'd find in the forgotten rack at a secondhand store. I'd always liked them best. Now they're just two dreary holes filled with fog. "Why do you even bother, Faye?" he mutters, leaning his thumb against the VOLUME UP button on the remote. "Stop buying the damn things. They're just flowers. They all die eventually."

I'm used to this. I *should* be used to this. The iceberg chill, the emotionless glances. *He's just tired. He's had a long day.* But that isn't true. He's been doing exactly this, all day, for dozens of days. *Nothing.*

For Huxley, every hour seems to stretch and weather his skin like a marathon in a blizzard. I want to pity him. I almost do.

I plod down the hallway into the back where our kitchen is and retrieve a garbage bag for the orchids, wishing I had someone to call, but everyone's sympathy for me expired weeks ago. I've tried to tell them that Huxley isn't well, hasn't been for a while, but they think *I'm* the sick one. They keep mentioning that place in Sweden, the one where all the hostages defended their captors. They're insane. They say I have a syndrome. But love is supposed to save, isn't it? How can it possibly be a syndrome?

I place each dead orchid into the bag and set it on the floor, beside all the others filled up with perished plants that I haven't gotten around to taking downstairs. *It wasn't always like this,* I tell myself. *Don't forget. Don't forget how it used to be.*

Lighting the stove, I set a pot on the burner and fill it with a can of tomato-vegetable soup from the Speedway down the block. It begins to simmer, spitting a red glob on my wrist. I reach to wipe it away and notice a small, nickel-sized bruise a few inches below. Another one a few inches under that. They trail down my arm like little yellowish-blue breadcrumbs, pulsating with flickers of pain.

Not again.

I think of Mandy, one of the other waitresses I usually work evenings with at Pete's. I think of her neon red lips, the way they sizzle like a "No Vacancy" sign when the diner's fluorescent lighting hits them just right. There's always a ruby smudge across her teeth when she speaks. "Faye, you gotta leave him," she told me when the bruises first appeared, while she wiped the sticky stains off plastic menus. "You're just gonna be all black and blue till you do something about it."

I stir the soup and ignore the throbbing in my arms. She doesn't get it. The problem is that I don't either. I can't explain where the bruises come from, just that every few days, I wake up with more. My legs are already spattered with eggplant-colored marks, while spots along my rib cage decorate my skin like a map of somewhere I've never been before.

Huxley hasn't mentioned them. *He's got to know*, I catch myself thinking as I sprinkle a pinch of salt into the soup. *But then again… why hasn't he asked me about them?* Maybe he's just not looking. There was a time when all he did was look. There was a time when he would guzzle down the sight of me, when I always found my face flushing because I could feel his eyes watching me from somewhere in the apartment. That was back then, back when he was still Huxley.

Some of him is still in there. When I say his name, he registers it in the form of a mere blink, and his face looks enough like the one of the man I traded everything for just a couple of years back, but something isn't the same. Something hasn't been right.

If he were still Huxley—that one, the old one—he would have held me at the first bruise. If he were still Huxley, he would have kissed every single swollen spot until they all vanished. If he were still Huxley, I wouldn't have to slather greasy makeup over my skin and promise Mandy that it isn't his fault.

But the thing is, that Huxley is gone.

He's turned into something sinister, something shadowy and venomous that invaded our home during the darkest part of night and swallowed him whole, and ever since this evil thing consumed him, everything around me has been decaying.

I dip a ladle into the tomato broth and bring it to my lips, but gag once the spoonful hits my tongue. The chunks of vegetable are all rotten with their skin peeling off. They float at the surface of the congealed soup like a heap of drowned corpses in shallow water.

I spit it back into the pot and I swear, laughter echoes from the front room.

The cracks in the walls are getting worse.

They inch from floor to ceiling in jagged patterns, spreading slowly across the old floral wallpaper like a skin disease. I reach out and trace one fracture, covering my fingertip in a smudge of velvety dust. "I'm going to call the maintenance man," I announce to nobody. There isn't anyone here to listen. Huxley is still asleep, and the outside streets of Bridgeport are still and dead, with the exception of a squeaky rumble from a damaged muffler ambling down our block.

It's early evening. The sky is a scorched purple, and my shift at Pete's starts in less than twenty minutes. I grip my jacket in one hand, knowing that I should leave if I want to catch the bus and avoid being late again, but my legs are sore and locked in place. I don't want to leave him here. Every time I come home, there's less of Huxley to be found.

It wasn't always like this.

My gaze drifts around the deteriorating front room—the only room, really, except for our utility kitchen, bathroom, and small bedroom—landing on a plastic red picture frame that rests on a chipped end table beside the door. I pick it up carefully, examining the thin photo strip inside. It's from our first date, two summers ago, that dive bar on South Halsted with a slanted floor and live music every night. I ordered a vodka cranberry, and Huxley teased me for drinking such a yuppie drink at a place like that, but he kept them coming on his tab. The air was wet with humidity and spilled booze, and the corners of our mouths were sticky with drink. When he leaned in to kiss me, he let his lips linger against mine, and his words breathed right into my mouth. "You taste so much like fruit; I'd probably never get scurvy. You taste like paradise."

Paradise.

He pulled me into the photo booth right after that, and in the pictures, you can still see the remnants of what he whispered all over my face. We look so giddy in black-and-white, with smiles too wide for our faces and bright eyes squinting through a film of vodka buzz. In the bottom snapshot, Huxley's mouth is warped, blurring as he said something else to me. I stare at his frozen, distorted lips, and try to remember the words. There's nothing. Just that one line, that one echo of *paradise*. The chemical smell in the booth, the burn of the igniting flash. Blinding and white-hot. My vision popped, and all I remember is that the room filled with spotty blue fireworks. I thought I was just falling in love.

I draw my fingers across the second image, letting my thumb settle where Huxley's face is all one big toothy smile. Something sharp bites it.

"Jesus!" I whip my hand back and notice a bead of poppy-red blooming from the pad of my thumb. *No. That can't be.* I glance back down at the frame and notice that the glass is chipped directly over each of Huxley's faces in the strip, all three of them and nowhere else. The middle one, with his devilish grin, is smeared with a drop of my blood.

My breath catches in my throat, and I glance at my watch. Eleven minutes until I should be punching in.

Sucking the tiny slice on my thumb, I wince at the unpleasant taste and reach for the doorknob to find it stiff. The lock is undone, but the knob won't budge. I try again and again, pulling and yanking, kicking the door, but it remains static, like a stage prop. *What the hell is going on?*

My watch feels heavy on my wrist. Nine minutes. I'm going to be fired if I don't start showing up on time. Then who's going to take care of us?

I glance over at the window, which looks out onto a side street from four stories up. Shaking away the pain that leaks from my thumb, I dash over to it and try in vain to slide it open. "I'm going to be late," I cry, banging on the glass, willing someone to turn his face up and hear me. Only a couple of people are outside, moving down the sidewalk obliviously. One has a pair of headphones smothering his ears, while another is yelling into her cell phone. The world has enough of its own shit to deal with before it realizes mine.

"Help me, *please!*" I press my hands against the glass and lean forward, hoping it will give, but it proves to be tougher than anything else in this apartment. *I'm going insane.* I begin to cry, slamming the window repeatedly, leaving watery red splotches where my thumb hits the glass.

Something cold is behind me now, waiting for my tantrum to subside. I take a deep breath and turn around, ashamed that Huxley has caught me like this. He says nothing, just stares at me with the smallest hint of bemusement.

"Didn't mean to wake you," I say, looking down at my thumb. The bleeding has stopped, and the little nick is barely even visible. "I was just trying to…"

"Shouldn't you be at work?" Huxley asks. His skin is becoming a sickly, famished yellow, and his face looks so translucent that I swear I can see the outline of his skull.

"The door's jammed," I tell him. "Same with the window. Everything's stuck."

"I'm sure it is." He moves slowly away from me. "You're already late, you know."

I look at my watch. He's right; my shift started a few minutes ago. "Hux." My voice comes out unevenly. "You look like you could use some fresh air. Do you want to come with me to Pete's?"

He takes a languid step toward the couch and squeezes the armrest to hold himself steady. He looks ready to pass out. I don't remember the last time I've seen him eat, but my own stomach churns at the reminder of food, so I imagine it wasn't anytime recently. "Please come with me, Hux. We can have some juicy hamburgers, some pie…you know we can't just hide in here forever. We're—it's falling apart."

Huxley makes a crackling noise, like an old radio trying to tune into the nearest station. I can only assume it's meant to be a laugh. "Oh?" He takes a step toward me. I've slept beside this man for two years, but my legs quiver. "You want to get out of here, Faye? You think this shitty, run-down building is the problem?"

"It *is* the problem," I insist, shifting my weight backward. This isn't a conversation I want to have right now, not while my shift is already taking place without me there to work it, but I don't know the next time I'll be in the presence of a lucid Huxley. "It's changing you," I keep going. "Something in here is."

He doesn't seem to hear me. Maybe the moment's already gone. He looks down at the floor and draws a long breath. The stench of bourbon and something else, something chemical, wafts from him. "Do you think you deserve better than me, Faye?"

"What?" Rage and confusion pile up in my stomach. I want to cry, to punch a wall, to break all the glass that's locking us in this goddamn trap of a house. "I've done nothing but stand *by* you, Huxley. I want to help. Don't you get it? I just want everything back the way it used to be. I miss the way you used to be, the way I used to—" Wet heat prickles me from the inside of my eyes. *No. Not now. Don't cry. Do anything but cry in front of him.*

Huxley snorts. "You're wrong, Faye. It's not me you want to save. It's *you*. You, poor little you, poor little Faye who traded a four-year-degree and family money and a strong name that would get you somewhere, anywhere but here. Anywhere but this trash heap cast off in the south side. What a fucking martyr you are, huh? Taking on a sad, waste of human flesh like me?"

"No," I sob. "No. You're not—"

"There's *nothing* left, Faye. Nothing and nobody."

"You're wrong." I sink down to the floor and press my fingers against my temples, trying not to listen. I am weak. I hate feeling so weak. How does he shut everything off so easily? What is in him that I can't have?

Huxley stands directly over me. "You think you can drag me out of here, into the shimmering part of Chicago, and we'll just escape this funk we've been festering in? You think the world's gonna show up and come to our aid, just like they're always helping those poor kids with bullets in their guts and the ones with cardboard signs on Michigan Avenue? Where *are* you, Faye? What do you think they're going to do for us?"

"This isn't the same," I whisper. "We're different."

"I get it," he says, gritting his teeth. "You think you'll shove me into this perfect mold you've created and then they'll notice us. Then you won't hurt anymore. But you're *wrong*."

I shake my head and look up at him. "I won't just let you disappear into this other *thing*, Huxley. I won't let you."

"Nobody *cares*, Faye! We're invisible. You've been staring at the flash for too long."

"What are you *talking* about?"

Huxley laughs again. This time the noise causes acid to rise in my stomach, all the way up to my throat. I feel my knees buckle as everything goes out of focus. I can see the fireworks again, but they're not blue, they're not like fireworks. They're black. They explode like smoke, like bombs. "You're *nothing*, Faye. You're *nothing to the world*. Nobody's going to save you. Not them—and not Huxley."

I swallow and blink my vision back to normal. "*What* are you?"

He opens his mouth again, but instead of laughing, a small black spot crawls out. Then another. Instantly, there are dozens of them, tiny and hairy, with eight microscopic legs, charging up and down his cheeks, flooding his eyelids and nostrils.

I let out a scream and crawl as quickly as I can toward the door, throwing all my weight against it this time. It swings open like it was never stuck in the first place. Pulling myself back up, I dash through the threshold and slam it, while Huxley calls out to me in a voice so steady and calm, you'd think the past twenty minutes hadn't happened.

"You're the one who locked yourself in this so-called paradise, Faye. Just like always."

Cherry is my favorite.

I devour every single bite, forking hunks of flaky crust and fruity globs into my mouth, barely bothering to savor the taste or the satisfying feeling of unspoiled food.

"You're eating that pie like you're a damn werewolf," Mandy says to me, sliding a paper napkin across the table in our booth. "It looks like you got blood all over your mouth."

"Cherry pie tastes a hell of a lot better than blood." I scoop the final bite into my mouth and swallow before I've completely finished chewing it, then wash it down with a swig of lukewarm Folger's.

"Good?" she asks me.

I nod.

"Great. I was able to convince Pete that your shift was an hour later than it actually is, so you owe me. I can't do this shit forever. I'm just one person."

"I know that," I say, wiping the red off my face.

"And so are you, Faye. *One person*. A human person. Not a fucking superhero or priest or whatever the hell you'd have to be to live with a man like him."

"Mandy, just drop it, please. I'm exhausted."

"I thought you overslept and that's why you were late. You're still tired? Groggy or something?"

"Or something, yeah." I yawn involuntarily. "Thanks for covering for me. I've got customers now, so we'll talk more on break."

She purses her lips, painted the same color as the pie filling. "Sure."

I tie my apron around my waist and head over to a short, plump older woman seated alone in one of the booths. The lamp suspended over her head illuminates every layer of foundation she's caked on her face to mask age spots. She watches me uncertainly and taps a manicured fingernail against the table. "What happened to the other one, the one with all that lipstick?"

"That would be Mandy," I tell her. "My name is Faye. I'll be taking care of you for the rest of the evening. I hope that's okay."

She shrugs. "It's fine with me." I offer her a sincere smile, relieved to be focusing on something else for a while. Sweat trickles down the nape of my neck, causing me to flinch and smear it away, just to make sure none of the droplets are spiders.

But that's silly. That was only a dream. It had to be.

"I suppose I'll have a slice of cherry pie," she says. "You've made it look so appealing just now."

My face flushes. "I—it's my favorite."

"We've got at least one thing in common." She beams. I swivel on my feet and head for the kitchen, but halt when I hear her call my name. She says it in a chiming voice, nothing like the swampy rasp I've gotten used to hearing from Huxley.

"Yes, ma'am?"

She reaches forward and snatches my wrist, just above where my bruise trail begins. She turns it over in her palm, exposing the marks, and lets out a heavy sigh. "It's getting worse, isn't it?"

I pull my arm back defensively. "These? I barely feel them. I'm such a klutz, always carrying too many more plates and trays than I should be, smacking into things…"

"Not the bruises." She releases me. "The thing in *him*."

I slowly sit down across from her and lay my hands flat against the table to keep them from shaking. "I'm not sure what you mean, ma'am."

She leans forward and takes both of them in her own. "Tell me the truth, dear. No more pretending. Was sleeping really what made you so late for work tonight?"

No. She's right. I haven't slept in days. It wasn't a dream. None of this is.

I inhale sharply, detecting that chemical odor again. "Do you— can you smell that?"

"Dear," she says. "It's your *pain*. The emotional kind. The kind that begins right here." She points at my chest, right where I can feel my heart thumping. "It's the pain that wears you down and contaminates your blood. The emotional kind. The kind that rots you from the inside out. I could smell it the second I walked in."

"What's going on?" I whisper.

"You *reek* of despair," she goes on. "And not just that, but hope, too."

"Hope?"

"Oh, the hope is the most wretched stink of all. It's got you clenched in place, plucking at your veins for sport."

I wince. "But it's…hope. It's all that keeps me going."

"May I tell you a secret, dear?" she says in a low voice. Before I can answer, she continues, "You only *think* it's hope that will save you. It sure looks the part, feels the part, doesn't it? But it's not. It's hope's malevolent, identical twin—fear. You can't give up, because what's the alternative? Come on, little girl. Do you really believe he's still inside there somewhere, or are you afraid of the fact that he probably isn't?"

I yank my hands out of hers. "With all due respect, ma'am, I *know* he's still in there, but he's infected. Maybe it's evil or maybe it's just sadness, I'm not sure, but it's alive and it's in him and it's struggling to survive. I'm watching him disappear like—" The sentence falls flat. I sound like I'm losing my mind. Embarrassed, I lower my head down and focus on a little metal spoon lying on the table. In the center is a sunken, sad face blinking up at me.

It takes a second for it to register that I'm looking at myself. I don't want to be this girl, not anymore. I fling the spoon off the table, sending it to the floor with a jarring clank. A few people in the diner turn their heads, Mandy included, but the old woman doesn't even flinch.

"I don't know why we're talking about any of this," I say finally. "I don't know *how* you know—do you know how to help him?"

She sighs and folds her hands together. "It depends on if he wants to help himself, or even be helped at all, for that matter."

"Of course he does," I say, but then, I'm not so sure. "If he won't help himself, then *I* will."

"How loyal of you," says the woman flatly. "But I suppose this is what you chose. Young people are always making decisions like this."

Mandy is still staring at me with her mouth stretched into a thin line that makes her lipstick look like a neon slash across her face. "Get up," she mouths. "Why are you just sitting there?"

"Ma'am, I should really be getting back to work." I stand up uneasily.

"I was like you," she tells me. "I was young. I thought I loved someone. I was ready to walk through a thousand torrential storms just to find some hint of, oh what do you call it? Paradise?"

The word makes me flinch. "That's pretty generic," I mutter.

"Because it's familiar. It's *heaven*. It's what everyone wants. It's the interchangeable promises they'll make you, the empty devotion they hand over stirred into something sweet. It's the poison itself that will someday rot you, just like I said."

"I'm so tired," I say. The room is getting too bright. My head is too heavy. How long has it been since I've been here? I haven't even gotten her damn pie yet. Mandy's going to yell. Pete's going to fire me. Huxley's going to—

"I can help you," the woman says suddenly. "You want to sleep again, right? You want the quiet, the peace of mind? Poor dear, you just want to be safe."

"I want *him*," I whine. "I just want him. No matter what."

She nods, then reaches into the pocket of her skirt and digs around. "Here we go. A natural remedy. A supplement for your troubles." She holds up a thumb-sized, black capsule between her fingers.

I squint at it. "Where'd you get this?"

She shakes her head. "Don't concern yourself with too much now, dear. It's just from the earth. It will restore things to a proper balance. From whence we came, we all return."

I nod and take it from her fingers, holding it up to the lamp. Inside is some sort of thick fluid, shimmering with little flecks of white and pink. "I'd love to be able to return. I'm nostalgic more than I'm afraid."

She smiles solemnly and touches my hand again. Her hand is warm and soft, like an oven mitt after removing a tray of cookies. Like the kind of grandma I never had growing up. Like the kind of grandma I'd like to be someday, if I ever make it there. "You always focus on the light, don't you, dear?" she whispers. "Even when it gets so bright it blinds you."

I stare at my funhouse reflection, distorted and mangled by the broken glass that fills the mirror. I try to smile, but it only makes me look like some sort of sideshow freak.

With one long breath, I pull my uniform dress over my head and kick it across the floor. My entire body is swollen in sprays of brown, yellow, purple, and blue. I run my fingers along them, trying to place the pain, searching my memory for a single instance when I remember feet and fists against my skin. Nothing. Instead, I have endless memories of Huxley's frigidness, slamming doors, cutting remarks, sleepless nights, tear-stained pillowcases. There's a bruise for every touchless moment.

I scamper across the cold wooden floor to my bureau and search around for something that will distract from my swollen flesh. Something sexy, something scandalous, something that reminds me of a time when my Friday nights were spent making out with Huxley in crowded concert venues, not plotting ways to exorcize demons from him.

I find a thin black slip, the hem lined with lace. *This should do.*

Huxley is rooted to the couch, perched upright like a display mannequin. I tip-toe around the room, keeping the black capsule tucked into my palm as I examine the area for any more traces of supernatural vermin.

None. Still, I know I have to act quickly.

I take a few steps around him so I'm blocking the television, then lean forward to shove his back against the couch. I straddle his lap so he can't move and whisper, "miss me?" He doesn't push me away as I'd expected, but instead, smiles menacingly and gives my hips a tight squeeze.

A dull pain shoots up my spine.

His hands crawl up my ribs, fingers finding every single bruise on my torso. As they press each one, a white flash rips through my eyes.

You need to grow a thicker skin, Faye. The flowers and food, your heart, everything will expire. Your blood is rotting, and I am rotten. You can't save anything. You're nothing.

You're nothing to the world.

His mouth is still, but the thoughts were in his voice, meant so harshly and loudly that I can feel them scraping their way inside, burrowing, flicking against my nerve endings.

I gulp back the pain, stretch my hand behind his neck, and fumble around to get the capsule directly between my fingers. The words are just tired reruns of conversations I've had with the monster, the monster that robbed me of him. The monster I'm going to murder.

I lean down slowly and press my chest to his to imitate a hug.

Then I slip the capsule into my mouth.

His hands slide up to my shoulders, resting briefly before moving to my neck. I feel his grip tighten again, and then my breath halts. Another flash. It almost feels good, this sudden rush. I can feel my head getting lighter, the pain beginning to fade, all of it.

Now. Before you float away. This time the thoughts are my own.

I smash my mouth to his, and once his lips part, I spit the capsule into his mouth, pushing it to the back of his throat with my tongue.

He reacts by sputtering a little and squeezes his hands even tighter. We're both choking now, but I keep my tongue in place so he can't resist swallowing the capsule. Finally, it rolls down his throat, and just before I'm gone, his hands drop from my neck.

I tumble backward onto the floor, coughing, and watch him jump up from the couch. He clutches his stomach and moans. "What the *hell* did you just do me?"

I crawl across the floor, away from him, toward the kitchen. "It's for your own good, Huxley," I manage between coughs. "It's going to get this thing out of you."

"It—burns!" he cries, dropping down to his knees. For a second, I'm terrified he will come at me on all fours, but instead he rocks to the side and collapses into a ball on the floor. "It hurts so much, Faye! How could you do this?"

"It's that *thing*," I insist. "It's killing both of us. I'm trying to save—"

Huxley lifts his head up suddenly and projectile vomits a wave of black tar against the wall. The floral wallpaper dissolves right beneath it. He shudders and makes a non-human noise, then spews another wave. The black bile seeps into the cracks that line the wall, sealing each one shut. I rub my neck and stare in bewilderment. *It's working. It's got to be working.*

He vomits again and again, until every crack in the front room wall has disappeared. Then he crumples back into a heap and begins to convulse. His head slams against the floor. The walls begin to ripple violently with him, like an earthquake tipping off the Richter scale. The television falls forward. The red frame on the table smashes to the floor. Every single lightbulb in the apartment goes out, then explodes one by one, pops of light flaring like a camera's flash.

Screaming, I scramble toward the kitchen doorway and crouch in the threshold, like I've been told to do in these kinds of emergencies. *These kinds of emergencies.* I realize that nobody has, in fact, ever prepared for *these* kinds of emergencies.

After about a minute, the walls stop shaking. One single light in the front room comes back on, glowing over Huxley as he lays splayed, face down, on the floor, still seizing.

"Hux?" I crawl toward him.

"Faye, help me," he slurs.

I roll him onto his back and let out a shriek. Frothy, pink saliva is foaming out of his mouth and mucus is gushing from his nose. There's blood. Not the black, demonic kind. Human blood. Huxley blood. I feel something wet against my hand and notice a trail of clear fluid oozing from his ear. He inhales and exhales unsteadily, gazing up at me with helpless blue eyes. The color of faded, broken-in denim.

"Hux, you're going to be okay," I barely whisper, but I don't know if I'm lying or not. His skin is cold, colder than usual. This doesn't make sense. Weren't things supposed to go back? Weren't we supposed to have peace and quiet?

I glance up, realizing everything has gone still, and a thick silence has coated the room.

"Faye, I'm so sorry," Huxley says. "I haven't been myself."

"I know," I say, lying down beside him. "But you are now. I have you."

"I can't see anything." His voice keeps getting quieter, and I have to strain my ears to hear what he's saying. I grab his hand and squeeze.

"Hux, I love you. I love you."

"I can't see anything," he repeats. "Are you still there?"

"Yes!" I shake his hand. "Feel that? I'm here."

"Don't leave me, please."

"Do you remember our first date, Hux?" I ask him. "That bar with the slanted floor? The vodka crans? The photo booth?"

He nods, sending a river of blood and spit down his chin. I place my head against his chest, listening to his heartbeat. It doesn't have a steady rhythm. Instead it feels like there are two hearts inside of him—one hammers alarmingly fast, while the other thuds erratically like a weak drum.

"Do you…remember what you said to me while we took those pictures?" I'm not sure why this matters to me right now. I know I'm losing him, and that we only have a few minutes left, if that. I should be doing something, but I could never explain this to any paramedic. Letting the tears spill out, I squeeze the fabric of his shirt and bury my face into his chest.

"The flash," he says. "You…had your eyes wide open. You told me…" he trails off, and I worry he's escaping from me for good. I jostle him slightly.

"Please, Hux. Say it."

"You told me that you didn't want to miss any of it. You wanted to see everything. All of it." He moves his head to one side, forcing a soggy cough that mists blood against the floor. "I told you…and you didn't listen, Faye, you didn't…"

"Huxley."

"You let it in," he wheezes finally. "You should have just shut your eyes and not let it in. Faye, *why did you let it in*?"

His shirt is soaking wet now, but I can't tell if it's from his blood or my tears. I let myself sob, loud and uncontrolled, while my body shakes and his heart quivers, until my eyes are finally dry and his heart is as still as the room.

The outside air is lined with serrated edges, keeping all in Bridgeport wedged into their homes like little dolls that have been tucked away now that playtime's over. I turn up the volume of the television to drown out the wailing of wind slamming into the windows.

On the screen is a vintage Julie Andrews, singing to a group of children in a meadow. I've seen the movie before, many times, but I never grow bored of watching the excitement dance in her eyes, in the children's eyes. Ignorance trills in their voices. Soon they'll understand that these songs won't keep them free.

A scratching nose erupts from inside my wall. Slow at first, like it merely wants to be noticed. Then the noise quickens. It gets louder, the sharp and high-pitched sound of claws dragging themselves up and down the drywall frantically. Sighing, I switch the television off and pull myself from the worn couch, following the noise, then placing my hand against the wall. A chemical smell seeps from behind a plastic red picture frame that hangs nearby.

The scratching continues, desperately, like it's beckoning me. "Shhh," I hush, stroking the wall tenderly. "It's okay. I'm here. I'm never leaving you."

I continue stroking the wall until the scratching stops.

It always does eventually.

XOXOX XOXOX XOXOX X

About the Author

Taro Turner grew up in the swirling swamps of northern Florida, where she was far more concerned about being taken by a demon than a human kidnapper. She was protected by her trusted closet monster and dead imaginary friend until she became old enough to look after herself. She received her Wiccaning at the age of 13, then her bachelor's of art in Creative Writing from Columbia College at the age of 22. You can find more of her strangeness at writtenbytaro.com.

CHRISTMAS IN CONNECTICUT

Robert Mayette

I 'm Joyful. It's still my name, that part won't change. You get to call yourself what you want when in the service of Santa. This is the Field. This is where we crashed.

Time feels like it's flown out of me, and though sunrises and sunsets would have come and gone, it's still Christmas Eve. It's still Christmas Eve because there are the gifts. Right there. That large now-orderly stack of broken packages and tattered burlap bags are them. And they are not where they're supposed to be. So, it must still be Christmas Eve.

When the night began, I was with Leela, Brazen, and Chompy. We'd stashed ourselves in the back of the sleigh. Only elves know that Santa takes naps during the night when he crosses the two big oceans, otherwise he'd never make it around the world without collapsing. Some elves like to reindeer surf when he's asleep. I don't think he'd mind it if he were awake, but no one wants to be the elf that took Santa off task. That happened once, in the '40s. Entire town of Duluth, Minnesota forgotten about because some jerk asked Santa about how to remember the names of the Great Lakes. The day after, the toys in assembly for next year were cleared off the entire stretches of workstations and all the elves wrote apology notes for everyone in Duluth.

They made me sign them all, of course.

I wish I could just sign something this time.

He was immediately asleep when Dasher and Dancer reared us up from the Azores; it was time to reindeer surf. I grabbed Leela's hand as we climbed over the front of the sleigh and down to the hitching, Chompy following behind on her side. She looked so scared, but I whispered that I'd done it a million times before. And we were both wearing slippers, so it's not like we'd fall to our deaths. Santa's had to rescue dozens of gently descending assistants over the years, and Brazen would raise the alarm if anything bad happened to us from his safe spot back in the gifts bound for Florida.

I took Comet, gave her Cupid. They snorted their displeasure beneath us, but they weren't the jack offs on the practice team who would bray until we were discovered. I held out my hand to Leela, and her fingers were warm within mine. Beneath us was a dark and faceless ocean, and above us a million points of light to steer a world by, and the gentle sound of sleigh bells rippling through the chill air. It was bliss, oneness with the night, with happiness, standing on the edge of possibility and dreamy conviction as the reindeer drifted up and down, up and down, like a raft traversing a wide, mighty river.

I'd brought some shot bottles of Drambuie with me, delicately handing one to Leela after tossing one back to Chompy. I crinkled my toes to clutch closer reindeer fur through the thin soles of my slippers when I took the first sip of mine. It was spicy warm and Heavenly, like it should be. We risked a few laughs and pratfalls, but I'm not a fool. Not half the one I appear to be. I kept an eye behind us, making sure that the white flowing folds around Santa's lips rose and fell in a regular pattern, and there was Brazen still, his head sticking out from the sacks, still looking at me pleadingly that we would finish having fun.

We were arriving in New England. Now Santa's a traditionalist, Navigation Elves like me have come to see. No stopping at the first town near shore. No. Each region at a time, however he's defined it, from one direction to the next. For this one, it was to be Southwest to Northeast, then round the whole of Canada, down the west side of the Americas, up and back until ending almost where we started in New York. Rembrandt's paintbrush never had such flourish. This all is why, when we first saw land, and Chompy said we should go back, I waved the thought away with my hand. Santa'd be out for another few minutes at least. He doesn't wake up until the reindeer have finished their first descent.

They were just about to begin descending. I looked at Leela and smiled, the lights of the anonymous towns beneath us catching in her long eyelashes, the sharp curves of her lips.

Then the sleigh lurched, and Santa woke with a gasp.

"Something's wrong," he said, dreamily and urgent.

Fire burst up from the start of the team, erupting from the hitching between Dasher and Dancer. The sleigh listed—I saw Leela keep her balance, but I slipped, the slippers keeping me airborne for only a moment before they gave out, and I clutched on to Comet's dressing to keep from falling. I scrambled for footing, Leela screamed, Santa snapped through the reins the sign to descend immediately. When I pushed myself back upright, there was Leela's already soot-marked face, the fire engulfing her side of the team front to back, her side splitting away, black and greasy, spiraling upwards like a greedy Icarus. She reached her hand out for mine. I shouted for her to jump, and I scuttled down Comet's near side, holding onto a tassel of angry bells, and reached out as far as I could, as far as the oceans, with every last inch of a three foot frame, and I just had her fingers—just had them—when the hitching between us snapped, and the fires spread to Cupid's dressing, and her eyes were breached by centuries of terror that could never find us at the North Pole, burst across her alone, fearful, anguished features when she disappeared into the rising phoenix with them, their entire side of the sled team fully broken off as a mad, flailing worm.

My eyes shot back to Santa, sputtering, stricken, blasted, before he vanished—just vanished—the reins tumbling into immediate convulsions in the night air. Brazen shouted out in fear, eyes wide, pointing ahead, and I turned to see the ground thundering up toward us, a hateful endless void, swallowing up my sight. And then stillness.

"Joyful?"

My hip screamed in pain. I felt my arm being shaken like it was in a snow wolf's maw, and my eyes shot open, but it was just Brazen.

"Joyful? You okay?"

Stars silhouetted his head. He looked dour, ragged, dirt- or soot-covered, despite the weak smile he donned upon seeing that I was stirring. Flames must have reached back to the sleigh, because the white cotton fringe on his hat was singed with a black streak running down the length.

The fire. "Leela," I said. "Did you find Leela?"

His eyes fell. "Oh, Joyful. Joyful, I'm sorry. The fire—they just were a streak of fire when I saw them all, Leela and Chompy in it both. Maybe. Maybe when it's daylight we can search for them. Maybe there's a smoke plume in all this blackness. Maybe they're still alive."

I felt a pain in my chest like I never have before.

"Maybe they vanished, too," continued Brazen. "Did you see Santa disappear? Maybe he pulled them out of the fires with him, and they're all okay."

"I just saw flames."

"And the reindeer, too, on that side."

"Not Dancer. I saw Dancer blasted apart."

"No, it's...It's..." He rubbed the back of his neck. "You don't study these things like I have. Santa's magic is ancient, before the days of fire. 'Blasted apart'? Unlikely."

"I saw what I saw."

He crossed his arms. "Not if Santa wished otherwise, you didn't. Not what you thought you saw."

Then I noticed the large white glowing disk resting at the center of his chest, what would have filled up his entire ribcage if he'd breathed it in. It passed through the tunic sleeves he crossed before him.

"The moon," I said, numb.

He turned to look behind him, but the white light stayed unflinchingly still. "Yes. Full tonight."

"I can see it through you."

His eyes widened, and he put a hand up before him to confirm it for himself. "What? What is this?"

I did the same test with my own. I was equally transparent. Not substance-less, though—the ground sure felt hard enough. I put my hand forward for him to take. "Help me up."

"What the hell is this?" he stammered. "Why are we see-through?"

"Just help me up," I snapped. "I think I broke something."

He took my hand and hoisted me. I couldn't stop my choppy gasps of pain, but it just hurt badly, my left hip and knee—I could put some weight on it.

We were in the middle of a large, open field. A tree line rested in every direction, a few hundred yards away, it seemed. In one direction, the oaks were crowned in yellow wavering light, marking the way to the nearest human village.

Gifts, mangled and distorted, were strewn everywhere. The sleigh had landed mostly upright, one rudder ripped off it, it resting at a painful angle upon the other. Most of the gifts that remained in the sacks were heaped up nearby it. Nothing stirred.

"What happened to the reindeer team on my side? I saw them crash at the same time as us."

"Didn't see them," said Brazen, picking up a raven-haired doll and brushing the dirt off of her. "Maybe they were picked up by Santa's disappearing magic as well." He snapped his fingers. "Maybe that's what happened to us! Why we're see-through. He tried, but... well, he tried once to bring us away, and almost...well, it will work later on."

"I don't know what happened to us. And I don't think you do, either."

He pinned the doll under his arm. "We should wait until morning. Someone's bound to find us, be looking for us. The sun has to come up eventually."

"What makes you think people will be looking?"

He pointed at the sleigh and the bundles of present-filled sacks. "I think people will know very early tomorrow morning that we've gone missing, Joyful. Don't you?"

I crossed my arms and took a deep, slow breath.

"Let's stay warm," he said after a moment. "It could be a long night."

There was some driftwood laying nearby that was cold but dry. We built a fire. We ended up on opposite sides, looking at each other through the flames, hunched, but I told myself that was normal when it was just two people in the middle of nowhere. It's like human businessmen when they're out at lunch. After a few moments, he turned on his back and looked up at the sky. That's when I saw the cut on his forehead.

"You've a nasty gash. I didn't see it before."

"I think it will be okay."

"There was a first aid kit on the sleigh. I'll go look for it."

"I searched for it earlier before I found you. It must have fallen out."

The fire was starting to sputter out after a few minutes.

"It's fine," he said. He set the raven-haired doll next to him on her back. She joined him looking up at the sky. "It's just a small cut."

"I'll go look for some more wood, then," I said.

I'd collected a few pieces of kindling in my arms when I saw it.

There, from out of some tall grass, one bell-clad slipper was pointing up at the heavens. I looked down at the identical ones I wore on my feet. I stepped closer, stepped closer to see my own blanched eyes, my own twisted neck, my own mouth opened in silent scream, physical, opaque, and very still.

I felt my throat tighten. "Brazen?" I called out loudly.

I heard his footsteps near. "What is it?"

"Look at this?"

He stepped forward to see, freezing in a gasp.

"Dead," I said, finally. "Dead!" I shoved the bundle of sticks at him. "Dead!" I grabbed one and was instantly beating him over the head. "Dead! Dead! We're fucking dead! We're see-through because we're dead!"

He crumpled into a ball, and I stopped myself and dropped the branch. After a few moments, I heard him sobbing. I let him cry, long and hard, and I did everything I could to not do the same, to not let anyone see me do the same. I thought of summer, when the ice would weaken in some places and arctic seals would come into the bay, and how happy they always looked. Always so happy. "Be like them," my mother once said to me. "See how happy-go-lucky they are?"

I crouched down next to him. "It's going to be okay."

He looked up at me, anguished. He grabbed the trim of my vest and pulled me near him. "Why is this happening? What's going on?"

I put my arm across his shoulders. "I don't know."

A few minutes later, we were back at the fire. It seemed like it would have gone out in the time we were gone, but it had stayed lit. I'd left all the wood I'd collected near my body, and I didn't feel like going back for it. "Let's just go to sleep," I said, and I don't think the words were fully out of my mouth before he was lying down next to the raven-haired doll, cuddling it in his arms, and the creases of his crow's feet softened in unconsciousness.

I'd trouble heeding my own advice, thoughts racing as they were, but I did eventually succumb for the desire to let my mind be washed away, forgetting. When sleep finally came, it came quickly.

I was jolted out of it by the sound of rustling and movement. It was still pitch night out, but I knew it was coming from the sleigh. Brazen awoke to the noise, too. The fire was still going, so I took out a lit branch that we could see by.

A thick black mass was hunched over one side of the sleigh, shifting and rolling in a wave of fur. It was digging through whatever was

"Bear," I whispered.

He nodded, adding, "But not white."

Brilliant, Brazen. "Why are we whispering," I said aloud. "What could it do to us now?" I walked over to the sleigh and rapped my knuckles on its sheen side. "Excuse me? This doesn't belong to you. Go away."

A set of eyes and a brown muzzle that licked its long teeth boiled up from out of the black mass, looked at me, and roared. Terror shot through me, and I stumbled backwards. The muzzle plunged back down into the wreck.

"That didn't work," said Brazen, helping me up. "We need to find something to scare him away."

"What do you think it's after?"

"There's the rack of candy canes and rum cake beneath the sled floorboards. I think it smells that."

"Bears eat that?"

"They eat anything. Help me find something."

We searched through the field, but apart from a light-up fire truck with a peculiarly large steering wheel on the back, there was nothing I could find. I called out to Brazen, but he was equally dumbfounded.

Then I was scratching my head when I saw it: the Phantonium Interspace Blaster. E-ticket item, this year's Tickle-Me-Furby-Pogs. We got a few dozen of them sent to the workshop last week—one of the advantages of having major contracts with the toy companies. It could make any noise you wanted, just say what you want into the speaker, pull the trigger, and get that. Say "duck"; get quacking. Say "cow"; get mooing. I padded over to it and picked the package up out of the dirt. Odd, though—it was much heavier than I remembered. The wrapping paper it had been in was mostly gone, but I saw the tag for the recipient, plucked it off, and shoved it into one of my pockets. Then I opened up the box and pulled it out.

There it was, exactly as it appeared to be, but—I tore it out of the Styrofoam—it was made of metal and was heavy in my hand. I turned it at all angles to see it from every side. It seemed a little darker in color, near black instead of red, and with sharper angles than I remembered. Felt like it might be tough to aim with small hands —good thing sounds have no targets—but I felt powerful holding it, like I could take on the world, like with one of these in my hand, I could do anything.

But when I looked at the pistol grip through my translucent fingers, I snapped out of it. I called out to Brazen that I'd found something and soon we were back at the sleigh.

"Oh, that should be perfect," he said. "But what noise would a bear not like?"

"I don't know." I pressed the red button on the side and heard the prompt-beep. "A sound that will scare a bear away." It gave its confirm twitter. "All right, let's see." I walked up near the sleigh and pointed the Phantonium Interspace Blaster up at the sky. I pulled the trigger.

Thunder, concentrated and boiled down into a loud, split second, broke from out of my hand. The force of the gun pushed me back, knocking me off my feet and the wind out of me. Instantly the black mass retreated from the sleigh, and Brazen called that it was running for the tree line.

"Well, you did it," he said, with a half-smile. "I don't think he'll be coming back."

"No," I said, finally catching my breath. "Probably not."

We went back to the fire, back to sleep. Brazen's doll still lay near the edge near the coals, but he'd lost interest in it now. And the Phantonium Interspace Blaster? I'd found something on it that looked like a safety, though there was never one on the model that we got in the workshop that day. I flipped it on and carefully tucked it into my inside vest pocket. It felt heavy, like it was pulling down my heart, but I was able to fall back to sleep.

A few hours later, I woke up. It was still pitch black out. I looked over at the fire—still lit and going, though neither of us were tending to it. Brazen was sitting at the edge of it, looking at the flames.

"Can't sleep?" I asked.

"No," he said. After a few moments, he asked, "Hey, Joyful?"

"Yeah?"

"If we're dead, then why am I getting really hungry?"

My stomach immediately started growling in agreement. I sat up. "Yeah. How is that?"

He looked at me with wide and curious eyes. "And shouldn't it be morning by now? I feel like I've slept the longest I ever had already."

"Me, too," I said. I got up and stretched like I never have before. Brazen motioned me to follow him.

The bear had made quite a mess in the sleigh—Santa would be especially furious, if he ever saw it—smashed lengths of candy canes everywhere and large globs of rum cake smeared all over. But that was only one of several compartments, and the rest were still tightly secured. Brazen, a Provisions Elf, had the combination for the lock that was securing it, and soon we were feasting on the best rum cake ever made by Mrs. Claus.

"Oh, that's good stuff," blurted Brazen through a full mouth.

I hummed my agreement.

"Hello?" came a voice from behind us.

We spun around, but it was just blackness in front of us. I fought back the urge to reach for the heavy Phantonium, instead calling "Who's there?"

We heard footsteps, a snap of a twig, and there in the very faintest edges of the firelight emerged a young boy, probably six or seven years old, in a sky-blue snorkel coat that went down to his knees. The coat's hood was pushed back, and his ears had reddened in the cold. In the V of his coat zipper were the tops of two white letters on a field of royal blue—some sport jersey of some kind. He carried an orange and black checkered backpack in one hand by its shoulder strap. "Who are you guys?" he asked, his eyes wide and fearful.

"Who... are we," I said. "Who are we, Brazen..."

I saw Brazen stiffen next to me. "We...are..."

The boy stepped forward, his face brightening. "You're Santa's Elves!"

The words jolted through me as if I heard them for the first time. "Well, yes! Yes, we are...that." I faltered as I turned to look at Brazen, still seeing the nasty, death-like gash across his forehead, the flickering of the fire behind him through his body.

"And you're helping, Santa, right?" asked the boy. "This is Christmas Eve?"

Brazen looked at me helplessly. "Yes, yes this is Christmas Eve," I said.

The boy laughed. "You two look really funny with those bells on your hats."

I looked again at Brazen—how his green cap had been blasted in the fire, almost unrecognizable. He studied me as well, taking in how hellish I looked. I was about to turn back to the boy to hopelessly agree with him again when Brazen tapped me on the shoulder and pointed to the side of the sleigh.

There in the shiny black lacquer, standing where Brazen and I were standing, were he and I as two smiling elves as dapper as we'd been when we got dressed that morning. No singe, no soot, not a blemish on Brazen's forehead, and both of us as opaque and solid as we'd been when we climbed aboard earlier that evening.

The reflected Brazen's smile stretched to Cheshire-cat proportions as the real, insubstantial one next to me began to grin. But then I noticed something else in the reflection. Standing there behind us, on the edge of the firelight, was the boy, but something had changed. His eyes were closed and his mouth was thin-lipped and as straight as the horizon in the Arctic. Two dark patches of red bloomed on his chest and hip.

My stomach seized. I knew what those patches were; they were in the unmistakable shapes of gunshot wounds. I looked at Brazen, and I could tell he understood what had happened, too.

Slowly, I turned back around to face the boy, and there he was: still smiling, eyes still bright and wide and full of wonder, his clothing unmarked.

"What's your name, son?" I called.

He took a few steps forward. "Jake," he said.

"Jake," I repeated. I straightened my bearing. "Jake, I'm Joyful, Navigation Elf, First Class. My friend is Brazen, Provisions Elf. No Class."

Jake laughed.

I burned with embarrassment. "I meant that seriously. Provision Elves don't have a classification sys—"

"Jake, would you like to see something really cool?" asked Brazen.

"Sure!" He came bounding forward.

"This is…um…" Brazen stepped aside and gestured at the wreck. "This is a 'Test Sleigh' that we sometimes try out. As you see, this test hasn't gone so well, so we'll report back to Santa that it had a few problems."

"Is everything okay?"

"Completely," I said. "We just need to straighten a few things up, and then write our report and everything will be fine."

"But it is Christmas Eve tonight, right?"

I rubbed the back of my neck. "It is, Jake. Everything's going to be fine."

"May we ask," said Brazen, "what you're doing out here in this field?"

Jake's eyes flashed with fear. "I'm not going to miss out on presents, am I?"

"No, no, no, no," soothed Brazen. "But it seems an odd place right now, for a boy of your age. I would have thought you'd be home in bed."

Jake looked perplexed, glanced down at the backpack he was carrying. "I...it is Christmas Eve, right?"

"It is," I said.

He scratched his head. "The last thing I remember is being at school." He set the backpack down in the grass, unzipped it, and pulled out a brown bag. "Look, here's my lunch."

I felt a sharp tightness in my throat, but I pushed it away and pulled out the biggest smile I could. "Let's not worry about it. Here—can you help us help Santa? As you can see, Brazen and I made a very big mess of things, and we need to start getting all the presents that are all over the place organized again. There has to be something in all this that's yours, too. It can be a game. You can help us find your gift from Santa."

Jake wore the biggest, most-thrilled, most-innocent smile I have ever seen in my life or ever hope to see. We began sorting all the battered, broken gifts with comments of his interspersed—"This one's wrapped nice, I wonder what it is?" or "My Mom says big bows on small things like this one usually means big bucks!"—indicating that whatever it was that made Brazen and I appear unaffected was equally spread to the cargo Santa carried. I felt my throat tighten again at that: whatever happened to the Big Man—if I had seen him in his last moments or not—he still had and used the power to make the crazy, insane, completely chaotic appear normal, good, right, and in full alignment with every child's wish on what Christmas should be.

We were at it for a few minutes when from out of the shadows Brazen and I heard another, "Hello?" This time a girl in a pink coat and My Little Pony backpack. The last thing she remembered was being on a swing. More came: two young boys who told us they'd last been sitting on the sidewalk curb; three more in their young teens who had been playing basketball.

When I looked at their reflections in the sleigh's side, all wore the blooms of red.

They just kept coming. They just kept coming, and they just kept helping. Occasionally, one would find a tag with his or her name— just the first name, but everyone instantly knew who it was for, though the first names had begun to double, triple, and quadruple up. We'd all stop as they opened it, and they'd play with it and with others for a few moments before setting it aside temporarily to help with the sorting. But as the night continued to stretch on, the work of sorting was becoming smaller and smaller, and the work of playing was growing more and more.

It was then that I saw Jake sitting alone at the fire. I walked toward him. "What's wrong, Jake?"

He turned to me, and he'd been crying recently. "Joyful, did I do something wrong?"

"What do you mean?"

He wiped an eye. "Well, I've been here the longest, as I can tell, and I still can't find a present from Santa for me."

"I'm sure there is one. There's plenty of presents still scattered around."

"But some kids have found two or three already."

"I'll help you look, will that help?"

Jake nodded.

"What did you ask Santa for? That will narrow down the size."

He smiled a little. "I only asked for one thing. A Phantonium Interspace Blaster —it's about this big, and—" I didn't hear the rest of his description. I reached into the pocket where I stuck the gift tag of the Blaster I had opened, and my heart sank when I read the name: *Jake*.

"Oh. Oh, Jake. I'm sorry," I said.

Jake looked puzzled.

"I opened that up by mistake earlier," I continued. "Before you arrived. I didn't mean to, but I thought that I could use it as a tool."

"Oh, then you have it?"

I felt the metallic device inside my inner vest pocket. It still felt like a heavy weight upon me—even heavier as I was hunched over to speak with him. I remember how angry it had looked a few hours before. "Yes. Yes, I do."

"Can I have it?"

I took a deep breath and slowly reached into my inner pocket, felt the cool metal handle of the pistol grip. But as I was withdrawing it, it started to feel lighter, warmer, and what came out of the folds of my clothes was the Phantonium Interspace Blaster as I'd originally known it from the workshop—full of lights, made of plastic, and seemingly innocent.

I was about to hand it to him, put it into his eager hands, when I said. "Wait. I should test it first." I pointed it up in the air, at an angle that I was sure whatever would blast out of it couldn't fall on another some distance away. I slowly pulled the trigger.

A tinny speaker said in sing-song: *Booga, booga, booga—go away, you stupid bear.*

Jake laughed. I did, too, nervously at first, and then with a full throat. I handed it to him, pointing to the button on it. "I used it earlier to scare a bear away. You can change the noise here."

"I kind of like it as-is," he said, pulling the trigger.

Booga, booga, booga—go away, you stupid bear.

He pulled it again.

Booga, booga, booga—go away, you stupid bear.

"Hey!" he called out, standing up. "Everyone! Look at what I got from Santa!" He ran into a small crowd that quickly formed around him.

Booga, booga, booga—go away, you stupid bear.

Away from the sounds of admiration, I turned back to the stack of presents to finish up the final bit of work.

I stopped when I saw Brazen looking at me, blankly at first, and then with a desperate look that said, *"No more. I can take it no more."*

Brazen wasn't going to have to worry about that too much longer, as we were going to run out of gifts soon. I looked at the children and wondered what would happen when the toys had all been opened, when they tired of them, when they realized that Christmas wasn't going to last forever—but their lives here just might.

This is the field. This is where we crashed.

‮)(ס‭(‭)(‮)(‭(‭)(‮)(‭(‭)(‮)(‭

About the Author

Robert Mayette is a writer of literary fiction, historical fiction, and fantasy, residing in Danbury, Connecticut. He is a lay scholar focused on medieval literature and early American writing with an emphasis on the works of Nathaniel Hawthorne. Rob is also a founding editor of the online journal *Read Short Fiction*. His own short fiction has appeared in various journals including *ESC! Magazine*, *The Battered Suitcase*, *MiPOesias*, and *Word Riot* and his most recent work appeared in the *My Peculiar Family* anthology. He is the father of young twin daughters that are the sum of all his joys when away from the desk. Please visit him at www.robertmayette.com.

THE DEPTHS

Elizabeth Allen

July, 1975

Hallie reached the beach house early on a Saturday evening after—counting pit stops—a thirteen-hour slog from Columbus. She killed the car's engine and exited slowly, allowing her achy legs to adjust to standing.

The place looked the same as it had fifteen years ago. Same battleship gray paint, peeling like a week-old sunburn. Same beach-version of a yard—pools of drifted sand, a few sparse tangles of scrub bushes. The side of the house that faced the road still bore the wood cut-out letters that read *Shore Thing*, typical of the goofy nautical names people liked to give such places.

Scaling the narrow steps on the right flank of the house, Hallie entered through the chipped, water-stained door. Yes, yes, all of this was familiar too—the living area with the attached kitchen, the two bedrooms and bathroom off a side hall. There were the inevitable half-hearted updates. The owners had put in a new couch and added white, faux-wood paneled walls. The ill-advised dark brown carpet that showed every grain of sand tracked in had been replaced by an equally iffy shag in a queasy green. A couple of big pink seashells spruced up the old glass-topped coffee and end tables.

These last items sparked a memory. When she was seven or maybe eight, Hallie had run into the corner of the coffee table. She and her sister, Gwen, had been tearing across the living room with Angie, a friend whose family lived in a tiny cottage next door. Hallie had dinged her thigh pretty good and howled at the pain. Gwen had commanded her to suck it up, as big sisters were prone to do. But

Angie had taken Hallie's hand and smiled at her. She'd said they should go down to the water and pack Hallie's leg in wet sand like a cast. They had stayed on the beach for a long time afterward, Angie tending to the wound with tiny, gentle hands.

"Hallie," the little girl had asked over and over, "can't we just stay out here?"

Looking past the tables now, Hallie saw the old sliding glass door, its bottom half milky with caked salt. She removed the aluminum pin lock, slid the glass panel, and eased out onto the back deck. In front of her, the Atlantic wavered in the waning sun. Here were the things that never changed, the moisture-laden air, the shriek of gulls, the ceaseless *ka-BOM!, ka-BOM!* of waves hitting the shore.

The back portion of the house sat high enough for Hallie to survey perhaps a mile in each direction. Seaglass Beach, halfway down the North Carolina coast, had always been a small, simple community. Hard-lined and painted white, gray, or brown, each of its waterfront homes stood above the sand on wooden stilts. To Hallie, they looked like the sepia photos she'd seen of old-timey beachgoers raising skirts above the surf.

Three flights of wooden stairs spilled down a grassy section of the dune to the shore below. In the corner of the top landing, a thin metal flagpole stood, a little rusty, but still straight and tall. Back when her family had rented the house, they'd been told about the custom of flying a flag when vacationers were in residence. There was a white flag with a simple drawing of a sandcastle always kept on a small shelf in the kitchen. Dad had been happy to play along but, being the eternal smartass, flew the flag upside down. "We're on vacation, gang!" he'd hoot as he popped open the first of about a thousand Rolling Rocks he'd quaff in the week they were seaside. "Up is down, and down is up."

Hallie went back inside and started to unpack: just a small suitcase, a beach bag, and a case of Smirnoff's vodka. She didn't want to be here alone. But since she was, the vodka was very important. Seven months ago, in the face-biting cold of an Ohio winter, she had made plans with her boyfriend. She'd looked forward to a week at the beach through every frozen morning and gray afternoon, through every shit day of her shit job and each lecture about moderation from her mother and her sister. Then, just two weeks before the trip, Cliff had called her at work on a Friday afternoon.

"Hal, I can't come. I mean, I'm not going to be able to get away, after all."

Her cheeks had started to burn. "Why not?"

"Work," he had murmured. "We're just...swamped."

Of course he had been lying. It had been the old girlfriend that had come back again. She had some kind of hold on him that Hallie could not match, apparently, no matter how many times the bitch hurt him.

When he'd confessed, when he'd come clean, she had lightened her tone. "Just come for the week. Just come and sit on the beach, then see how you feel." But he could not be moved.

"Hal," he had said and sighed so deeply. "Hal, sometimes things change. I am still your friend."

She had sobbed for a few moments. When she had spoken again, the words had come out in a dangerous croak. "You know what I'll do."

"Hallie."

"Say you'll come, or I will."

"Did you take your medicine today?"

"*Say you'll come.*"

"Look, we're not doing this anymore." There had been a pause and a slow exhaling. "You...do what you have to do, if you're so determined."

She'd cut herself that night at home, short parallel slices, a slow meting out of pain. Slick blood had gleamed on her arm as she ignored the ringing phone, sure to be her mom or sister. It would be just like Cliff to call and tell them about her threats. "You've got to do something about her," he'd bray into the phone, as her mother would whine distress and her sister would cluck her tongue. A regular barnyard of disdain.

Cliff wasn't coming, but she hadn't cancelled the beach house. She had the time off from work, and she knew the way to Seaglass. When the week came, she went. Just her, with her clothes, her Valium and her vodka. Of course, her mother and her sister had tried to talk her out of it. When that didn't work, Gwen had made her promise to call when she got to the beach and every day she was there.

Now, Hallie wanted to get at least the first call out of the way. She picked up the receiver of the gold princess phone on the desk in the living room and placed it to her ear. No dialtone. *So sorry, ladies.* At least her mother and Gwen couldn't bother her. She figured she could call later in the week, find a payphone or something.

In the kitchen, she cracked open a bottle of Smirnoff's and poured herself a drink in the first glass she found in the cupboard, a faded Flintstones jelly jar. Immediately, she thought of her dad's tradition with the initial bit of vacation alcohol. Turning her gaze to the back of the kitchen, she noticed a little shelf above the sink. Sure enough, there was a white sandcastle flag folded there. It looked too new to be one they'd flown years ago, and the castle was slightly different, but it would serve. Hallie carried the flag out the sliding door and to the rusting pole on the top deck. She was feeling pretty good, considering. *I'm on vacation, and I will, by God, make it official.* She attached the flag to the rope and sent it skyward, upside down of course. "Up is down, motherfuckers," she said to no one, "and down is up."

Hallie followed the flag ceremony with a couple more drinks and some Valium. As she saw it, the whole mess with Cliff was pretty much a Scarlett O'Hara deal: *I can't think about it right now. I'll think about it tomorrow.* In her mind, there was no better prescription for putting off thinking about something than vodka, pills, and hours in front of the TV.

She woke the next morning to the sound of knuckles on wood. She slid her head off the couch cushion, staggered down the short hall, and opened the door. On the other side was a boy—thirteen or fourteen, by the look of his slight frame. He wore wire-rim glasses and a slightly pained smile, and he had a canvas toolbag slung over one shoulder.

"Ma'am? You Miz Gregg?"

"Yeah, that's me."

"My name is Pete Showalter. I was asked by the rental company to come and nail down a coupla loose boards on your deck?"

Hallie blinked and stared at him. "Boards?"

"Yes, ma'am. On your deck?"

"Oh. Okay."

The boy looked at his feet. "Well, I'll just go around to the beach side and come up from there, but I wanted to let you know I'd be here for a couple minutes. That all right?"

"You don't have to walk all the way around, you know. You can cut through the house if you want."

"You sure, ma'am? I don't want to track anything in…" He lifted one workboot to check for dirt.

"It's not my carpet."

"Alrighty then." The boy entered, then trudged through the living room, slid the pin from the glass door, and took a step out. He stopped.

"Something wrong?" Hallie asked.

"You…got somethin' here. On your deck."

She moved up behind him and saw two small piles of red and pink gore. Hallie gasped. Something had been slaughtered, disemboweled right there.

Pete frowned at the globs, then plunged a fist into one of them and came up with a handful. Hallie forced herself to look a bit closer. It didn't smell like rotting meat, she decided. It was certainly slimy and shiny, but it looked more like frilly-edged ribbons. "What the hell?" she murmured.

"It's seaweed," Pete said lightly.

"Red and pink seaweed?"

"Seaweed comes in all kinds of colors."

"You like seaweed, do you, Pete?"

"You could say that, ma'am. I study marine biology at Duke."

"I thought you fixed loose boards on decks."

Pete grinned. "Sometimes I handyman on weekends for extra cash. But mostly I'm a college student."

"Wait…How old are you exactly?"

"I'm small, but I'm twenty-two next week." Pete gazed around the upper deck area, then in one corner found a little plastic sand pail sitting by a faded child's sunbonnet, likely left by an earlier family of renters. He scooped up the piles of goo, using his hand to herd them into the container. "Was this here when you woke up this morning?"

"As far as I know."

"Well, that's unusual. It's a kind of red algae."

"Oh." Hallie stared at him. "Is that bad?"

"What I mean is that it's a deep-water algae. And it's odd that it's here. This type is common to the Gulf of Mexico, not these waters."

"What the hell is it doing on my deck?"

"I really can't tell you." Pete looked toward the stairs. "Well, let me get at those boards, then." Leaving the pail, he ambled around the deck with his toolbag, while Hallie lingered by the sliding door and looked out over the water. Ten minutes later, the boy smiled at her. "All done."

Hallie could feel the boy's eyes skim over her. Flirting, she thought at first. But no, he was looking at the cut marks on her arms, laid bare by the tank top she was wearing. She turned away quickly and passed back through to the living room. "Look, I'm going to get myself a cocktail. You want one?"

"Oh no, ma'am." Pete said, picking up the pail and following her. "I do not indulge. But thank you for your hospitality."

Hallie sniffed. "And you call yourself a college student." There was still a half full bottle of Smirnoff's on the kitchen counter. She grabbed the jelly jar glass, splashed some vodka into it and held it up for Pete to see. "Pretty classy, huh?"

Pete smiled shyly. "I like those Flintstones. You bet." Then he hoisted the pail. "You mind if I take this?"

"Petey," she said, taking a sip of vodka and moving closer to him, "you can take anything you want. *Mi casa es su casa, and mi gross deck goo es su gross deck goo.* You're welcome here anytime."

The boy's face reddened, and he slipped past her, sidling to the door. "Alrighty then. Thank you, ma'am. You have a good day now." He left, and there was a frantic clatter on the wood stairs. Out the window, she saw him bolt to a baby blue Volkswagen in the driveway.

It was early evening when Hallie decided she should call Cliff. It would be right about now, rock-solid vodka logic told her, that he'd be realizing his mistake and starting to miss her. They could still salvage the week if he knew she would forgive him. She shifted her drink to her left hand and picked up the phone receiver. Dead. She'd forgotten.

Hallie found a payphone at the Piggly Wiggly about a half a mile back on the main road. Three rings brought a woman's voice, high and woozy, as if she'd been interrupted while laughing. "Hello?"

It was a short conversation, a wholly unpleasant back and forth, then some vague threat from the girlfriend about calling the police. Hallie beat the girl to the hanging up part and pushed the door of the phone booth open. In that single small movement, a row of raised, peach-colored slashes on her lower left arm, her oldest scars, shimmered like satin in the failing light. She started to walk back to the house, deliberate in her steps along the gravel shoulder. She surprised herself, not thinking of Cliff now, but of Ryan—her first serious boyfriend, the instigator of the scars.

They'd been sophomores at Ohio University and fallen hard for each other. She hadn't hade many friends, but it didn't matter when Ryan was around. Her classes had been hard, she had been flunking Econ 101 and not keeping up with her bio labs. Her mom would phone her to crab at her about wasting their money. But she had been able face it all with Ryan. Only with Ryan. Then one day he had said she was getting too clingy, too needy. Just like that. *Much too clingy. Much too needy.* He had started making plans without her. Finally, he'd broken it off. She was exhausting, he had told her, just too much work. He said he needed someone easier to be with.

Like *she* wasn't tired. Like *she* didn't need things to be easy.

When it was over, when the rejection was complete, she had to do something to ease the pain. She had felt compelled to replace that inner ache with something she could see—so efficiently done with a nice, shiny, sharp steak knife swiped from the cafeteria. She remembered that first time, being scared, but discovering how necessary it felt when the teeth of the blade had bit into her arm, how essential it had been to drain the exquisite poison of her misery.

Her roommate had found her, blood twining down her arms, streaks of burgundy staining her shirt and jeans. That had started the whole grand opera: her mother's constant worrying and the medication and the visits to Dr. Morton Willis. God, so excruciating, how hard he had tried to be cool, with his bell-bottom cords and his feathered hair and his acoustic guitar on which he strummed achy, cornball tunes, Bread and Carpenters and Seals & Crofts, between appointments. He had been the one who so helpfully had told her she was her own worst enemy. He had been the one who chirped the good news. Life is worth living! Don't seek a permanent solution to a temporary problem! Have a nice day! (*Smiley face!*)

What nobody got, not her sister or her mom or even the tiresome Dr. Willis, was that she hadn't been trying to kill herself. She simply had wanted to get some of the hurt out—or maybe just be the one to decide where she hurt and why.

After the incident, Hallie didn't return to OU. She had picked up clerical jobs, and somehow managed to bluff her way into the tiny marketing department at Kitchen-Brite Appliances in Columbus. And there had been other men. And it had been all so much work. She had run hot and cold, sometimes in rapid succession, babbling like a game show host and running around town one day, then taking to her bed, too low to lift her head the next. When she felt a guy start to pull away, she'd get even more anxious. Sometimes she forgot to take her pills, or took too many. Sometimes she cut.

She'd thought Cliff would be different.

Back at the house, she cracked open the second bottle of Smirnoff's and spent the rest of the evening in front of the TV in the bedroom, wondering if the Valium would be overkill. She still had no appetite. By the time the 11 o'clock news ended, she could feel herself sliding into unconsciousness again. She had turned over to click off the bedside lamp when she heard it.

A steady thumping.

As if someone was coming up the stairs from the beach.

Thump...thump.

It grew heavier and quicker, then stopped. Hallie realized she was holding her breath and let it out. Maybe it was Pete the fix-it guy? A minute or so passed, and then she heard what sounded like soft footfalls on the top deck. She forced herself to the window and peeked from behind the edge of the curtain in time to see just the top part of a dark shape disappear down the first flight of steps. Then the regular thumping resumed. Whoever it was, he was leaving.

It might have been just a neighbor, she assured herself. Edging back into the bed, she reached for the little bottle on the bedside table. Maybe just one Valium, she thought, to make sure of some sleep.

Hallie drank all the next day and ate very little. By 10 p.m., she was sitting in the little upholstered rocker by the sliding glass door with the curtain drawn. She had watched a rerun of *Medical Center*, and now the news was on. Just as the weather report started, she heard it again. *Thump…thump.* She got up, crawled behind the chair, and nudged the edge of the curtain aside.

There was a child, standing right there on her deck.

Hallie could see her in profile as she faced the glass door. She looked to be seven or eight, bone thin and drenched, as if she'd just come from a swim. Her white-blond hair curled in tiny tendrils just past her shoulders, with a small bit of sheer green seaweed tangled amid the strands. She was wearing a swimsuit, which might have been pink at one time. Even in the poor light of the deck, Hallie could see the suit was very dirty and worn. It had rows of tiny ruffles in the back, like the one Hallie wore when she was little. Looking at her face, she felt the pinch of the familiar.

Hallie emitted a small groan, and the girl jerked toward the faint sound as if it had been a clash of cymbals. Her eyes were very large, and the pupils were dilated into two perfect black circles, the size of M&Ms. Her skin was nearly translucent, and Hallie could see the veins at her temples and in her neck and arms. It reminded her of the inside of abalone shells, streaked with blue, green, and pink, and different depending on which way the light struck them.

What the hell? Hallie gripped the jelly glass in her hand. Maybe the girl had snuck away from her house to go down to the beach? Or, *Jesus*, maybe she'd fallen off a boat. Then again, maybe her parents had just abandoned her. There were plenty of poor folks just a short way inland. She certainly looked as if she hadn't been fed or taken care of. Hallie started to think that she should open the door and help, but something in her hesitated.

Her right leg began to ache from all the crouching, and she shifted her position slightly. Drawn by the movement, the girl moved closer. Her eyes grew even more huge, wet and bulging from their sockets, and her mouth dropped open, gaping impossibly wide. There was nothing in there, Hallie saw, just an endless black maw. The blue-and green-veined stick that was the girl's arm reached toward her, tiny fingers splayed with what looked like opalescent webbing between them at their bases.

"Jesus!" Hallie shrieked and fell back onto the carpet, the Smirnoff's in the jelly glass flying everywhere. The curtain flounced back into place, mercifully blocking her view of the deck. She puffed air through her nostrils like a steam locomotive gathering speed—too terrified to move, but at that moment, deathly certain that whatever the thing was would find a way in. She shook and puffed for another five minutes before she could work up enough nerve to peek on the opposite edge of the curtain. If she was still out there, Hallie couldn't see her.

Then, faintly, she heard the thumping again. Hallie pictured the girl heading back down the stairs, back to the beach, but she didn't really know where she was going. Or what, exactly, she was.

Hallie didn't call the police, but didn't take any Valium, either. If the bony girl-thing decided to come back, she didn't want to be so doped up she couldn't run or scream or something. But she wasn't going to do without the reassurance of Comrade Smirnoff. She crouched on the sofa in the living room and kept the bottle handy, drifting off, then jerking awake at least a dozen times through the night.

Finally, harsh sunlight intruded around the outer edges of the curtain on the sliding glass door. Rising tenderly from the couch, Hallie opened the curtain a few inches and squinted at the beach. The girl last night, *that thing*, had scared the shit out of her, but there was more to it than that. Somehow, it felt familiar. She realized she was still holding the vodka bottle and reached to place it on the coffee table in front of the couch. The glass table.

Then it clicked. The girl, that thing, looked like Angie. *Maybe it's her daughter*, Hallie mused. *Couldn't that be possible? Maybe they live nearby.*

Who might know that? Who still lived here who would've been around back in 1960? There was that lady from two doors down, the one in the white house who used to come around with homemade blueberry pies and jars of Methodist Women's Club salted peanuts for sale. She had even babysat for Hallie and her sister a couple of times when their parents wanted dinner out alone. What was her name? Betty? Bertha? She'd seemed like a beach lifer.

Hallie threw a light, long-sleeved shirt over the tissue-thin Ohio U T-shirt and jean cut-offs from the day before. Nobody gave a shit what anybody looked like at the beach, which worked just swell for her. Her head hummed as she pushed open the screen door on the side of the house. She descended the stairs and headed for the white house. The road was empty, the day again as hot as piss water for... whatever time it was. She didn't have her watch, but the sun was already pretty high.

She reached the lady's house—or what she hoped was the lady's house—and rapped on the aluminum frame of the screen door. "Anybody home?"

There was a short pause, then a silver-headed, heavyset woman in a faded housecoat and knee-high hose appeared. She cocked her head like a parrot and squinted at her. "Yes?"

"Um, hi. I'm not sure if you remember me. I'm Hallie. Hallie Gregg? My family used to come down here every year for a while. Two doors that way?" She jabbed a thumb toward her left.

"Er...I don't know..."

"We were the Greggs? From Ohio? You used to come and sell us food. You babysat my sister Gwen and me a couple of times?"

"Well, good night! I'm gettin' old. How long ago was that?"

"The last time we were here was fifteen years ago."

"Long ago as all that? Doesn't seem possible."

"I'm sorry to bother you, but I just wanted to ask you something... gosh this is awful, but I forgot your name."

"Bertie," she said, opening the screen door. "C'mon in. You want some iced tea, honey?"

"Miz Bertie." Hallie smiled. "Thanks. I'd love some."

The old woman led her into the kitchen and motioned for her to sit at her aluminum and Formica kitchen table.

"I'm sorry to come unannounced," Hallie said, "but my phone's on the fritz."

Bertie placed a glass of tea in front of her and took a seat. "That's all right. I enjoy the company. Now, what you been up to, dear?"

Hallie took a sip of the tea, sweet enough to make her teeth sing. "Oh, not too much. Just working and stuff. I'm still in Ohio."

"I see," Miz Bertie said. "How are your mom and dad and that nice sister of yours?" She dug into her pocketbook and pulled out a pack of Pall Malls and some matches.

"Gwen's fine. She's married now, and she's got two little boys. Mom's okay, too." Hallie moved a bit in her seat. "But I'm afraid my dad passed away. It's been almost five years. Cancer."

"Have mercy," Miz Bertie breathed, lighting the cigarette. "What kind?"

"Lung."

"Mmph." She took a hit off the Pall Mall, and her eyes followed the smoke as it wandered across the space between them. "Well, that certainly is too bad. He was a good man."

They stared at each other a bit, then Miz Bertie sniffed. "It has been a while, hasn't it? But I can still see you girls racin' around the beach." Her face broke into a wide smile, and she barked out a phlegmy laugh. "'Member how you and Gwen and Angie used to run into the water and bob up and down? Then you'd plop yourselves on the sand and spend hours on those castles."

"You remember Angie then."

Bertie's smile faded. "Well, she lived in the house right betwixt mine and your rental. At any rate, I ain't likely to forget that child."

Hallie pictured Angie's little hands blurring over the sand with her own, building castles for their imaginary families—huge, adventurous, improbably rich, yet somehow devoid of parents. Then they'd stand back and watch as the incoming tide destroyed their work, dismantling their dreams bit by bit. Angie, so slight she might just as easily have washed away. Angie, facing the ocean, planting her feet deep into the wet sand and waving goodbye.

"Miz Bertie," Hallie murmured. "Do you ever…hear from Angie? I mean, does she still come back here?"

Bertie's entire body sagged, and she dropped her head toward the Pall Malls on her lap. "Oh honey, it's been a long, long time. You didn't hear what happened to her?"

A bit of ice snaked up Hallie's spine. "No. What happened? Where is she?"

"She died, the poor little lamb. Fourteen years ago, so it must have been the summer after your family stopped comin' here."

"We wanted to come back. We did. It's just that my dad, he lost his job. We couldn't afford it anymore, and we…" Hallie swallowed hard. "How did she die?"

"She drowned, darlin.' Angie was playing down on the beach and her mama, she was watchin' her. Then she went up to the house to take some chicken out of the oven, and when she come back, the child was far out into the water—still had her sunbonnet on and still holdin' her little sand pail." Miz Bertie's eyes, large and brown as a Jersey cow, grew moist and her voice cracked a bit. "She called and called. She saw her head go under and then…nothin'. That woman couldn't swim worth a dang, so she called the rescue station right quick. Then she went for a few neighbors. I was one. We all searched, but we couldn't find her anywhere."

"But they found her eventually, didn't they?"

"They never did. Never even found the things she had with her— the bonnet and the pail. The coast guard and the rescue station folks searched up and down the coastline. They never found that child."

The sweet tea curdled in Hallie's stomach. *What* had been standing on her deck these past two nights?

"You all right, honey?" Miz Bertie asked in a kind voice. "It's terrible news no matter how long it's been. You girls were such good friends."

"It's okay. It's just…so sad. What happened to her parents?"

"Moved away. Can't really blame them. It'd be hard to wake up every day and look out over the thing that took your daughter. But then…I sometimes questioned whether they wanted her at all." Bertie took a slow drag on her Pall Mall. "They were…hard…hard people, and Angie was so soft and dear. Y'know, some folks just ain't cut out to be parents." Miz Bertie's cow eyes stared off, past Hallie, toward a window that faced Angie's old house.

Hallie forced down one more sip of tea, then thanked the old lady and headed back to the house. It was strange, she thought. Over the years, Angie had made an appearance in her mind only sporadically, maybe when she saw the ocean on TV or photos of Gwen's kids playing in the sand. In reality, they'd been together only a few weeks each summer, maybe two or three months in all. There had never been any contact—no letters, no phone calls—in between.

But how she'd died, the circumstances of her death, brought an immediate sense of profound loss. Hallie had been so young; she'd had no sense at the time what their friendship must have meant to Angie. But now Hallie could see it for what it was. It meant everything to know that she might have been, in some way, someone's lifeline, the bright spot of her existence, her joy. She'd never conjured any love like that since.

Outside now, in the bright, unambiguous sunshine, she reached the only conclusion she could about what she had seen: she'd gone out of her head. She recalled the one bit of advice from Dr. Willis that seemed even a little useful: *Don't let your mind create a situation that isn't really there.* Angie had seemed real, but she'd been concocted from Hallie's own ingredients: the mess with Cliff, the sentimental journey to the old beach rental, the vodka, the Valium. All things considered, she'd cooked up a pretty good ghost. Had scared the hell out of her, anyway.

What she needed to do was to keep a clear head, stay away from the Valium and give the Smirnoff's a rest, just for a night. She'd walk to the store, maybe get a six of Little Kings Cream Ale, even a bottle of wine. But just one. Those would have to do for today.

By 9, she had more or less stuck to her pledge. Okay, Hallie noted, it had been four Little Kings over the course of the day, but they were so ridiculously small. And it was two glasses of rosé, but she felt completely fine. She was nibbling a small turkey sandwich when she heard sounds on her deck. Bracing herself, she peeked from behind the curtain to see a small dog sniffing at the door.

Hallie exhaled. *Okay, I can handle a dachshund.*

Swishing the curtain aside, she unlocked the door and slid it open. The sharp-nosed intruder was on the sandwich right away. Beyond him, on the steps, a dark shape appeared. "Bismarck! Gol' dang it, dog! You come when you're told!"

It was Pete, stomping toward the dog but smiling broadly. He scooped the animal up in his arms. "Well, what do you think of that? Look whose house he decided to invade! He's got a mind of his own, like all wiener dogs."

Like all wieners, Hallie thought, giving Bismarck's back a polite pet. "It's alright. No harm done."

Pete's smile faded. "Miz Gregg? Do you feel alright? You look… very tired."

"I haven't been sleeping."

"Usually the beach is where folks sleep best. The tide, it tends to calm most people."

"I guess I'm not most people."

"Say, since I ran into you, let me ask. Would you like to go to the movies with me and my girl? We're going to see *Jaws* tomorrow night, the 7:30 p.m. show up at the Star Cinema."

"I don't think so, Pete."

"You sure? Terror on the beach!"

No. No more terror required at this time, thank you. "I'm sure. So, did you ever figure out how that pile of red algae got on my deck?"

"I didn't." Pete frowned a bit. "It shouldn't have been there."

"No, it shouldn't." *But, you know, sometimes stuff happens, and there's no explanation. Just a fluke. Just a goddamned fluke of nature. Nothing more.*

The two stood awkwardly for a moment, the dog panting between them. "Well, alrighty then," Pete said. "Good to see you. You try and get some sleep now. Fix you some warm milk—that always makes me drop right off." He held up one of the dog's plump paws and wiggled it. "Say good-bye, Bismarck."

Hallie gave the dog a weak wave and smiled. Standing there, listening to the two make their way back down the stairs, she didn't find her deck all that scary. *Sweet Pete, quite the coincidence he engineered.* She pictured him pushing Bismarck up the steps so he could follow and pretend to be mad. Next, she supposed, he'd be fixing her up with one of his pimply-faced student friends.

Hallie leaned on a railing and sniffed the night air with pleasure. A light breeze riffled through the seagrass on the dunes, and the sky was full of stars. She remembered how her family would come out here and look at the night sky. Her parents knew nothing about astronomy, but she and Gwen would pick out the different constellations and planets they'd learned about in school, and point them out.

She was outside maybe ten minutes when she noticed something moving on the dune next to the deck. The seagrass bent this way and that, and Hallie half-expected to see Bismarck snuffling back toward her. Instead, a pale figure crouched, then scuttled—like a crab— up the sand. It reached the railing and crawled through, making amazingly quick progress.

It was her.

Hallie didn't scream and didn't run back into the house. She found herself unable to move. *Maybe if I'm still, she won't see me.* Her eyes combed the girl's face, searching for Angie, the person she'd spent so much time with as a child. The girl, the thing, was wasted, almost skeletal, but now that she knew what she was looking for, Hallie could see her friend—even down to the small mark on her left cheek.

"Angie?" she whispered.

The child said nothing. Instead, she reached out a single spindly arm again and pointed toward the beach.

Hallie, though numb with terror, heard herself ask, "How…how did you know I was here?"

The girl motioned toward the upside-down sand castle flag undulating in the soft breeze. Then she looked back at Hallie, searched for her hand, and made contact.

Hallie cringed, but it was all the movement she could muster. The child's hand was smooth, wet, almost weightless, but solid. This was no ghost. She was real. Somehow, in some way she couldn't fathom, her friend still lived. Hallie felt the grip on her hand grow tighter. Then the girl tried to move forward, to head down the stairs toward the beach, just as she had led Hallie out of the house on so many mornings. Hallie still couldn't move—almost couldn't breathe—so her hand stayed where it was. The girl grew frantic now, lunging ahead, trying with her tiny body to drag her friend down the steps.

Hallie felt only the slightest pull.

Going nowhere, the girl emitted a grunt and looked back at Hallie. In an instant, it was the face from hell again, from the depths, the eyes alarmingly huge and the gaping maw yawning black and endless.

As if a spectator to the scene, Hallie heard herself shriek and saw their hands break apart. The deck, the railing, the starry sky all pinwheeled in front of her and then, with the *thunk* of flesh-covered bone meeting planked wood, it all stopped.

Hallie woke to screaming. Her first thought was that she was still shrieking, still falling with Angie—still gaping, still pulling—by her side. When she was able to lift her head, she saw that she had fainted—and spent the night—on the deck. Small shadows darted and interfered with each other on the wood boards, and she realized several gulls were congregating overhead. About a foot away rested the sad remains of her turkey sandwich. The gulls made tentative attempts to get closer to the food but were unsure how big of a threat she posed. Each try was met with more screaming, as if they were trying to egg each other on. Hallie stood, with effort, and tossed the sandwich over the deck railing. Sensing a safer bet now, the gulls lunged at the prize.

She shivered in the morning air. The wind had picked up overnight, and it shot the flag straight out from the pole. She recalled the white twig of an arm, a webbed index finger spiked upward. The flag—that's how Angie knew she was there. Who else flew a damn sand castle flag upside down? Only ridiculous, pathetic Hallie.

It was starting already, the noxious fog starting its creep behind her eyes, the start of the next inexorable slide down. In a few days, she would have to head back to Ohio, lonely, with nothing but the shit job. Would she do what she always did, take to her bed and draw her vodka and Valium to her? Would she find a nice, sharp knife in her kitchen?

Would anyone care? Anyone, that is, except for her mother and sister, who *had* to care, even when they'd long grown weary of that occupation?

Angie cared. She was still a child—tiny, weak—but she had done more than Hallie had, seen things she could only guess at. Her mind reeling, Hallie pictured Angie in what was now her natural habitat, Angie in a crazy, color-saturated cartoon, wafting through boundless walls of water, wandering the ocean floor, big pink plants and bright-orange coral and fish in brilliant blues and yellows all around, strange and beautiful flora and fauna the dirtbound never see. Perhaps plumbing the depths of the Gulf of Mexico, a bit of algae had stuck to her. This she brought with her, to leave on the doorstep of her childhood friend, a sign that there was much more out there than most people ever cared to think about. Angie desperately wanted to show her another way to live. Hallie's life—her stupid, empty life—had shown her nothing good.

Still light-headed, she went inside and stretched out on the couch. It was mid-afternoon when she woke again. She showered. She fixed her hair and put on a simple cotton dress. She took her time. She did not rush. When she was ready, she grabbed a chilled bottle of Smirnoff's and set up a folding chair on the top tier of the deck. Then she took a serrated steak knife from the kitchen drawer and sat down outside to wait for Angie.

By the time the girl made her way up the steps, Hallie was very drunk and her arms dripped crimson. Angie came to her side silently and reached for one of her hands. She seemed to examine Hallie's arm, and as she did, her face became soft and sad. She shook her head as if to say, *Please, no more.* Then she touched her index finger to her cheek, to the small scar there.

Through her fog, Hallie remembered. There had been a cut on Angie's cheek the last summer they played together. It was precisely the size of the row of tiny diamonds on her mother's wedding ring. Hallie recalled how Angie wanted to stay out on the beach all day. *Keep swimming,* she said, *keep building castles, stay outside, don't go inside. Inside is where bad things happen. Everything, everyone too close together.*

The years melted away, the chasm of time closed. They were again two girls on the beach, huddled together on a big striped towel, collecting seaweed, building castles destined for destruction. And at last, they were alike, even more than when they'd been small. Now they both knew loneliness. They both knew hurt. They both realized the brutal shortcomings of the world—this dry and arid wasteland right here. It was just too much work, and the people in it not worthy of them.

This time Hallie let Angie lead her off the chair. Her head swimming, she followed the girl down the stairs, step by step. She walked with her over the bumpy edge of the closest dune and over the cool sand that the outgoing tide had kissed just hours before. Soon they stood on the water's edge, the moon small but bright, plating everything in silver-blue. Hallie inched toward the water, felt the warm surge flood over her feet.

Now she knew what Angie wanted.

It seemed too big a step, and at the same time, so small a gesture no one might notice. Leaving would be such a relief, but Hallie was not so far gone that she couldn't see the finality of such an act.

In that moment, the world split in two. The wet and the dry. The light and the dark. The good parts and the bad parts. Up was down and down was up. Reason and emotion, divorced but still speaking, conversed between themselves.

I can't think about this today. I'll think about it tomorrow.

It is past midnight. It's already tomorrow.

Will anything be different in a day, a week, a year?

Nothing different. Just more of the same.

I'm scared.

You are not alone.

Am I ready?

Follow her.

Angie was almost past the breakers. Hallie watched her roll, sleek as an otter, in the waves, moving toward the open sea.

Stepping further into the tepid surf, Hallie didn't feel the water much. She was instead focused on Angie. She kept going. It was a slow march and her arms were raised, like a shell-shocked prisoner in surrender. She was nearly up to her shoulders when a wave broke over her, churning up much cooler water and a tangle of seaweed that laced itself around her waist. Her body felt heavy and inert, already succumbing. She thought of the water, taking her, covering her. Would she exist like Angie? Would she exist at all?

Another breaker swept over her head and it was like waking. The two halves of her mind joined again. *Wait! Wait! Think about this. Come back another night. You can't do this. You're not ready.*

Hallie thought these words, then realized she was speaking them too. Angie, treading in the deeper water, her tiny blonde head just visible above the waves, gave no sign that she'd heard. The surf was quiet, but the storm between Hallie's ears shrieked without ceasing. "I'm sorry!" she screamed. "I can't—I can't do this. I'm going back! I'm going back!"

She turned and started to slog back toward shore. She could see the yellow lights in the houses on the beach, the serrated line of rooftops under the moonlit sky. Angie was on her in seconds.

Now in her element, the feeble child became strong, a sinewy creature of the deep. Her arms became like iron-braced tentacles, wrapping themselves about Hallie's body. Angie drove her head close and placed her mouth at Hallie's ear, croaking a promise she couldn't make out but understood completely. This, the touch of one who loved her, who would never leave her, was what she had asked for, what she had always wanted.

Hallie felt the cold water start to deaden her limbs as Angie dragged her away from the shoreline.

XOXOX XOXOX XOXOX XC

About the Author

Elizabeth (Betsy) Allen holds a bachelor's degree in journalism from The Ohio State University, as well as a master's degree in English and an MFA in fiction writing from George Mason University. Somewhere in between those degrees, Allen worked in corporate marketing communications, public relations, and freelance writing and editing. She currently serves as a creative writing instructor for Writopia in Washington, D.C. Allen's fiction publishing credits include several short stories published in various genre anthologies, including *Twisted Yarns, Strangely Funny,* and *Southern Haunts.* She also is the co-author (with her brother Ben Small) of the graphic novel trilogy, *The End of Gath,* and is currently revising a novel that began as her MFA thesis project. At home in Alexandria, Virginia, Allen lives with her husband and two rarely cooperative but (fortunately for them) cute dogs. In her spare time, she indulges a tragic crossword puzzle addiction and frets about her two grown children and grandson. Find her on Facebook or Twitter (@WriterMuse).

HEROES

Jackie Logsted

My sister is a legend.

I've always thought so, but believe me, it's more than a younger brother thing; I can't remember a time when I didn't. When we were in elementary school, there were these huge trees in our backyard. Big and winding, twisting around each other, reaching for the sky. It was her idea to climb them. I was the one who fell. She threw herself down after me. "If you fall, I fall," she told me. She's never stopped telling me. I don't think she ever will. We'll be in rockers and she'll be screaming through my hearing aid, "If you fall, I fall!" When I was in middle school and getting picked on by some eighth graders, she told me that if they were ever bothering me, she was a call away.

The first time I called her, she showed up a period later to give the "little assholes" a piece of her mind. She rode there on her bike. From the high school. A mile away. In freshman year, I had my first relationship. He broke my heart. That's an understatement; he ripped me to pieces. I was in my room the night it happened, practically crying the soul out of my body. I didn't even know eyes could hold so much water. I'm not much of a crier; my friends like to joke that I'm "empty inside" since I'm not exactly the most transparent about my emotions. My sister came in, her hair wildly thrown on top of her head, a basket of white sheets in her arms. She put the basket down on the ground and lay next to me, both of us leaning against the light-yellow walls. I put my head on her shoulder and she played with my hair. After an hour, I got up to get some water and that was that. She spent the next two weeks covertly checking up on me when she was supposed to be finishing her college essays. Mom didn't like that very much, but Karen would say that "Mom can deal." She hasn't said that in a while.

I don't tell her how highly I think of her. I don't think I have to.

We live in one of those cookie-cutter neighborhoods where nothing bad ever happens. Houses face each other in a long cul-de-sac with our house at the tip, looking over everything that goes on around us. Behind our house is a forest that goes all the way to the school; you get the big, winding trees, some space, and then the world falls away. But the thing about our neighborhood is that no one ever talks to each other, and no one's really invested in each other's lives. We get holiday cards and wave if we drive by, maybe a little small talk here and there, but no one *really* talks to each other. It was always just me and Karen and Mom and Dad. That was always what it was until it wasn't.

Last August, right before the school year, Mom sat me and Karen down and told us she had cancer. Dad couldn't even stand to be in the room; I found him a while later, sitting alone in his study. He didn't say anything, and neither did I. Karen had to leave for college five days later. She's always been the one to take care of anything that needed taking care of. For the first time, I was the one left to deal with things. Less than a month later, Dad got sick, too. Some congenital thing. I don't even know.

Mom's first round of chemo was a week or so after Karen left, and every day was the same after that. Wake up. Check in on the two of them to make sure nothing went bump in the middle of the night. Brush teeth. Clothes. Ask if they needed anything. Kiss them goodbye. Go to school. Come back. And so on.

I was doing pretty badly in my classes, but I didn't tell Mom and Dad. When they asked about this test and that test, I told them it was fine, or I was still waiting to hear back. That made them pretty happy. Classes were awful. If Karen was around, she'd have made me tell them the second she realized what was going on, which would have been the first one, but she wasn't around. The pity was the worst thing for me. I couldn't handle the looks. But my friends were pretty good about everything. They'd skip with me.

The first few weeks, that's all I really did. Go to school, leave, come home, sleep, go to school, leave, come home, not sleep. We were in math one day. Our teacher was rambling on about cosines and angles, and I was sitting with my friends. I couldn't stop tapping my pencil. They were always around me now. Maybe they always were. I was in the middle, Jack behind me, Kyle to the left, and Ian to the right. And we all just got up at once. Everyone watched us go. But it's public school, so no one can do anything about it. It was one of the best moments of that whole time. In a regular week, it'd be no big deal; people skip class all the time. That week, it made me feel like a legend. After the first time, it was like that all the time. I could hear Karen's voice in my head, but it was just a voice.

I honestly can't remember a lot of what happened during those first weeks. It's all kind of a blur. I'd go out with the boys and do whatever. These are guys that I've spent my whole life with who I never really got to know until then. Ian is much more of an asshole than everyone thinks, Kyle is much less of an asshole than everyone thinks, and Jack is the guy you never know you need until you do. I can't remember what everyone thought of us before, but right then, everyone loved us. There are a few reasons why that was true. I had all of these people around me all the time but it got so fucking lonely. I still skipped classes, but I stopped skipping school with them after about a month, and they understood. They still went out at night, but I didn't join them. It didn't feel right not to be at home anymore.

I remember the first time I visited her in the hospital. The world stopped. I made excuses not to go back.

I got home one day after trying to visit her again. Dad was at work when school got out, and instead of crossing the street and walking through the woods that led to our house, I went in the other direction. I walked to the hospital from the school (only about a mile, give or take), made it all the way to her floor, all the way to her closed door, but still couldn't make it in the room. The first time I visited was with Dad. We stood there and looked at her while she slept. After the first time, this was the closest I ever got to being back in that room.

When I got outside, I saw that Jack had tried to get in touch with me a few times. I smiled, but put my phone away. I walked back the long way: through town, past the school, down the cul-de-sac, and to my house, at which I opened the door, knocking over two brand-new stacks of fruit baskets.

When someone's sick who you don't know too well, what do you do? Send a fruit basket. A muffin basket. A lemon meringue pie. What people forget is that if everyone believes the common courtesy is to send a fruit basket, we end up with forty-six fruit baskets. It was frustrating how ingenuine it was, but it was ingenuine because we didn't really know each other. I don't think most of our neighbors know our last name. And I never really cared about that before. I didn't care that my neighbors didn't care, because I didn't care that much either. You smile at your neighbors when you see them, but you don't have to really know them. Right now, though? I wish I did. I wish they knew us, too.

We were getting the baskets every day. At first, Mom would take them to the kitchen with feigned enthusiasm every morning, like clockwork. After a while, she stopped picking them up, and the stack grew right inside the door like that for weeks. On this day, I took them out one-by-one to the front yard, and lined them up on the curb.

Another week, and I got my first letter from Karen. It was always our thing, the letters. We started it when she went to sleep-away camp when I was in second grade, and from that point, whenever we were apart, we swore off any other mode of communication (plus Karen tried not to use cell phones, despite Mom's wishes). She sounded worried, but mostly like herself. *Bubba!!! How are you?!! In psych my professor told us about these kids that pulled social experiments in elevators and I'm thinking of you!!* Standard stuff. We kept corresponding like that for a while without talking about what was going on. I started telling her what life was like over here. Her letters started coming less frequently.

Once, I got home from school early—math was last period; I hadn't been in that room for weeks—and I was headed to the kitchen when I heard Mom and Dad in the study. She was crying. She never cries. "It makes me feel guilty," she'd say, laughing. That was Mom all over. The kind of person that would laugh when she was talking about crying. "It makes people feel bad. And the *last* thing I need right now is people feeling bad for me." They felt guilty about everything, especially Mom. I stopped to listen; she was choking out sentences to Dad. "He shouldn't be taking care of us; we should be taking care of him. Who's taking care of him?" I went up to my room, but I could hear her from there. I snuck out the window.

Onto the roof below my room, down the driveway, past the big trees, and into the woods behind our house. I pushed myself and pushed myself further and further away from the house until I couldn't see the lights of the cul-de-sac. I could only see the lights in the sky, and the trees towering over me. I stopped running in the middle of all those trees when I couldn't push myself anymore, and all of this angry energy was tensed up behind my eyes and in my fists. I was breathing heavy and fast. And then I was crying before I knew I was crying. And my phone started ringing.

I had a moment where I looked at it and kept looking at it. I almost didn't answer, but then I did.

"Hello?"

"Bubba?"

She was crying. How did I know she would be crying?

It was raining, and I watched a camera pan from my face to the top of my head to the top of the sky. Miles and radio waves away, the moment I fall, Karen falls, too.

Karen came back for Thanksgiving. For the past eleven weeks, Mom had been through three treatments of chemo, two weeks' worth of puking, eighty-eight days barely stepping foot outside our house, but between the two of them, Karen looked worse.

She left for a few more weeks and came home for Winter Break. She didn't go back.

Parents always say when they have more than one kid, that they could "never, *ever*, pick a favorite. It's not possible!" But I was Mom's, and Karen was Dad's. It wasn't by a large margin: the two of them loved us more than anything, there's no question. It never bothered either of us. It was just how it was. I was Mom's because of how similar we were. She'd say our hearts were "linked." Karen was Dad's because she was his first. Karen always thought Dad got sick because his heart broke when Mom did. I think Dad got sick because Karen left.

The first weekend Karen was back for good, we got an old green wheelbarrow and cleared out fallen sticks from the big trees in our backyard. When I was six, and she jumped out of those trees after me, all I could think was, "Man. She's a superhero." And ten years later, I'm looking at her tossing in branches, and her skin's got color again, and her eyes look like they used to. And she smiles at me and I know that she still is.

I don't know what's going to happen next. And I don't know what will happen after that, and after that, and after that. But who ever does? Eventually Karen will go back to college. And I want that for her. But right now I need her here, and I can see she needs to be here, too.

)O)O)( )O)O)( )O)O)( )(

About the Author

Jackie Logsted is a seventeen-year-old high school student in Western Connecticut. After publishing her first nine books—*The Sisters 8* Series—with her parents, she stepped out of the publishing world to focus on school, her music, her writing, and her other creative ambitions. She has continued to write and create a lot, recently earning herself a finalist position in a poetry contest for her piece "Godly." With "Heroes," Logsted steps back into the publishing world and could not be more excited to see where it takes her. This is her first solo publication.

THE MATING HABITS OF THE LATE-ADOPTING SMOKER

Dorianne Emmerton

Anna shivered, her coat too light for the early winter. She blew out a stream of smoke, rolled her cigarette between her fingers and shared a glance with the gray-faced man beside her. Wordlessly, they agreed that it was cold and nicotine was good.

Three months ago, Anna didn't smoke. It was unusual to start in your late twenties, she knew. You were supposed to start as a teenager, before you knew better. Anna had known better until recently.

For her twenty-seventh birthday, there was a party at a chic downtown lounge. Her best friend gave her a framed picture of the two of them back in university, Jennifer's pale, round face mugging for the camera while Anna smiled sweetly under tiny sister locks.

Monique didn't bring anything. The Facebook event listing had said "no presents," but Monique would have brought a gift anyway, except she had promised to stop antagonizing Istvan. Anna's boyfriend didn't like her friendship with her ex and was surly to Monique, even though she and Anna had broken up a decade ago.

Sometimes Anna teasingly called him "Istvan The Green-Eyed Monster." She tried to sound as if his jealousy was cute instead of annoying. She never asked him if he would feel differently if Monique were a man.

At her party, he'd looked gorgeous in a blue striped dress shirt with French cuffs. He'd given her a topaz necklace, and everyone sang "Happy Birthday," and she didn't pay for a drink all night. Earlier in the day, she had Skyped with her father and opened the present that had come in the mail: a beautiful statuette of a scorpion, her astrological sign. She didn't hear from her mother, but she hadn't heard from her mother since she was nineteen.

A few days later, she stopped being able to sleep.

She roamed her apartment at night, or Istvan's apartment if she was staying there. At first, she had kissed him goodnight, claiming she wasn't tired yet and would read for a bit. Night after night, she'd finish a book and start another, then grow bored and wander. Pacing out on the balcony, opening all the cupboards in the kitchen, excavating every closet before putting everything back the way she had found it, until dawn lit up the sky.

After two sleepless weeks, Anna decided to fight it. She went to bed with Istvan and initiated sex, energetic couplings that wore him out. But she didn't get worn out. She stared at his back as he slept.

She tried drinking a bottle of wine before bed every night. Then she tried a bottle of wine and a joint. She still couldn't sleep, but she liked how she felt.

One morning over breakfast, Istvan asked, "Did you finish that merlot?"

"Yes," she answered. "I was up for a while after you went to bed."

He squinted at her. "You look it," he said. "Tired. Your eyes have bags."

"Gee, thanks. You really know how to flatter a girl."

"Maybe you should see a doctor."

Her doctor prescribed medication. It didn't work, but she felt wonderful after a bottle of wine and a joint and a sleeping pill. She started leaving the apartment, walking around the streets at 1 a.m., 3 a.m., 5 a.m. Her feet barely felt the pavement. The city was so lit up, it was never too dark to see.

She saw raccoons fighting over the flesh of a dog that lay dead in the street where a car had hit it. The blood smelled like musky copper with an undertone of rare steak. She saw a man, a glint of metal tucked into his waistband, chasing after a woman wearing torn clothes. Over brunch on the weekends, Istvan talked about renting a cottage for a couple of weeks next summer, and did she know Mexx was having a sale?

She dumped him. She never slept. She walked all day and night.

Objects on the street were alive. Railings, garbage cans, telephone poles: everything had a shine, a glimmer of sentience. When she saw a thing that shone brighter than the rest, she talked to it. The object never answered back in words, but she could feel a pulse that grew stronger or weaker depending on what she said. She took stronger as a "yes" and weaker as a "no." She asked a telephone pole if the woman running the other night had been raped by the man. The pole pulsed stronger. She asked if the woman was still alive. The pole pulsed weaker.

One day she was talking to a park bench about the people who used it as a bed when she heard a young boy ask, "Why is that woman talking to a bench?"

His mother answered, "She has some mental health issues, dear. It's not polite to stare."

Anna pulled herself together. She returned home, took a shower, dressed in clean clothes, and went to work.

Apparently, she hadn't been at the office in weeks, hadn't called or emailed. They presented her with a payout. If she didn't want to accept, she could lawyer up—but she was out of a job either way. She took the check. It would only last a month or two. She had to snap out of this, get some sleep and a new job. But when she returned to her neighborhood, there was a dead pigeon on the sidewalk. She dropped to her knees to sniff it.

How many days had it been since she'd closed her eyes for more than a blink? Fifteen at least, maybe twenty, maybe more. In her living room, where objects did not communicate, she decided to see a psychiatrist if she did not sleep before the month was up. A few hours later, day turned into night, and the throbbing in her veins led her back out into the street. She forgot all about seeing a shrink.

One gloomy afternoon, while walking, she heard her name called out in Jennifer's voice. She hadn't seen her best friend since her birthday party. Had Istvan spoken to Jennifer, told her about the drinking and drugs? Istvan didn't know she no longer tried to trick her body into sleeping with substances.

"Anna, wait!" Jennifer yelled.

Anna sped up and took a series of turns. She couldn't get lost in this city, but she could lose people.

She discovered a twenty-four-hour coffee shop with a smoking section cordoned off beside the building. The nights were getting colder, and it was a good place to warm up during her walks. The pallid faces of the regulars became familiar to her, and she became familiar to them. An improbably skinny woman offered Anna a cigarette, and she accepted, her first smoke. It tasted bad but also good, like the first time eating mouldy French cheese. That initial hit of nicotine cleared the murk from her memory: it had been three months since her birthday party. Almost three months since she had slept. Two months since she lost her job.

She bought a pack of cigarettes.

Back at home, Anna looked in the full-length mirror. Her hair had noticeable streaks of grey twisted through her locks—that seemed new. Her skin was leathery in texture, like those white women who tan too much, except without the orange sheen. No, not orange: she looked distinctly ashy. She worked a small pile of moisturizer into her face.

She had lost a lot of weight, since she didn't eat anymore. Her comfort food used to be peanut butter and jam sandwiches, but they made her feel sick now. Peanuts loaded up with oil and pulverized, fruit loaded up with sugar and pulverized. Processed food; factories farting polluted smoke into the air to mass-produce enough to feed too many humans. Why not eat the protein that was easily available everywhere? She went walking and salivated at every dead squirrel.

At the coffee shop again, she smoked her fifth cigarette of the evening. She went inside between each for the warmth, but it was so much effort: going inside, sitting down, drinking a coffee, getting up, coming outside, smoking a cigarette. It was all so much work. Maybe she should go home.

When had she last paid her rent? She didn't want the landlord to change the locks, not with all her stuff there. She should still have money for one more month.

Anna had to go back, write a check, drop it off in the building's mailbox. She raised her hand to drop her cigarette, but the gray-faced man beside her said, "Don't you want to finish that." It was phrased like a question, but it wasn't delivered like one.

She *did* want to finish. A deep inhale burnt her lungs pleasurably, sent tingles down through her torso. She looked at the man to thank him with her eyes. His eyes, she noticed, had pupils like vertical slits. Her gaze still locked with his, she took another drag and thought she could feel movement in her own eyes. Like her pupils had adjusted to match.

Anna grew bold in where she ventured, especially after midnight. Nobody seemed to notice her presence, except for the gray, gaunt men and women at the coffee shop. She was invisible in the dark, except to her own kind.

This was her kind now: the people other people didn't see. One night Anna tested her theory, feeling fearless. Her heart didn't even change pace as she followed a man who was clearly on the lookout for followers—down the street and up the stairs of a building, silently slipping in the door behind him. In a dank apartment, he opened his bag to display automatic weapons. The men there gave him a stack of cash, and Anna counted it along with him. She stayed behind after he left to hear the group plan a drive-by shooting. The next night, she arrived at the appointed address to watch the murders happen, bodies strewn across the concrete driveway. She crept up and lapped at the warm blood with her elongated tongue.

At the coffee shop, the regulars sniffed her, smelled her meal, and smiled in approval. A gray man, probably the same one she smoked with last night, offered her a cigarillo. She accepted, and they stepped outside.

"A good night for you," he murmured, his voice a low hiss, but clearly audible to Anna's ears.

"Yesss," she agreed, noticing that she lingered on the end of the word. They finished smoking in companionable silence. When they re-entered the coffee shop, the man did not use his hands to open the door. He pushed it with a scaly tail that emerged from the slit in the bottom of his trench coat.

Under the fluorescent lights of the bathroom, she looked in the mirror. Her bones were even more pronounced than last time she had looked; she was a gaunt woman. She pushed her hand down the back of her pants to discover that her tail bone had grown a few inches. She could wag it.

Anna left the bathroom and ordered a coffee. Coffee, blood and cigarettes was all she needed; at least now she understood her new means of survival.

The sun came up in the sky. She decided to go to her apartment.

Istvan and Jennifer were in her living room.

"What is thisssss?" she whispered.

"We're worried about you," said Istvan.

"What's going on?" asked Jennifer. "I haven't heard from you in forever. You don't answer your phone, texts, emails, Facebook messages, nothing. I'm pretty sure you ignored me in person the other day. On purpose!"

"I'm fine," said Anna. "I've just changed some of my priorities."

"Obviously," said Istvan. "But your new priorities aren't so healthy."

"You don't look great," added Jennifer.

"How much wine are you drinking these days?" asked Istvan.

"Why didn't I get my apartment keys back when I dumped you?" Anna bared her teeth at him. "Give them. Now."

"Monique's worried, too," said Jennifer, and Istvan frowned. Anna took this opportunity to advance, pushing her nose up under Istvan's earlobe, her breath on his neck. He still wore expensive cologne. It was hard to smell his meat underneath.

"What are you doing?" Jennifer squealed.

Istvan didn't say anything, didn't move. She pressed her teeth lightly into his skin. They used to do this in bed. In the days before insomnia, she would fall into a sated sleep along with him, afterward. She should have known things were changing when she no longer felt lulled by their post-coital embrace. She should have had an idea after the time she found herself cleaning his skin from beneath her fingernails with her tongue.

Her tongue was forked now, the product of a slow metamorphosis that had started way back then. She flicked its two tips against Istvan's tender neck. He didn't flinch, but a tear fell down his cheek.

Jennifer started talking at a breakneck speed. "We've been friends for a million years, and you were there for me when my Dad was sick, when my cat died, and you watered my plants while I was on vacation, I love you and if something's wrong you can tell me, I will always be there for you, like you have been for me..."

Anna could vaguely recall all the things Jennifer mentioned. The cat who had cancer, the father who had cancer, the jade and spider plants. But Jennifer also smelled delicious. She was a fat woman with a lot of juicy bits that would be good to sink your teeth into.

Who should she eat first? Her best friend or her boyfriend? She hadn't known that she would evolve to this level, but now she was glad to have such significant victims for her first kills.

Anna reached up under Istvan's shirt, scratching his back like she used to in bed. Her nails were talons now, an inch long each and thick like the claw end of a hammer. Jennifer turned for the door, but Anna caught her with her other hand and pulled them both in close. Their hearts were beating at three or four times the placid pace of Anna's own. The harder their blood rushed, the better it smelled.

There was a knock on the door. Jennifer sobbed.

"Are you expecting sssssomeone?" Anna hissed.

"Yes!" Jennifer said. "Monique, she, she you know, cares too. Istvan didn't want her here, but I did, so I said I'd text if things were going really badly, and she shouldn't come, but I—I—I never texted."

Not even fear for her own life could stop Jennifer from talking too much.

Monique was here. Would the addition of a third person who was still human bolster them to try an attack, an escape? Could she defeat three, even with her enhanced strength? And if she won, could she eat three people? She wouldn't want any of their flesh to go to waste. They were the three people in the world closest to her, after all.

Her freezer would keep the leftovers fresh.

Anna pulled Istvan and Jennifer around the wall so they couldn't be seen from the front door. Jennifer sobbed. Anna cut a hole in the seam of her sagging jeans with the diamond-sharp tip of her tail. The tail, now fully grown, wrapped around Jennifer's arm and pressed the tip to her throat.

"Make another sssound and you will die firssst," Anna hissed. "Besssties forever!" she added with a grin, displaying her jagged teeth. Then she called out, in an approximation of her old, full-throated voice, "Come in!"

The door opened with a creak and shut with a click. The soft sound of Monique's footsteps came closer. With Istvan firm in one hand and Jennifer held with her tail, Anna's free hand snapped out to catch her former girlfriend in an instant. But Monique didn't look scared. The tight curls of her red hair bounced as she looked Anna up and down. Monique smiled, her top two teeth showing adorably. Anna had always loved that smile.

Couldn't Monique see what was going on, Jennifer's fear, Istvan in shock? Anna opened her mouth and blew fetid breath at Monique. She just smiled more. Anna sniffed all around Monique's face, her neck, the row of buttons down her shirt, her crotch. She smelled good, but not good like food. The others smelled like a meal. Monique smelled like a garden after a rain shower.

Anna dropped her tail and arms, freeing her two captives.

Jennifer started crying again.

"Go!" Anna snarled.

Jennifer fled from the apartment.

Monique stepped forward and caressed Anna's scaly cheek, staring into her eyes. Anna saw the pupils across from hers lengthen and thin until Monique's were as vertical as Anna's. A thin, forked tongue slipped out of Monique's smile, and Anna saw that her two top teeth still protruded adorably, but they were now razor sharp and dripping with saliva.

Istvan was standing frozen, his face blank. Anna hissed in his direction, but her heart was no longer in it. She was glad that he was terrified, but she was not going to eat his face. Not today.

"Should we keep him for a meal later?" she asked Monique.

"No," was the firm answer. Monique grabbed Istvan's face in her talons, only an inch between them. "You had a horrible fight with Anna today. She insulted your pride, and now you hate her and never want to see her again. Jennifer was here with you for a short time, but had a breakdown. You're afraid for her mental health. Now go."

Istvan stumbled out the door. The two women circled each other, sniffing and laughing breathy, high pitched laughs.

"When did you change?" asked Anna, wondering if they had been going through the same thing at the same time.

"Long before I met you," answered Monique. "I'll show you how to hide it, how to switch between our disguise, and our true form. This will be easy; you have always been an excellent learner."

"Did you...give it to me? Some kind of sexually transmitted infection that's been dormant all this time?"

"Blame your mother for that. She was a late changer, too. She had you long before she had any inkling."

Anna stopped moving, suddenly filled with that old hurt, the emotional weight of her teenage devastation. Her tail withdrew up into her spine, her talons, teeth and tongue reformed to their human shape.

"Is that why she left?" Anna slumped into a chair.

Monique also transformed, once again wearing the pale skin and arched eyebrows that Anna used to wake up beside. Monique sat on the arm of the chair and took Anna's hand into her own. "I'm sorry. I should have planned out how to tell you better. There's been enough time—I've been waiting so long! Watching you date Istvan, that's been unpleasant. He's not good enough to be an appetizer. Not for you."

"My mother?" Anna asked.

"I'll take you to her. She's been waiting too, ever since I found her and told her that you were one of us. When she left your family, she was hoping that the gene wouldn't pass on, but by the time I sniffed her out, she had come to her senses and was glad to hear the news. She wants you back in her life.

"I wasn't sure myself when we started dating; the smell was so faint. Maybe you were just a carrier and would never hatch. It was when we went spelunking that I knew."

Anna chuckled reflexively. The word "spelunking" had always made her laugh, especially after their date in the caves, back in university.

Some jocks in the cafeteria had made a crack about "spelunking," referring to sex between two women, and Monique and Anna had adopted it as a pet term. One weekend, they took a trip and stayed at a B&B near a touristy cave location, the same place where the movie *Quest for Fire* had been filmed. They snuck in illegally after hours, and touched each other, surrounded by damp rock.

"Remember the flashlights?" asked Monique now, stroking her hand, her arm, her hair.

"No," answered Anna.

"Exactly."

Anna remembered that they hadn't taken flashlights. But she had still been able to see.

"You let me break up with you?" Anna asked.

Monique shrugged. "You were pretty determined. I could wait." She bent over, speaking her words hot in Anna's ear. "Lizards live a long, long time."

"You're not like the coffee shop people," Anna stated.

"Those sallow fools? No. You are like me, like your mother, full of color, of fire and glory. Those salamanders have no potential, so they are sucking yours up with every smoky breath you take in their dismal place. They still eat like you have until now, lapping at the remnants of death like a starving puppy dog. But you are ready for more. You are ready to hunt."

Monique stood and grew up, up, up, easily seven feet tall. Her skin retracted to display iridescent green scales, like a coating of emeralds. Anna stared at the ridge of Monique's brow so far above her and willed herself to look the same, not gray but brilliant green. Monique reached a talon down to Anna, who took it, and stood, and grew.

She caught up to Monique, and both their heads brushed the ceiling, their human-sized clothes ripping to pieces. They put their mouths together, breathing humid air back and forth, licking pointed teeth. They sunk their claws into each other and lay down heavily, destroying the furniture with the thrashing of their limbs.

"What do we do now?" asked Anna in the aftermath. Then she confessed, "I'm hungry."

"You will never sleep again," Monique promised, nuzzling the tiny orifice of her ear. "But you will eat. There are many bad people in the world. Tell me about one of them."

Anna told her about the telephone pole confirming the man she had seen was a rapist and a murderer. She could remember what he smelled like.

He was Anna and Monique's first real meal together.

✕◯✕◯✕ ✕◯✕◯✕ ✕◯✕◯✕ ✕

About the Author

Dorianne Emmerton is a theater reviewer, radio show host, and writer. Recent publications include stories in the anthology *Friend. Follow. Text #storiesFromLivingOnline* and Issue #1 of *Beer and Butter Tarts*, as well as a personal essay in *A Family by Any Other Name: Exploring Queer Relationships*. She is currently working on a science fiction collaboration with Ottawa band Saturnfly. She lives in Toronto.

STIKINI

Travis D. Roberson

The hooting came in the middle of the night and echoed through the hotel room. Lloyd lifted his head from the pillow. For a long time now, his mind had been drifting through the strange purgatory between consciousness and sleep, where time moves like a shadow and the world seems a fog. But the hooting brought him out of it.

One lonesome bar of moonlight slipped through the curtains, illuminating what little bit was left inside the Jim Beam bottle on the bedside table, highlighting the naked shoulder of the Seminole girl sleeping next to him. She hadn't drunk nearly as much as he had, and she seemed completely undisturbed by the hooting, as if it weren't there at all.

He pulled open the bedside table's drawer, took out the Beretta resting inside, and racked a bullet into the chamber. He walked over to the window, made a small opening in the curtains, and took a peek. It was quiet again. The hooting had stopped.

Lloyd scanned the street down below, all awash in the grainy orange of streetlamp.

Nothing.

He let the curtain go and made for the bed but stopped. Had he heard it again?

He pulled back the curtain. Down below, across the street, stood what looked like a woman. Her defining qualities were obscured in silhouette, but Lloyd could see she was short and stout, maybe old. She was staring up at him, but she didn't move. He kept his eyes on her.

A raspy voice came from the bed. "What're you doing?"

"There's a lady out here," Lloyd said.

"So?"

"You hear that owl earlier?"

"Huh?"

"Few minutes ago. There was an owl. Sounded like it was right outside the window."

"You're drunk, man."

"She's still there. Just starin' at me."

"Probably cuz you're staring at her."

"No," he said. "There's somethin' that ain't right about it."

"You sure whiskey's the only thing you've had tonight?"

"Come here an' look at her."

She sighed. Lloyd heard her footsteps coming across the carpet. She pressed her naked body against his back, wrapped an arm across his chest, and propped her head against his shoulder.

"Where?" she said.

"Right—shit." Lloyd ripped the curtains open all the way. His head snapped in every direction, looking for the woman.

The girl, laughing, went back to bed. "You need some sleep."

"Yeah."

Lloyd stayed at the window, holding the Beretta and watching. After a while, he got back into bed, put the gun away, and closed his eyes. As his mind began to slip back into that quaint interim it had occupied earlier, he thought he heard the hooting once more.

He woke sometime in the late afternoon, his stomach weak and his breath rank with yesterday's whiskey. He turned over. The girl was gone, rumples in the sheets the only remaining proof of her existence. He tried hard to remember her name. Something with an L. Lisa?

He reached over and grabbed his cigarettes off the bedside table. He lit one and laid there, smoking and wondering if what he'd seen last night was just a conjuration of his mind or something more.

He'd made it his job and his purpose to run down the darkness in the world. Not the criminals and the drug dealers, but the more unnatural hauntings, the things that existed beyond the limits and comprehensions of mortal man. The things that shifted in shadow and used darkness as a camouflage to continue their existence in a time when man had turned its eyes from such grim realities and stories. The things that claimed home and right to the world long before humanity had taken its current form, the forebears and progeny of metaphysical and mythological gloom.

It was a pursuit he had started some time ago. It had shattered his grasp on the world and opened a hideous door to a new concept of what the world bore and what roamed through it. He'd hunted darkness to its depths, and it had driven him further down whiskey bottles and to the tethers of his sanity. It was becoming hard to know what was real and what was a product of his brain playing tricks. The things Lloyd hunted had given him a third eye, something that glimpsed beyond the veil of the natural world—but often times it seemed filtered through a kaleidoscope lens.

When the sky turned pink and orange with the sunset, Lloyd gathered up his things and left the hotel room, going out into the Florida heat. He'd been to Florida before but never this far south. He'd come here to hunt down what most would call a ghost, but what he simply considered a nuisance.

It was its own world down here, nearly its own country. He didn't care for it, didn't care for Florida much at all. Beyond a guise of beaches, sunshine, and orange trees was a land haunted and inhabited by too many strange things. Florida came with its very own skeletons, its unique breed of demons.

Lloyd loaded his things into the truck, dropped the Beretta into the glove box, and pulled out onto the main road. He pointed the truck north and headed out, back home to Alabama.

The truck's headlights cut a path through otherwise impenetrable darkness, swerving a little every time Lloyd reached for the Jim Beam. The sharp fumes of the bourbon provided momentary relief from the heavy stench of swamp that managed to infiltrate the inside of the truck even with the windows up. Sad country tunes were coming from the radio, songs that made Lloyd feel closer to home.

This continued a while, until something began to interrupt the twangy guitars and voices singing in thick drawls. He reached over to the radio and turned the volume knob until the music was a fuzzy whisper and listened.

The hum of the truck's engine.

A nocturnal symphony of crickets and frogs.

Then, there it was.

Hooting, loud as ever, as if it were right behind Lloyd's ear, bouncing around in his skull.

He kept listening, kept driving. The hooting faded back into the night, and everything with it went silent, as if the sounds of the entire region had been abruptly devoured through a vacuum.

Lloyd kept his eyes on the road ahead, listening to the silence—listening to nothing. Even with such attentiveness and focus on the road, he never saw the owl coming. It appeared in the glow of the headlights, wings spread, gliding towards the windshield.

Lloyd shouted and jerked the steering wheel, throwing the truck into the tall sawgrass and swamp water that bordered the road. He threw the truck in park, reached under the seat where he had the shotgun strapped, and brought it into his hands. He popped open the truck door and pumped the shotgun as he stepped outside.

Swamp water splashed over his boots as he marched toward the road. He walked into the red haze of the truck's brake lights and scanned the darkness. Out in the middle of the road, standing perfectly still, was the woman he had seen from the hotel window, cloaked once again in night's shadow.

She stayed there, watching him.

Lloyd aimed, fired.

Sparks sprayed from the road where the shotgun blast blew a hole into the concrete. The woman was gone.

Lloyd heard the hooting behind him, spun around, pumping the shotgun, but nothing. The vacancy of night. He heard a peculiar sound, looked up, and saw an owl fleeing across the sky, moving too fast to hit. He lowered the shotgun and walked back to the truck.

Jim Beam was spilled all over the seat as a result of his abrupt maneuvers behind the wheel. He swore under his breath, sitting down in a puddle of bourbon, and closed the door. He set the shotgun across his lap and fished a cigarette out of his shirt pocket.

Once he had the cigarette lit, he took a long drag on it, leaned his head back, and closed his eyes. Six years he'd been hunting the creatures that subsisted in the void between reality and whatever waited beyond life's end. He'd convinced himself that he had a relatively broad understanding of these entities, but he rethought that now. Whatever was hunting him, he had never encountered such a thing before.

Lloyd opened his eyes. Pressed against the window was the face of the old woman, her eyes shining through the darkness. Eyes that weren't human: sharp yellow eyes belonging to that of an owl.

Lloyd leapt back as a talon-tipped hand smacked the window. He fired the shotgun. The window exploded into a torrent of shards, flinging in every direction like a belligerent downpour of hail. The woman tore away from the truck, shrieking with a noise that was neither animal nor human.

Lloyd reached behind him and opened the passenger door. He stumbled out onto the road, where the woman was doubled over and still shrieking. The sound tore through Lloyd's ears, scrambling his thoughts and senses. The woman staggered into the headlights.

Where the shotgun blast hadn't mutilated her, Lloyd saw brown skin speckled with age. Her hair dangled over her face in long, tangled streaks of silver. She shuffled towards Lloyd, those owl eyes catching him again.

For a moment, there was no more shrieking. The woman's mouth opened, and behind her teeth and tongue, Lloyd saw what looked like a beak. The shrieking came louder now, a sharp and unforgiving explosion of noise that knocked Lloyd backward. He felt something slash his neck, followed by the slithering warmth of blood.

The shrieking died away. Lloyd turned to the sky and saw an owl moving toward the moon as it was gradually revealed through a curtain of clouds.

Lloyd pulled the truck into the bar's gravel parking lot. Warm air rushed through the opening where the window had been. There were still shards of glass that Lloyd hadn't cared to clean up littering the floorboard.

He parked near the front door, took the Beretta out of the glove box, stuck it in the back of his pants—not bothering to hide it—and went inside.

There she was, pouring a shot of whiskey from behind the bar: the Seminole girl that had shared his bed two nights ago. The shot she poured was for the only other person in the bar, a sad-looking old man—the only type found inside a bar at two in the afternoon.

Lloyd took a seat on the end farthest from the old man. The way she looked at him, Lloyd knew she remembered who he was.

"You look like hell."

"Yeah. Well. I feel even worse."

"How'd you get that?" She tapped her finger against the side of her neck.

Lloyd raised his finger to the bandage. He'd almost forgotten it was there. "It'd take a bit of explainin'."

"Uh-huh. Bourbon?"

"No. Not right now."

"Well, I'm working right now. Anything else you want is gonna have to wait."

"Yeah," Lloyd said, "you look real busy."

"Did you come here just to piss me off?"

"No. Look, I'm sorry. The other night—you mentioned somethin' to me 'bout your grandad. You remember that?"

She gave him a strange look. "Yeah. Why?"

"I think I might need to talk to him."

She laughed a little. "You know, when I said he was a medicine man, I didn't mean he waves sticks around and scares off ghosts and shit, right?"

Lloyd leaned forward and took her wrist. "Please. I just wanna talk to him."

She drew back from him. "Shit, man. You sure you're all right?"

"I don't really know anymore."

Lloyd was right: her name *was* Lisa. They took her car onto the reservation, down a narrow, unpaved road carved through a maze of swamp and cedar trees, and arrived at an ordinary trailer resting beneath the dismal shade of a palm tree.

Lloyd got out and followed her up the trailer's steps. She rapped on the door, and it opened shortly after. An old man with long gray hair and skin like worn leather stood before them.

"Grandpa," she said, "this is the guy I called from the bar about. His name's—"

"Lloyd," he said, holding his hand out to the old man. "Lloyd Barnes."

"Most people around here call me Gran," he said, shaking Lloyd's hand. "Come on. Come inside."

Lloyd followed Lisa into the trailer. They took a seat on a worn-out couch, and Gran eased into a recliner on the other side of a cluttered coffee table.

"I don't usually discuss my practices with people outside the reservation, but I'm doing it as a favor to my granddaughter."

"I appreciate it," Lloyd said.

"So what is it? Drinking?"

Lloyd shook his head. "No. Nothin' like that." He looked up at Gran. "You know anythin' 'bout owls?"

"Owls?"

Lloyd nodded. "Owls."

He described to Gran the woman he had seen outside the hotel, the hooting that had followed him, and his experience out on the road.

"Jesus, man," Lisa said. "I think you're having a mental breakdown or something."

Gran raised his hand to her and walked over to the window. He pulled open a space in the blinds and watched outside for a while before returning to the recliner. The sternness in his face had retreated and been replaced by a look of discomfort and fear.

"What brought you here?" he asked. "To Florida?"

"I was after somethin'."

"You've been walking a line through dark things. Things I don't think you understand."

"I might not understand 'em, but I know they ain't good. I know they shouldn't be here."

"What started you on this...mission? To get rid of the world's darkness?"

Lloyd stayed silent for a while. He felt Gran's and Lisa's eyes on him.

"I served in 'Nam. I saw somethin' when I was over there. Somethin' I still can't rightly explain. I watched this thing kill men—men that had exchanged fire with Viet Congs and dodged land mines. Killed 'em like they were nothin' at all. Like they were just deer or somethin'. Ever since then, I knew there were things out there in the world more vicious—more deadly—than anythin' the war had ever shown me. More dangerous than any man."

"You think you can hunt these things?"

"I've done all right so far."

"You were chasing the darkness then. But now it's chasing you."

"I just need to know what it is," Lloyd said. "How to get rid of it."

"I can't say its name out loud. That'll bring it to my door."

Lloyd reached into his back pocket and pulled out a crumpled receipt from a liquor store. He unfurled it and laid it amongst the clutter on the coffee table.

"Write it down then."

Gran stared at him for a moment, sighed, and pulled the piece of paper closer. Lisa dug a pen out of her purse and handed it over to her grandfather. Gran leaned in and wrote something down on the receipt. He handed it back to Lloyd.

Lloyd examined the word scribbled in blue ink:

STIKINI

Lloyd folded the receipt and slid it back into his pocket. "So," he said, "how do I get rid of it?"

"I don't know how you brought it on you," Gran said, "but it's looking for a heart. That's what they go after, what they feed on. They take the shape of the person they used to be. They wear their past selves like shells. To get rid of it, you have to get rid of a piece of who it once was."

"How do you reckon I do that?"

"You have one advantage," Gran said. "You've hurt it."

"Any place I should start lookin'?"

"You're the hunter, aren't you? Track it like you would any wounded animal."

Lisa drove Lloyd back to the bar. Before he got in his truck she said to him, "I don't really know what the hell's going on. But if you don't end up dead in the next few days, you come and get a drink on me or something. You're in a bad way, man."

Lloyd brought the truck to the side of the road. He could hear glass from last night's encounter crunch beneath the tires as the truck slowed to a stop. He unstrapped the shotgun, made sure the Beretta was sturdy in his pants, and got out.

He walked to the other side of the road and set off through the sawgrass in the direction he saw the owl fly the night before. The sun was sinking into the western rim of the world, casting an orange glow that made everything seem on fire.

Lloyd carried a flashlight in his pocket for when it got dark, but didn't need it to find droplets of blood scattered through the sawgrass. He followed the trail the droplets made, moving in zig-zag patterns, sometimes turning around and going the direction he'd come only to turn around again. Eventually, he came to gaps in the brush where it had been trampled down and coated in blood.

He followed these clearings as daylight finally surrendered to darkness. Weak clouds streaked across the sky like strands of cigarette smoke, the moon glowing with a strange electric quality that gave a certain halogen haze to the sky.

He took the flashlight out of his pocket and clicked it on. The trail of blood shimmered in the beam of light, leading Lloyd to a large oak tree draped in moss.

The tree seemed out of place among all the sawgrass and occasional palms. He knew this was the place he needed to be. He clicked the flashlight off, a wide swath of moonlight falling upon the oak as if it were the centerpiece in a stage play.

Lloyd only waited a few minutes before he saw the woman. She came crawling out of the grass on her hands and knees, shuffling under the shade of the oak. She seemed completely unaware of Lloyd's presence.

He watched as her mouth wrenched open and a narrow hook-shaped beak slid out past her lips. The beak opened, and the woman started to make retching sounds. A cascade of blood spilled from the beak, and following it came a winding, sinuous pile of intestines. Lungs and other such organs followed, until there was a giant mound of viscera and innards piled before the woman like some grotesque vigil to death itself.

One last thing came from the beak.

Lloyd recognized it as a heart.

The woman caught it in her hand, a hand that now looked more like a bird's foot, the fingers transformed into talons. She carried the heart and placed it in a hole in the center of the oak.

Lloyd knelt down in the sawgrass and watched the woman carry each piece of herself to the tree, placing the organs in a circle around the tree's base, hanging the intestines from the branches as if they were ornaments.

"All right," Lloyd mumbled to himself. He kept his eyes on the woman, pumped the shotgun, and rose to his feet. "Wait—"

He spun around. The woman stood before him. She raised an elongated, feathered limb and brought her talons across Lloyd's face. He toppled backward and dropped the shotgun. He pawed the ground for it, blood spilling into his eyes and blinding him.

The shrieking started. Lloyd gasped as he felt the talons stab into his chest. They pushed through his skin, tunneling through the muscle and to the bone, going toward his heart. He would have cried out, but he was silenced as the woman's beak pushed into his mouth.

He choked and gagged on the beak. It stretched his mouth wide as it pushed further down his throat. He felt immobilized, slowly choking as the talons progressed to his heart, blinded by his own blood. He wondered if this was how it was always destined to go, finally hunted himself. He just wished it wasn't so painful.

No.

He gained control of his arm, thrust it underneath him, and wrapped his fingers around the Beretta. He pulled it loose and placed it against what he believed to be the creature's head and pulled the trigger.

The creature howled. He felt blood and feathers rain down on his face. The beak was out of his mouth and the talons left his chest. He scrambled to his feet and wiped the blood from his eyes.

The creature was before him, more birdlike than human now, staggering and shrieking, blood spilling down its face.

Lloyd unloaded another round into it. It shrieked louder and stumbled backward. He spun around and ran for the oak tree. He saw the shotgun laying in the grass and dropped down to grab it.

Talons caught him in the shoulder. He screamed and kept screaming as they tore down the length of his back. He fell forward. The talons closed around his head, slicing through his scalp and bearing down on his skull.

He could see the oak tree with one eye. He stretched his arm out before him, taking hopeful aim at the hole in the center of the tree where the heart rested. He fired.

The creature went to shrieking again. Its talons pulled from Lloyd's head. He rolled over and watched the avian qualities fade from the creature, returning to the woman it had once been.

The woman continued shrieking as Lloyd watched the color drain from her skin, fading to a sort of sickly gray. The skin withered and ripped, and soon there was no shrieking at all, just a pile of bone and feathers.

Lloyd returned slowly to his feet. He fought against the temptation to fall back down. He turned around and looked at the tree. The organs and entrails decorating it were gone.

Lloyd nodded, turned, and set out for the truck.

He was somewhere far from lucidity when he pulled the truck up to the bar. He looked into the rear-view mirror and took assessment of the deep slashes in his face and the dried blood that left him more red than white.

He opened the truck door and got out slowly, the blood from the slashes in his back making him stick to the seat. He hobbled toward the bar and through the door. It didn't seem open yet, but she was there, rinsing out glasses and setting things up.

She saw him coming toward her, her mouth hanging open as she watched him slump against the bar, and collapse onto one of the stools.

Lloyd looked up at her. "Reckon I'll take that drink now."

XOXOX XOXOX XOXOX X

About the Author

Travis D. Roberson grew up in Central Florida. His work has been featured in *Ontologica, The Eunoia Review, Title Goes Here:, Local Ghosts,* Zimbell House Publishing's *Dark Monsters,* and a few other places. He was the third-place award recipient in the 2011 Porter Fleming Literary Competition.

THE FATE OF THE WORMS

Page Sullivan

The sound of falling rain on the windshield is white noise, blurring my thoughts along with the dripping, painted picture of the outside world. The rain draws out life. Worms led to die, sun-dried on petrichor-scented pavement. Drops persistently fall on my car, making that hollow sound. Water determined to lure the living things with beating hearts out of the belly of the metal-shelled beast with gasoline running through its veins. The rain's slippery fingers strike my umbrella. Sounds of a drum circle surround my house. Maybe if the liquid, jeweled fingerprints of rain did lure us out to face true humanity instead of what it has become, we'd be unable to hide behind an idolized image, under man-made skies, far from the truth.

Our fate would be no better than that of the worms.

XXXX XXXX XXXX X

About the Author

Page Sonnet Sullivan is 14 years old and created her first collection, *Song Poems*, a micro-chapbook, through the Origami Poems Project at the age of six. She is the youngest member of Ocean State Poets. Page has read her work at Newport Public Library's Summer Solstice Open Mic and Java Madness Coffee House. Page's essay, "The True Spirit of Christmas," won Third Place in The Newport Daily News's 2015 Holiday Spirit Essay Contest and was subsequently published.

Ignorance Is

Rhonda Zimlich

Steadying herself near the edge of the fire escape on the fourteenth floor, Rainy Marriski dared to look down at the place she guessed she would hit, a grey rectangle of sidewalk darker than the neighboring sections.

Her stomach lurched at the smallness of the street below. Gripping the railing, she lifted her eyes to the horizon, scanning the erect blocks of skyscrapers and the silvery harbor beyond, and fought the tug of a sudden updraft, her wings tucked close to her back.

Yes, she had wings. Giant, awkward, cumbersome. Each wing was more than six feet long with a featherless span of mottled, flesh-colored latex. When she extended them—which she rarely did—they stretched across the room. They protruded above her head by a foot when she stood straight. The membranes trailed behind her like a veil, as close to a bridal train as she might ever know.

What if the wind caught her wings just so? What if she were strong enough to pull their span outward against the fall, to at least glide? But the reality of her predicament crept back. She was a freak of science now; that was all she could be. When she climbed out on the ledge, she knew she was done pretending. She had lost the hope of flight. She had lost many things. But she still clung to curiosity. As morbid and terrifying as it had become, curiosity seemed to be the one thing she had left.

Sharp gusts of wind came in sporadic bursts, then fell to hushed whirls as the sounds of the traffic below filled the audible void. The cold, smog-choked air of the city pulled and pushed at her form. Tears chilled as soon as they formed then rolled downward to match the numbness of Rainy's cheeks. The railing where her hands gripped had become slick with her palm sweat. Her fingers ached. She returned to the idea over and over again of surrendering to the urge to let go. She felt fleeting optimism to overcome and allow her desire to fly to replace the regret and terror. But success might be worse now. She had climbed out onto the ledge following a sense of escape, not to take to the air—and certainly to be gone before Gary would return. But once out on the ledge, she found herself fixed with fear and gripped with heartache. Or maybe she remained fixed to the railing because she held onto the thin chance that flight was still possible, and that she had climbed out on the ledge for one last great attempt. Of course she had.

A distant shrill and clang of breaking glass and crashing steel startled Rainy. The noise was uncanny. Two cars had collided at an intersection out of sight. The sound came from somewhere far below her on the busy streets of downtown San Diego. Horns blared in the distance. Rainy imagined distraught drivers, their fear and shock shifting to anger at one another, at themselves, elevated heart rates taking on the cadence of rage as their alarm turned to fury. She wished that she could see them, that they could see her.

Another crash of glass brought everything back.

A white plate slipped from the waiter's hand just as he turned to set it on the table. It landed with a shattering racket that froze the other restaurant patrons mid-mingle.

"I am *so* sorry," the waiter apologized. He bent to gather the fragments of broken china from the floor near Rainy's feet, taking extra care to pinch at the slivers of porcelain that had fallen into the cracks of the concrete veranda.

"It's nothing." Rainy smiled, forgiving the slip. She hoped her date would notice her kind patience.

"I will return with another plate of nigiri." The man tipped toward her and Gary before he turned toward the kitchen and sped away as a busboy arrived with a short broom.

They were having dinner at a sushi bar in La Jolla, a quaint coastal community near the University of California campus. They sat outside on the veranda overlooking the inky-blue Pacific. The ocean breeze was cool, but the sake was warm.

"You're lovely. You know that?" Gary cooed as he poured her another cup of sake. He reached across the table to move a strand of hair from Rainy's eyes. "Too pretty to be a pediatric nurse. All of your boy patients will fall in love with you."

"I think boys are more likely to move to general practitioners before puberty. They tend to leave pediatrics long before girls." Rainy sipped the warm rice drink, enjoying its low burn as it slid down her throat. "It's a macho thing for young boys, I think."

"So is conquest." Gary smiled. "For young boys, I mean. I was one, once." He laughed with a lightness she enjoyed. His eyes sparkled at her.

Rainy enjoyed the conversation as much as the company. Being very new in nursing school, she worked a late shift at the hospital as a switch board operator and slept long hours during the day, between class schedules. She had no social life and no family, since her dad had passed last year. When she wasn't sleeping or in class, she found herself reading for long hours or watching too much television. It was nice to have companionship for a change. It was flattering to have one-on one time with a prestigious doctor. The fact that Gary was also good-looking made the deal a little sweeter. Glasses clinked and cheeks flushed.

The waiter returned with a plate of nigiri and placed it in the center of the table without interrupting the conversation. Gary plucked a smooth rectangle of salmon from the plate with his chopsticks and popped the fish and rice in her mouth.

"What if you could do something amazing?" He grinned like a cat.

Typical—ask a question like that and without a fair chance to respond. She smiled as she chewed, the flavor of salmon taking her back to her childhood in Seattle. But she pushed the thought away. The pain of her dad's absence would not mix well with this moment.

"Mmm…" she managed.

Gary didn't seem to need her response anyway. "I have been working on new patches of myelin sheathing at the base, molecular level of nerves. It's pretty amazing what we can do with stem cells, though I wouldn't let the word out just yet." He offered another piece of nigiri.

Rainy covered her mouth with her napkin, pretending to still chew a bit.

"Stem cell research will be a tangle of controversy in the new millennium, I'm sure of it. But the 1990s are all about me."

"I see." Rainy, playing along, cocked an eyebrow.

He tipped his head and said, "Curiosity is in our nature, and I intend to exploit that to its fullest capacity. No matter what happens, you can't stifle curiosity."

"And what are you curious about, Doctor?" she asked.

"There's this new organic compound that actually fuses inorganic connections to nerves." He made joining gestures with his hands that Rainy found provocative. "I'm sure you've heard some of the talk about bionics. They're able to get connective tissues to fuse with internal prosthetics made of coral. Have you heard of that?"

"I have. Well, a little." She sipped the sake again, feeling lightheaded from its effect and a little embarrassed that she wasn't more up to date on stem cell research; she was studying to be a nurse through a local community college and was just moving beyond the basics. Rainy had done quite well in most of her bio courses, but the specifics of stem cell research and bionics was beyond her scope. She wondered if Gary could sense that. It didn't matter though. He had a chiseled jaw and deep, brown eyes that penetrated her. She could learn about prosthetics for next time. Tonight was all about anatomy for her. Besides, Gary seemed content to be doing all the talking.

They had gone out a few times before, but this time was different. When he had approached her, he was urgent and even seemed a little flushed. Rainy read his haste as sexual frustration. She didn't mind. She was quite attracted to his intellect and to his physique—tall, broad shoulders and fit. It had also been quite a while since Rainy was interested in someone. Their few earlier dates had already packed more than a spark for her. She only hoped to not come across as too eager. So here they were. Rainy teetered between coy and willing. She was confident that her balancing act was coming off well, and that maybe she would take Gary home with her after dinner.

"Well, let me spare you the tedious details." He smirked, topping off Rainy's sake again.

His curvy mouth was irresistible.

"Let's just say that this newest technology has bionics at such a high level of operation that prosthetic fingers can grasp paintbrushes, allowing some of my patients to create elaborate works of art… even paint their own toenails. This will revolutionize bionics!" Gary clapped his hands with a bang.

Rainy looked around to see if anyone was looking at them.

He lowered his voice. "The first thing I should make very clear is how important it is that we keep a wrap on what I have planned." He sipped his sake.

"Meaning?" Rainy leaned in allowing just enough rise in her eyebrow to seem interested but not enough to show her eagerness.

"Let's just say that ignorance is bliss. Besides, there will be plenty to say once we reveal what I have been able to do…what *we* have been able to do…*after* we have done it."

"So, ignorance is bliss?" Rainy asked. "That's hardly a medical perspective."

"*Contraire.*" Gary smiled, reaching his hand up again to brush away her hair, only this time he rested his fingers on Rainy's cheek for a small second. "So smart," he sighed.

Her heart skipped.

"I'm sure you've heard about the physics of bumble bees?"

"What do bumble bees have to do with bionics?"

"Bumble bees have to do with impossibilities and ignorance being bliss and the miracles of nature." He downed his sake and launched into what he had been building up to. "Bumble bees don't know their own limitations. They don't know that their tiny wings are too small for their bulky bodies. They don't know that the laws of physics deny them their birthright of flying. But, bumble bees don't care about physics. They fly. They fly regardless! And they excel at it."

"Nice," Rainy said. "One of the most brilliant medical minds of the end of this century and you want to anthropomorphize bees. I can see you've thought this all out."

"Don't be like that," Gary sat back in his chair and pouted like a spoiled child not getting a favorite toy.

"Sorry, it's the sake." She gave her best eye-bat and tipped her head. Rainy could play, too, and she was enjoying the extra attention. Besides that, he had once given her a sample of a new opiate, something to give her a little insight into what might be available to pain victims. Rainy was more than willing to see what other treats might come her way if she played along. "Please continue."

"Well, most bees—in fact most insects in the family *Apidea*—are not supposed to be able to fly by the laws of physics…*our* laws. Their wings are too small for their large bodies, as I have already said. And yet they fly." He paused and took a bite of his food.

Utensils clanked and dishes clattered. Up until then, Rainy had really been enjoying herself, and she wanted it to continue. Maybe it was the sake taking over, or maybe she was feeling lonely or disappointed in nursing school, or a hundred other things. She reached her hand across the table and took his. She slipped her foot up next to his calf, just to make her intentions clear.

"Tell me how this relates to bionics," she purred, stroking his knuckles with her thumb.

Gary furrowed his brow. "I'm not sure I should continue."

Rainy felt the sting of rejection. Embarrassed, she pulled her hand back and sat upright.

But Gary relented. His tone softened a bit, and he reached forward and now took her hand in both of his. "I'll tell you, but I need you to promise me you can keep a secret."

"I can. I can." Rainy leaned toward him, pleading with her tone.

Holding her hands tighter, his words came in an urgent whisper. "How would *you* like to fly?"

Feeling dizzier, Rainy gave herself to his words and his grasp. Right then, she would have promised Gary anything. She would have flown over the moon for him, with or without wings.

Wings.

She awoke to the sound of breaking glass. A slanted room through her blurred vision challenged her to make sense of recent events.

Only a blink and the pain registered in her neck, back, shoulders, wings—well, not really in her wings.

Rainy had been sleeping as she did, doing her best to maintain her Elephant Man pose, half upright on the chaise lounge in her dilapidated hotel room. The morning light clawed her eyes. She squeezed her eyelids shut against the arrival of this new day. She did not want to wake up. She forced her eyes open again. She groaned, fighting the reality of waking. She hated waking each new day to find that her circumstances were not some nightmare, a product of her restless sleep.

"Damn clumsy things," Rainy cursed her wings. Scattered shards, remnants of her water glass, came into focus on the floor; a quick jolt in her dream or a readjustment and her wings took out whatever was within a few feet of them. She made a mental note to not sleep with a glass of water nearby. As long as she had to wake up, she might as well wake up to order instead of chaos.

It was the same each day for Rainy; she returned to her hell and her nightmare with each new dawn. And each time she awoke, she fought it until she sat forward, her prosthetic wings unfurling behind her. Only after the world came into focus would she accept her predicament, if only for another sixteen hours or so.

At least she had a button. She pressed it. The pain subsided and the sharpness of the lines in the room softened. Once, Gary had told her that the button was linked to morphine, along with some other goodies. Rainy didn't care anymore what was in the I.V., as long as it did the trick, as long as it killed the pain in her body, in her heart. And it did. Mostly.

Next, she would look for her morning meal. Today, a delivery of day-old bagels and cold coffee sat on the table near the door. There was lox too, which meant that Gary would not return that day. He skipped a visit when he provided protein in the morning.

Typical, Rainy thought as she dragged herself across the room. She gripped the pole of the I.V. station, moving it with her as she walked, the tips of her wings trailing on the ground just behind her, pulling shards of glass along the wet floor.

This wasn't like a bad haircut that would grow out. It wasn't like a tattoo that Rainy could pay an expensive plastic surgeon to remove. Her wings were very permanent now. They weighed forty pounds and were anchored to her shoulder blades, vertebrae and backs of her ribs with stainless steel pins and rivets. Rainy's scapula had been rebuilt with extensions that protruded from her body. The network of diodes, wires and devices controlling her wings was cumbersome and difficult to haul around, so Gary had designed a special belt with a pack that could be anchored to the center of her lower back and secured with a harness. She removed the belt when sleeping or when Gary wasn't around, which was most of the time now. She let the tangle of wires and cables hang free, dragging around behind her. Gary said the belt was for flight, or if she ever wanted to leave the hotel room. She never wanted to leave the hotel room and she had never flown.

The room was on the 14th floor of an abandoned hotel in the penthouse suite of a once popular tourist area in downtown San Diego. She had a view of the old waterfront. The newer section of town was just to the south, where great skyscrapers were being erected by the dozens. Hungry developers and their greedy contracts swirled through the waterfront district like pesky seagulls. But just a mile in, the old downtown section was quiet. Gary called this part of town "perfect," telling Rainy that this hotel in particular had just the right altitude and seclusion. Rainy did not wonder about his need for privacy. Here, she could scream as loud as she needed, and it would startle only the pigeons. There was no rescue and little release.

The relief Rainy got came from the drugs. These were given so that she could operate within a tolerable level of pain. The side effects were inhibiting at best and quite debilitating. Rainy did not mind. She had become like Gary's well behaved lab rat, patiently awaiting her next treat, smacking her button whenever the moment called for it. Any minute now; she could feel it coming on again. When there were additional surgeries or major adjustments, she welcomed the rewards of stronger drugs and larger doses. Rainy looked forward to such times but not just for the drugs. During those times, Gary would stay longer, sometimes even for days. There was an additional room with a nice bed. Gary would bring chess. Rainy had come to anticipate those additional surgeries, each new "perfection" bringing them one step closer to the miracle of flight, and her closer to him, if only temporarily.

It was hard for her to understand, but she still wanted to make Gary happy. More than anything, she wanted to please him. She wanted to fly, she still told herself. She wanted to do something amazing, to be a part of something extraordinary. She had certain fears, sure. But there was also a sense of dignity that came with something of this magnitude. Her dad thought she should just find a comfortable place in life. He thought nursing school was a waste of time, and that she ought to find a nice man and settle down. This would show her dad how wrong he had been, that she would do something astonishing. She would fly! She still believed she would, too, though she had long since given up on the exercises and the physical therapy Gary had prescribed for her to perform in his absence. What was the use once the drugs subdued her anyway?

Once Rainy had her bagel and cold coffee, she sat on a stool near a cluttered table. Her shoulders hunched and her wings slouched. Rainy pulled her feet up onto the crossbar between the stool legs. She cupped her bagel and nibbled mouse-like, resting her elbows on her bent knees, all the while staring across the room at one particular item as if her gaze could penetrate it, evaporate it, or make it less real.

The door.

A strange urge came over Rainy to swoop a sheet around her wings like a grand cloak and make for the elevator. She played the fantasy out, telling herself that she would gain superhero notoriety and fame, if even on foot. She looked to where the tether of an I.V. needle was taped to her arm; she imagined removing it herself. She had seen Gary do it so many times, so it was nothing for her to match his motions. She remembered the procedure from nursing school, and she was sure she could hold steady. *A natural*, her teachers had said. If only she could get over the queasy feeling she often felt with needles.

As her attention returned to the door, she rubbed at the needle in her arm. Then, she sat upright, pulling at the tape and tearing it from her flesh. Some of the hair came off with the adhesive, and

Rainy winced, became dizzy, then slumped back under the weight of her wings. Feeling seized by exhaustion, Rainy thought back to when she first came through the operation. Her medical attendant had called her *Angelita*. She closed her eyes and tried to remember his face while she rubbed the soreness from her arm. Her head swirled into darkness.

Angelita. Angelita, de grandes alas.

The upright post of the glass I.V. had toppled before Gary could catch it, and the I.V. bottle hit the floor with a crash. Rainy's body spasmed in an involuntary jolt on the gurney, and her wing caught the lead.

"Try to move them slowly," Gary growled. The young Latino orderly rushed into the room and righted the I.V. post. He moved quickly to change the bottle and clean the spill. Rainy caught him sneaking a glimpse at her. Something about his glance made her feel ashamed. The young man's eyes fell to the floor as he turned to leave the room and he spoke the soft words: *Angelita, de grandes alas.*

She fought the bleary haze that held her, but she could not clearly discern her whereabouts as she crawled out of her drug-induced haze. The walls were sterile-white, yet she had the sense that the place was not a new facility. It was hospital-like, that much she knew from the sounds and smells. Some places had that air about them. It smelled of Lysol and bleach and other attempts to wash away things soiled.

"Where am I…" she slurred.

"Somewhere where I can take good care of you," she heard Gary explaining. He said something about *fine medical care* and *free from prying eyes*. Rainy remembered the eyes of the young orderly. They were a piercing brown, and she thought she detected a look of horror. But she was heavily drugged. He could have just been annoyed to have to clean up her mess.

The next day, she had better clarity. She was in a convalescent home of sorts. She was by herself for the first few days. She learned the orderly's name: Emilio. He was kind but only spoke to her in Spanish. After what Rainy thought was the third day, she was moved to a new room.

"Your roommate is named Marta," Gary explained. "It is more than convenient that she is blind; it is also to your advantage. But Marta is a paranoid schizophrenic. She keeps to herself and is harmless, but stay alert. She's a superstitious old *Bruja*."

"Sounds like a match made in heaven," Rainy tried to joke through the pain and grogginess.

Gary explained, "There are limits on space. Besides, I think Marta will be a perfect companion. She spends a great deal of time in prayer, which you may find soothing."

This last statement gave Rainy pause. Gary knew she had no religious feelings. How could she benefit from listening to incantations and prayer rants? She found herself annoyed by his assumption and welcomed the injection he offered. Already she knew she could not function without this kind of help from him.

True to Gary's description, Marta spent most of her time praying in her corner on her knees on the stark white linoleum, begging her *Bendito Dios* to bring her insight and to deliver her from this hell. She counted her prayers on a rosary that she fingered. It was a beautiful set of glass beads with an intricate glass crucifix that Rainy thought was quite lovely. She felt bad that Marta could not see the exquisiteness of the piece, though maybe one day long ago she could.

Rainy did not have much clarity during that time, but she remembered Marta. She remembered Emilio, too. He called her *Angelita*. He was kind and gentle, but his eyes would never look at Rainy after that first day. Soon Rainy became convinced she was in Mexico. It made sense, if she gave it much thought. The U.S. would not tolerate this type of experiment.

"Don't call this an experiment," Gary warned, holding her hard against the gurney. Her wings pressed down next to her spine and shoulders, and she stifled a scream. "Experiments are for grad students and veterinarians. You are my opus."

He released her, and she shuddered. Rainy felt like a monster, not an opus. Once she had been a vision of loveliness before him, and now she was his hideous mistake, though he would never admit it. Not yet.

She was uncertain about the number of corrective surgeries and additional medications. The medication was not a problem. Rainy never minded the morphine, but that wasn't the drug then. She had been given a cocktail of steroids and stimulants, coupled with some pretty hefty opiates and barbiturates. It was enough to sedate a horse. She was almost sure of it.

In time, Gary brought some free weights to help her build her strength. He had started working on a physical therapy program. But she couldn't do anything without the drugs. That much hadn't changed. For a while, anything with Codeine was off limits because it would stir her deepest dreams. The nightmares would wake Marta, the poor blind fool that she was. Marta would start wailing and praying. This would set into motion a recipe for sleeplessness that was disruptive to the entire process.

"It might be time to move you to another facility," Gary said one afternoon. "This one will have windows and a view." He paused and smiled, holding her juice cup and straw to her mouth so she could sip without lifting her arms to the chore. They had been working out her trapezoids and deltoids, and her arms had become fatigued. "A view can be a great inspiration."

Rainy drank the juice and frowned. "This hasn't worked the way you thought," she drooled between sips.

The menace in Gary's quiet stare ignited a thermal flicker in his eyes. He let go of the cup, and the juice spilled all down the front of Rainy's gown, a cold liquid filling the gap between her gown and her breasts, then running along her ribs and sides. Rainy gasped but didn't dare move.

Gary got up without a word. He left the room and did not start shouting for Emilio until he was at the far end of the hallway.

Soon, Emilio arrived with a towel to sponge up the moisture and remove the cup.

Rainy asked for a sedative. She whispered, "*mas morfina, por favor...por favor.*" This much, she had learned during her Mexican *rehabilitación*.

And then the great grey time came when she did not remember being introduced to Marta, only that she had always been there: a permanent fixture in the chaos of the indiscernible; when she did not remember the change in the room, the new wing extensions, Emilio replaced by a small woman with dark eyes who looked at the floor when she came and went.

A painful memory split her vision: Rainy heard the rosary spill onto the floor and become a thousand tiny, pinging balls of glass. Its beads scattered, bouncing in the midnight darkness with only their patter to describe the collapse.

"*¡Bestia!*" Marta screamed at her. "*¡Bestia! ¡Demonia! ¡Diabla del infierno!*"

The first contact with the wings had been an accident. Marta had walked too near to Rainy, bumping into her wings. Marta screamed as her hands felt along, gripping the leading edge of Rainy's left wing.

Rainy cried in anguish as the older woman tugged in disbelief at the enormous apertures anchored to Rainy's back. The pins responded to the surprise contact in the dark, sending searing pain into Rainy. She called out with agony.

Marta reached out her hands, proxies for her absent vision; her mouth fell agape as her hands described the enormous wing anchored to Rainy's skeletal structure.

The wing twitched mechanically as the pain in Rainy's spine triggered a reflex. In an instant, both wings fluttered like an injured bird trying to loosen itself from a snare.

Marta came unhinged.

"*¡Diabla! ¡Bestia! ¡Bestia!*" Marta carried on like that, screaming her demon words, until the orderly came and took her away down the hall. Echoes of her attempts at "*exorcismo*" ricocheted off the distant walls.

It was the first time Rainy considered herself as such: *Bestia*. She saw herself in this new hideous form. What had she done? How had it come to this? She thought she had always been so practical, so very well measured in her actions and intentions. And yet, there she was: disfigured, forever altered. *¡Bestia!*

The orderly had flipped the light switch and left Rainy exposed in the harsh, fluorescent glare. A crack in the smooth wall caught her eye, and she stared at it until her eyes watered to blindness or until the injection took her away. She could not remember which came first.

When Gary came, Rainy asked about the new place, the place with the windows. "What kind of a view?"

"It's on the 14th floor of the old Cortez in downtown San Diego. You know the place." He even seemed to smile at her eagerness to go along with the move. "The building itself is unoccupied. Well, besides a few vagrants who keep to the lower floor. I've worked out a deal to have the top floor—the penthouse suite—all for you."

"Is it safe to move me?" She thought she should ask.

"Certainly." He now sat at the edge of the bed, a familiar softness returning to his tone. "You have been stable for quite some time. I am only trying to build your strength and manage your pain at this point." He smiled.

For a moment, Rainy let her guard down, and she relaxed. She felt more comfortable with Gary then she had since before the operation, though she wasn't certain why. She took a deep breath.

"Gary?" She waited.

Gary had reached down for a medical bag and had pulled out a few items. He drew a digital thermometer out and placed it in her ear.

"I can bring you take-out from the Gaslamp District," Gary continued, not detecting her change. "I know how much you love that Greek place on 7th."

"Gary?" she said again.

"Yes." He centered his gaze on her face.

She felt a flutter. He still held a bit of the charm for her, and she longed to not ask her question but to instead just hold onto the moment. It had been so long since she felt comfort in his presence. Still, there was an edge to the bitterness that scraped through her need, so she pressed, "Is the operation reversible?"

Gary pulled back. "We've come too far for that sort of talk now."

"I've become your guinea pig. I didn't sign up for this." Rainy didn't try to hide the resentment from her tone.

"Don't be like that." Gary looked into her eyes, touching her face with his hand.

Rainy rubbed the injection site where the track marks had started to scar.

"Besides," he cooed. "There's still the miracle of changing the world...of being the one to fly!" He removed her hand from her track marks then wrapped her arm in the blood pressure cuff and began to squeeze its bladder to check her vitals. A blood vessel in his forehead seemed to pulse with his squeezes. "Remember when we first started down this road, we were going to make medical history together." His brow furrowed on the word "together."

Gary was always so certain. Everything he did was calculated. Strategic.

"We are not together. I don't even know where I am, and you are certainly not here with me." Rainy felt the inflated blood pressure band begin to lose air as Gary watched the clock. She could feel her pulse register in the cuff, in her arm, through her neck and shoulders, and she even thought she could feel it in her wings.

"I can be with you more. I have to make some changes." He looked at the clock then back to her. "We *are* in this together. Start to finish. I promise you that."

He stuck a tongue depressor in her mouth and pressed hard while looking into her throat. His other hand came to her neck and gripped around her gullet. He then locked eyes with her and pressed harder on her tongue with the flat, dry stick. His tone shifted to a throaty rumble. "I have to say, I am a bit frustrated that your enthusiasm has waned."

Fear held Rainy motionless. The hand on her neck clawed around to the base of her skull.

Gary whispered, "You should have thought this through when you were busy turning cartwheels over this project. Don't forget *you* wanted this. You were eager for this."

Gary let go and removed the tongue depressor. He got up and walked away.

Rainy breathed deep but stifled a gag. She rubbed her neck. Still shocked, she whispered, "How am I supposed to be enthusiastic about being a freak?"

"What makes you think you are a freak?" His tone shifted to mock empathy. He turned to look at her, his expression smacking of that same sway he presented when they had shared a sushi dinner so long ago. If Gary thought she was a freak—even for a second—Rainy would never have known it, still to this day. Rainy was his work of art, his opus and his masterpiece. Even if he had started to have doubts in the procedure, as she had, he would never let on. Instead, he would bring her to a lovely nest with a tempting perch and lofty view. He was taking his directions from nature then, manipulating them to suit his needs through fine tuning and inquiry. That was the great backbone of medical science, strong enough to support bionic prosthetics, and indeed prosthetic wings.

Gary returned to her side with another needle and a quick prick sent her to sleep.

Another memory came to her: A vial of blood lay broken on the counter. Rainy watched its contents seep out onto the countertop. A lattice of small, red spider webs spread into the pattern of the nearby paper towel.

"Crap!" Gary spun on his heel.

"Is that going to be a problem?" Rainy nodded at the paper towel and blood.

Gary mumbled as he moved to fetch another vial. He returned and smiled at her then, washing his hands in the sink by her gurney before he continued.

He talked as he washed his hands. "Did you know that it was only a little over a hundred years ago when maternity patients in Vienna had mortality rates upwards of sixty-three percent because the attending physicians refused to wash their hands when moving from cadavers to obstetrics?"

He returned to her side and took out a new syringe. Rainy could feel Gary's heat as he drew the blood, smell his aftershave, sterile like the walls of the convalescent hospital. She watched his hand, steady and sure as he talked.

"It was a heretic named Semmelwies who discovered that the intervention of soap and water could decrease mortality rates by as much as fifty-four percent there in Vienna. Do you know what they did to him?" Gary was so close now, she could smell his breath, feel the warmth of it against her face. She leaned back onto her wings and felt a searing pain all the way down her sciatic nerve. "They put him in a mental hospital." He leaned back and then stood. The emotion was plain on his face now as his brow contracted. "He died in that mental hospital."

Rainy knew the story. She remembered it from a nursing course on hygiene. But there was more to it, to this hero heretic with clean hands. The part that Gary neglected to mention was that Semmelwies's colleagues, the ones who called him a heretic, were too clouded by their own medical prejudice and pride to see what he was saying. History saw it; Rainy could see it, too. None of those doctors could admit that they had a hand in the deaths of thousands of mothers and infants. The cause had to be disease, and not practice. Certainly not the responsibility of physicians. But they would not see it, just as Gary could not see his shortcomings. To Gary, these wings would have to work. As with Semmelwies, someone else might get credit for Gary's findings and work. In the case of Semmelwies, Louis Pasteur came along and now school kids know his name, and Semmelwies—for anyone who knows anything about him at all— remains a heretic to historical references.

He moved to her I.V. A clear saline solution hung near her bed, intended only to keep her hydrated and offer additional supplements that she couldn't otherwise get in food—and also where he could administer her drugs.

She heard the cap pop off the newest needle before she saw it, long and sharp and catching the light just so, a shiny beacon in the hell of her existence.

"What are you giving me?"

"Something to help you relax so that I can sort some things out," he said as he moved to the tube and inserted the needle.

And then the world went black.

When she woke up, she was in that hotel room. There was no Marta. Had she been real? What about Emilio, that young orderly not yet wise enough to be afraid of decisions that lead to lifelong disappointment? Rainy had been his *Angelita* with wings unimaginable. And the woman that came after Emilio; she could not look at her, and Marta could not see her…and Rainy could not yet see. She could not yet see the world for what it had become: a great trap. That room and its walls, the view outside, the harbor with the ships coming and going and even the far horizon with its glorious sunsets and soaring pelicans floating in V-shaped lines—all of it—her vast cage.

Rainy stood and turned, her wings knocking something from a tabletop. When she looked down upon the broken item, a memory crashed upon her through the broken picture frame lying on the floor. Lines of cracked glass skewed the image: a sliced photograph of a stern-faced, older man with a silver beard trapped beneath the fractured glass. His left eye was obscured by tiny shards; his right eye matched those of the young girl with him in the photo. An adolescent version of Rainy, wrapped in the older man's arms. She smiled through the glittering splinters. The picture of her and her dad was the only thing Rainy had from her old life, before Gary. Before the wings.

Rainy kicked aside the broken picture, and the pieces of glass jingled as the photo and its frame separated and spread out across the floor.

Slumping on her stool, Rainy pulled the I.V. needle out of her arm. She wished she would have pulled it faster, because the motion made her light-headed and made the room swim. But—a few deep breaths—and the deed was done. She placed a cotton ball over the point where the I.V. needle had come out of her skin. Then she taped the cotton in place and took several more intentional breaths.

The door swirled into focus.

"See," Rainy said out loud. "If I can do this, I can go out."

She stood, securing the belt and harness. She stuffed the pack with all the wires, diodes and batteries, and wrapped it around her waist. She reached for the bed sheet.

In her hands, the cotton was soothing and soft. She held up the cloth, then draped it around herself, concealing as much of the wings as possible, and securing it at the nape of her neck. She took a long look in the mirror. The room swam as she turned to check all angles of the sheet's fit.

Somehow the sheet looked just fine, even though Rainy did not. She looked ominous, like a prize-winning costume at Halloween. Her skin was pale and her eyes were sunken, outlined in dark circles. She had done her best these last few months to get her weight down, having given up two meals per day for supplements and a beverage that Gary had developed for weight loss. His chemical therapy program had also taken its toll; she could see it in her hair. The once vibrant chestnut color had faded to a dull, mousey brown, and it had thinned. Her image made her sad, and she touched her face under her eyes where the dark color showed the outline of her skull beneath. Hollow bones were not an option. The changes in her diet were necessary.

"Who?" was all she could say before the tears came, but she pushed it away.

Rubbing the spot on her arm where she had removed the I.V., she longed for her button. She grabbed a bottle of pills and stuffed them into the pack with the wires. Then, she set out the door, grabbing the old, metal hotel room key from the hook before she left.

Rainy shattered the fetters that bound her. She pried the bars from her cage and donned her new identity as she moved toward the elevator. She thought she understood what Gary intended when he first started. Everything was leading toward her making that even greater leap, that final exodus from her strange nest, a reintroduction, of sorts, to society. But she would have to go this way, and she would show him what she could do, even without flight. In a sense, he had pushed her to do this. She could not blame Gary. Parental birds often go to strange measures to encourage their young to fly, even acts of brutality.

The elevator opened and she clambered in. She pulled her wings in around her. The button panel was dingy, and the metal was tarnished and old. But the button for 14 was rubbed shiny and new from excessive and recent use. She pressed the button marked 'L,' also worn clean, and started the descent into the unknown. Her stomach sank, but she insisted to herself that it was just anticipation… anticipation and hope. She must have still had some hope then. She stood as tall as she could and lifted her head to watch the lights count down her floors:

12. A sense of eagerness began to mount. She hadn't come up with a plan.

11. She thought if she had money she would go to the deli up on A Street.

10. Maybe just going out to the street would be enough.

9. She needed a pill.

8. She noticed that the dirty panel had three buttons that were worn clean: The 14th floor, the 7th floor, and the 1st floor. She pushed the 7.

The elevator stopped, and the doors opened with a rickety shudder.

Rainy peered down a long, sterile hallway, punctuated with closed doors. The floors were stark linoleum, and the walls were painted a sterile white. Rainy could detect a slight smell of Lysol and bleach. She stepped from the elevator and walked up the hall in careful steps. Silence overwhelmed her, and yet she continued. She looked into a small window set in one of the doors. She saw a dark room with what appeared to be an exam table. Rainy shook it off, but a strange thought had started to creep into her mind; it had yet to fully form. She crossed the hall and looked into another small window in a door. The window was blocked by something covering it from the inside. She tried the handle, afraid she was meddling, but too curious about her developing thoughts to ignore the impulse. The handle gave, and she pulled the door open.

Rainy's eyes burned at once as the smell of rancid meat overpowered her senses. She gagged and covered her mouth. She started to turn away, but stopped.

The large room spanning before her had been gutted of furniture and familiar interior features. Rainy saw—amidst wires, diodes and batteries—a dozen pairs of prosthetic wings, each made of artificial, fleshy, mottled gray material. Wings much like her own. Some dangled from hooks along exposed rafters. Others were lying on examination tables near collections of surgical instruments and medical equipment, and one set was crumpled on the floor against the wall.

They were each just like Rainy's wings, with one distinct difference: each hanging version had a human spinal column attached to it.

The spinal columns were in varying stages of rot, and each had a different set of hardware attached. But there were no bodies—at least no *complete bodies*. There were only wings, and vertebrae, and the thick, putrid smell of decay.

As she turned to run, Rainy's eye caught on a simple crucifix hanging on the wall near the door. Marta's!

She rushed back to the elevator and pressed the call button over and over until the doors opened with a slow *whoosh*. Inside, she pressed the 14ᵗʰ floor button, abandoning her idea to venture outside.

Back upstairs, she threw the stool against the window, shattering the great glass wall that separated her from the fire escape ledge, knowing her wings would not fit through the tiny window. Glass exploded: Tiny shards and enormous pieces, all razor sharp and devastating. Rainy saw it all so clearly. Before climbing out onto the fire escape, she knew what Gary had been trying to make her see all along. It was plain then, how well-played this entire affair had been. She would fly, one way or another. Even if his experiment was deemed a modern-day Frankenstein nightmare, it would make people wonder about possibilities. You can't stifle curiosity, they would say, just as Gary had said on that fateful night of bliss so long ago.

Once outside, she had time to think it through, standing there on the ledge of the 14ᵗʰ floor of the El Cortez. She had to be the one to initiate it in the beginning, just as she had to be the one to climb out onto the ledge. He could never put her there himself. Not directly. How many others had sat across dinner tables just like that one, sharing sake and having that same conversation?

How would you *like to fly?*

How fine-tuned that performance had become! She'd played right into it, eating the seeds from his hand like a starving starling! She had seen him over those last few months, adjusting the network of wires and connections on her wings and back, and she knew he had a talent for minute details, for working backward to achieve his objective. She was certain of it. What she was uncertain of, and what made her sick to imagine, was how many had come before her.

Gary's words echoed in her head and in hear heart: *Ignorance is bliss.*

Just like the bumblebee, Rainy could never know that she could not fly.

A pair of doves landed on the railing near her. She looked from them to her feet. This was the first time she recognized the pain in her sliced toes and heels, blood seeping from small glass cuts. She felt the mounting sting and burn from the unseen recesses of her soles. A trail of red marked the path she had taken from window and along the ledge.

Rainy had a fleeting thought that she could stay, climb off her perch and find help, survive long enough to see the man brought to justice. At least there would be no more victims, no visits with other young nursing students or co-eds or waitresses, whoever they were. No more trips to Mexico or sushi bars and no future occupants here on the 14th floor. Maybe Gary already had another prospect. Maybe she was lovely, too. Charming and smart—but only smart enough. And hopeful—but only hopeful enough. And then the great lie of the entire ordeal stripped the last bit of her sanity and so she spread her huge wings, holding their span wide, the latex taut against the wind gusts and the pain.

Rainy leaned forward, the cold updraft taking her breath away. She stretched her large wings further, spreading them to their greatest, most glorious length for the first time.

Then she let go.

)(O)(O)( )(O)(O)( )(O)(O)( )(

About the Author

Rhonda Zimlich is an MFA student in Fiction at Vermont College of Fine Arts, as well as an illustrator, poet, photographer, and aspiring novelist. Even though she was born in sunny Southern California, she loves living in the rainy Pacific Northwest with her husband, twin daughters, and mischievous black cats, Athena and Osiris. When she's not writing, Rhonda is an avid runner. Her fiction has appeared in places such as *Icarus Down Review, Acorn Review, Crow Pie*, and also in an award-winning video game called *Cart Life*.

BLACK-HOODED CALLER

Pablo Patiño

I've been having dreams, recurring dreams, about a man in a black hood staring at me while I sleep. I try to scream—only what comes is just a faint huffing noise—and Jenny, my wife, tells me to go back to sleep.

She wasn't quite as calm a few days ago. The middle of the night. The bedroom was dark. By the entrance, a cluster of light shaped itself into a ball then took on the form of a shadowy man in a long robe and cowl. He hurtled through the air, straight at me. I pulled the pillow out from under Jenny's head and threw it at him. It landed on top of our dresser. Broke a few knick-knacks and a little perfume bottle. I turned to Jenny, who smacked me on the head *to wake you*, she said, but I told her I was already awake.

Full disclosure—the visits started shortly after my biopsy turned up positive for lymphoma. It's been two weeks since my last chemo treatment. I'm aware that these visits are a manifestation of fears that are taking on new forms in my head, but knowing *why* they're happening doesn't *stop* them from happening. Some dense corner of my left brain refuses to get on board with the rest of my logical mind. It's got to do with the way I was brought up, the reason I still go to church. I often tell myself there is no one there, but there's a stubborn whisper that wastes no time in answering me back, "Are you sure?"

After dinner, I scratched the back of my head below my ear and came back with a wad of hair between my fingers. I slipped my hand in my pocket, telling Jenny I was jumping in the shower. I hadn't washed my hair in days—nor taken a shower for that matter—and there was just *no delaying it any further*, as Jenny put it.

I held the shower head over my shoulders, and the water slid warmly down the arch of my body. I reluctantly moved the spray over my head, and the water hit forcefully, finding its way to my scalp.

My hair began to fall off in clumps.

I picked up the loose strands and dumped them in the garbage pail, then dried myself off and stepped closer to the mirror. My fingers made shiny, winding rings on the steamy surface of the glass; my palm made an even wider sweep. I saw myself. Not completely bald—not entirely. I looked so different.

There was a cold rush—like the window had been opened—only the window was closed. I began to tremble, and for a minute, my head started to spin. Nauseous, I gripped the sink for balance and forced my head toward it. I closed my eyes and took deep breaths until the spinning subsided. When I finally looked back up into the mirror, I saw a dark mass move behind me.

I turned my head, but it was gone. I put on a T-shirt and sweats, wrapped my head with a towel, and walked into the bedroom.

"Are you okay? I thought you drowned in there," Jenny said.

"I'm cold." I checked the windows. It was starting to rain; there was a smattering of raindrops outside.

In bed, Jenny looked up from her cell phone. "Take the towel off. You're being silly," she said in a softer tone.

I did.

"It's an improvement. You should've done this years ago." She was trying to maintain her cool for both of us.

I appreciated the effort. "Can you shave me?"

She inspected my head. "What if I cut you? Esteban, call your mom."

"You're right." I agreed, a bit too fast and with a false cheeriness. She wasn't kidding. My mother was a beautician. It was how Jenny and I met; Jenny's mother was a regular at the shop. I told Jenny I wouldn't be long. Mom was only a twenty-minute drive.

I'd told Mom about my condition the day I found out. She didn't know why I needed to see her that night, so I expected surprise as I walked in with my baseball cap and only a few patches of hair under it.

"I lost my hair." I took off my cap and walked into the kitchen.

She walked over to me without saying a word; she held my face in her hands and gave me a kiss on the forehead.

"Stop it." I took a deep breath. "You're gonna make me cry."

She took a few seconds and told me she was making coffee.

"*Después.* Can you shave me first? I brought the shaving cream and the razor."

"I shaved your father's head when he got his treatment." She pulled the coffee pot from the cabinet and set it on the counter.

After my father died, she'd opened the beauty parlor with the insurance settlement. Women from the neighborhood—tall, dark, light, with straight or curly hair—talked about daughters and their boyfriends, misguided love affairs, letting rice breathe before it gets mushy, and the latest scrapes from Isabel or Silvia, the heroines from their favorite telenovelas. I heard it all in the back storage room by the side entrance, the TV on the old vanity table assuring them their conversations would be drowned out. Except when they lowered their voices, my ears perked up ever so firm.

"Mom, you remember the man with the black hood?"

"*¿Qué dices?*"

"The man you told the ladies about, the man you said took Dad."

She'd finished shaving me and was drying my head with the towel.

"I overheard you talking at the beauty shop. You were talking to the German lady with the thick accent."

"She was Russian. Mrs. Svetna."

"Dad was very sick. The tumors were visible on his neck and under his arms. You were in the kitchen, right about where you are now, and you saw a man in the bedroom standing by Dad."

"Mrs. Svetna called him The Angel of Death. Why bring this up?"

"I have to," I said.

"Why?"

"Because he's come for me."

She sat back in her chair.

"He comes at night. He's by my bedside when I open my eyes. Sometimes he's just a blur. Sometimes he's fully there, as real as you are right now."

I could smell coffee brewing in the pot.

She placed an empty mug in front of me. "Some people can see him," she said. "Some can't. I don't know why. You get it from my side of the family."

"Tell me about that day."

She thought about it. "I was cooking."

"Was he sick then?"

"Yes."

She poured me coffee.

"Your dad was sleeping in the bedroom, the door open. I was stirring the soup with the heavy copper spoon your grandma gave us when I saw him. A black shadow that grew from the floor until he was the shape of a man, a giant man, stretching his arms out toward your father. I yelled and threw that big spoon across the hallway, banged the door so loud your father got up. I ran in and couldn't find that evil thing, but I knew he was still around. 'You're not taking him,' I screamed. 'I'm not letting you take him!' Your father held me and quieted me down. I hid the spoon under my pillow when we went to bed."

"The big spoon! I thought that was for me."

She chuckled. "You were my little altar boy. Father Moises would have used it on me if I ever tried it on you."

"Father Moises?" The name brought back the heavy musty scent of incense, the solemn drama of the organ. Father Moises was a man of God.

"You know," she said, "I begged your father to come to church with me."

"That wasn't going to happen."

"Why us? We're good people. I loved your father. I asked Father Moises to come by one day when your dad was asleep. Father Moises blessed every room in the house, the kitchen, the bathroom, your room, but we were afraid to go in your dad's room. Then, while we were standing in front of that closed door wondering if we should go in, your dad opens it, and in the most polite way you could imagine (your dad was an educated man), he asked Father Moises to leave. Esteban, how do you ask a priest to leave?"

"Dad was an atheist."

"I wanted Father Moises to finish the job. Your father said he didn't mean to be rude. He wanted to hold on to..."

"His dignity."

"Esteban, what good is dignity? It didn't save him."

"Father Moises couldn't have saved him either."

"How do you know? You don't know."

"Can I have a little more coffee?"

I didn't stay long after that. The rain had cleaned my car to a shine. I sat in the driver's seat, drenched.

My seventh birthday. At our old house in Queens, it was getting late and my friends had already left the party. Dad had his back to the dining room window as the rain pelted the glass. He had one hand on the couch for support and the other on the gift he was holding. He pushed me to unwrap the present. "Open it, Esteban."

I unwrapped his present, thinking it was a book. It was a diary.

"I know how much you like to write," he said—the English teacher talking.

I hugged him, trying not to hurt him. He was so light.

A few days later, I walked in his bedroom. I was so excited to read him something I'd written, but he was asleep. On his dresser was his own notebook. I opened it. Browsing through the pages, I noticed he had sketched a silhouette, a penciled figure of a man in black with a cowl draped loosely over a skull.

By then, the cancer had spread. Dad was grotesque. His neck had swollen, and he could hardly speak from the pain medications. "Esteban?" he muttered, opening his eyes.

I closed the notebook and ran out of the room.

Jenny was reading in the bedroom when I got back. "If you tell me I look better bald, I'm moving back in with my mom." I took my cap off and showed her my perfectly smooth dome.

"How *is* your mom?" She sat up on her pillow and put the book on the night stand.

"She's good. We got to talking about the shop. I told her about my nightly visits." I undressed to my shorts and T-shirt and slipped inside the covers next to her.

"It's more common than you think. I see it at the hospital. It's called Hypnogogia or sleep paralysis."

"Hypnogogia?"

"A neurological condition; you're not awake and you're not asleep. You want to scream, but you can't. That's because your brain has turned off all motor neurons in your spinal column, preventing any movement, except for your eyes. That's why you can't yell when you want to. You just happen to be asleep."

"REM," I said.

"What?"

"Rapid Eye Movement. You're not the only one with a master's degree, you know," though hers was in clinical psychology so this was right up her alley. "And another thing."

"Yes?"

I leaned closer to her. "You know, you're really cute when you get nerdy."

"Never mind your crazy visions." She broke a smile. "We'll see the oncologist tomorrow, and he'll tell us…"

I pushed closer and kissed her gently. As I pulled back, we looked at each other, acknowledging my sudden suggestion. I whispered, "Let's not talk about this anymore."

She leaned back on her pillow and, moving her arms around my neck, said, "Yes, Mr. Bald-Headed Stranger, you can have your way with me, but be quick before my husband gets back."

We both laughed, and I put out the lights

"The lesions have reduced," said Doctor Singh.

I sat up on the exam table, scrunching my butt on the wax paper, trying to get comfortable. The bright lights amplified the smallness of the room.

"We'll need to do a bone marrow biopsy. It's standard procedure, so don't go thinking the worst."

"Another test?" I asked.

"Just to rule out any possibility of complications."

I stared at the floor in a daze.

"Look at me," he said. "You have to stay positive. You have to fight." He handed me a brochure from the stack neatly piled on his desk. The brochure promoted a conference on mind-body therapies focusing on visualization and imagery.

"Really?" Jenny helped herself to one of the brochures and skimmed through it. "Will this be replacing the chemo?"

"These are adjunctive therapies." He nodded, trying to thwart her sarcasm.

"There's no real medical evidence to back any of this up," she said.

He straightened his back and looked at her. "You would agree that stress and fear can be harmful to your health. Studies back that up. There's a reason why most heart attacks occur on Mondays."

"That much I'll give you," she said.

"Then why is it hard to believe the opposite is true? Some people use religious imagery, others make up their own symbols, their own metaphors as they go along. It gives them hope, makes them stronger. I'm treating a patient who came to visualize a beautiful meadow with a flowing stream. She felt cool water and hard stones under her feet. The stream was crystal clear and shallow, and, every once in a while, she'd spot a black stone in the mix and toss it away. These were the malignant cells. She had an advanced condition when she came in. It was a struggle for a while."

"Did she get better?" I asked.

"She's in complete remission now."

Jenny's leg began to twitch.

"We shouldn't take any giant leaps," he said, "but what harm can it do?"

"I'll think about it." I folded the brochure and tucked it into my back pocket. "Thank you."

Jenny tossed the brochure back on his desk, toppling his perfect little stack.

I held the door for Jenny as we walked out of the office into the parking lot. She turned to me as we got in the car. "Where'd you get this quack, anyway?"

"Me? I thought you got him." We laughed, easing into our seats. The truth was Dr. Singh had come highly recommended by a co-worker; Singh had treated her uncle.

It was eight o'clock when we left his office, because we had made a late appointment to accommodate our working schedules. I was exhausted by the time we got home. I hadn't done anything extraneous, but I felt as if I'd run a mile. We went right to bed. I fell asleep shortly after my head hit the pillow.

A little past four in the morning. My eyes opened. I lifted my head slightly to get a look at the alarm clock on the night stand. The room was dark. Jenny was sound asleep. I turned and saw him. He was standing beside me by the edge of the bed. A faint, pale light came from inside the hood. Two eyes stared at me, yellow and lifeless.

Before I could move, he pressed his hand on my chest. His fingers pinned me hard against the mattress. The pain was unbearable. I squirmed to get lose, trying to move my arms. I screamed.

Jenny sat up. "Are you okay?"

"Jenny, he attacked me!"

She flicked the lamp on her night stand. "You were dreaming again!"

"No!" I pulled up my T-shirt. "See how red it is?"

"That's it. You're seeing someone. I know exactly who you need to see. I'll call him tomorrow."

I left the lights on till daylight.

Jenny made an appointment with a psychologist within two days, her former professor at NYU. Three years had gone by since she'd sat in his classroom, but they had kept in touch. According to her, he was brilliant, even though he was constantly getting in trouble with the administration for his unorthodox views. He'd agreed to see me as a favor to her.

He looked to be in his mid-sixties. His name was Steven Miller. I remember thinking, *you can't get more American than that*, though he was more Indiana Jones than Brady Bunch. The nurse walked me into his office and told me he'd be right in. I sat in a chair facing his desk.

Diplomas lined the back wall in symmetrical harmony, the bigger ones encased in gold frames. Very impressive.

The left side wall told you the real story. Photos, mostly in color, scattered randomly in frames of different sizes. There he was, floating down the Amazon in an old river boat, and in the Himalayas, walking side by side with Buddhist monks. There were a few photos in India. I couldn't place the temple, but the statues were definitely from there as far as I could tell.

I had waited but two minutes when he walked in. Lean and solid, his grey-brown hair pushed back to shoulder length. You could tell he worked out and was possibly a runner.

I got the feeling he was going to move things along at a rapid pace.

After the usual get-to-know-each-other chatter, he asked, "So, what brings you here?"

I wasn't sure how to approach it. "I'm having trouble sleeping."

He didn't respond.

I was suddenly wishing I hadn't agreed to this. "Jenny didn't tell you?"

"She did, but I'd like to hear it from you."

I took a deep breath. I had no choice. I was about to tell a complete stranger I'm fighting a demon, or an evil spirit, or the Angel of Death himself who keeps requesting my company and won't take no for an answer. "At night, I see a man in a black hood by the foot of my bed, sometimes standing right beside me."

"You do realize you're dreaming," he said.

"He seems so real. The other night, he attacked me and pushed his bony fingers on my chest. I haven't been able to sleep too well since then."

"When did you first start seeing him?"

"In a sketch, a drawing. I was a kid. Now he stands in front of me at night. He's angry, insistent."

"Ever since you were diagnosed, correct?"

"I know. He's simply a manifestation of what's been happening, but..."

"You're still afraid," he said.

"Please tell me he's not real."

"He's not," he said, "but in a way, he is." He found a cigarette in his desk drawer and lit it with a silver lighter he pulled out of his pocket; the lighter was beautifully engraved with the outline of an encrusted wolf's head. "Are you a religious man?"

"I'm not sure," I answered.

"You don't believe in God?"

"Honestly, I don't know, and this is coming from a once devout altar boy."

"You either believe or you don't."

"It's not that simple," I told him.

"I see." He chuffed out a soft gray cloud. "It's harder *not* to believe, isn't it? After so many years, you're fully vested."

"Can we get back to the man in the black hood?"

"We've never stopped…angels, demons, evil spirits, men in black hoods, and yes, even God Himself, ideas that have been around for thousands of years; once you open the door to one, you open the door to all."

"You're not going to tell me to ignore him. I've already tried that."

He took a long puff of his cigarette. "No, my suggestion is to do the opposite. Take him on. Fight him."

I looked at him to make sure he was serious.

He was.

"Look," he said. "Right now, you need a plan of action, correct? We can figure out the why later. You look jittery, you have bags under your eyes. You're a mess."

"Yeah, thanks."

"Don't be so quick to get rid of him next time. Talk to him. The more you engage him, the more you'll see him for what he is, something imagined."

"That could be dangerous," I told him.

"How so?"

"What if he's not entirely a dream?"

"You really do believe, don't you?"

"I'm beginning to think that maybe I do more than I let on."

"Ok, let's use that." He took another puff. "Do you know the absolute sure way of defeating a demon?"

"I didn't know there was a sure way."

"To cast him out, you must first get him to say his name. In your case, though, I'd say pulling the hood off would be the equivalent. Once you get a look at who you're dealing with, he's lost his power. It's the fear of the unknown that we're dealing with here."

"That's easier said than done."

"Here's your backup." He got up from his chair and went to the credenza behind him, unlocked the top drawer and began to rummage through its contents until he found a square cedar box about 12 by 12 inches. "Here it is." He laid it on his desk and opened the lid to reveal a wooden crucifix resting on a cushion of silk. Excited, he took the crucifix out of the box. "Look at how beautiful it is!" he said, quickly regaining his composure, settling his tone a few decibels so as not to disturb the figure of Jesus with his eyes surprisingly still closed. "You can say I'm a collector of ancient artifacts. This wooden cross belonged to El Conde de Consuegra in the province of Toledo, Southern Spain. You can see the cross held by El Conde himself on your left. I took that picture of the old man about five years ago." He pointed to a picture of an older gentleman holding the cross. Next to that hung a large oil painting of a knight on horseback leading his army of crusaders against an opposing force. "That's a distant relative of El Conde on the oil painting. I eventually persuaded El Conde to part with the cross. He had bills to pay, just like the rest of us. It dates back to the 13th century. Can you imagine this same cross I'm holding at the head of an army of valiant Christian soldiers battling legions of invaders out of their beloved home?"

"Can I hold it?"

"Of course you can." He gave it to me.

It was made of wood, the same as the box. "It feels so light."

"And yet it's such a powerful object, don't you agree?"

"Yes." I *did* certainly agree.

"Take it with you. Have it with you tonight."

"You're giving it to me?"

"I'm lending it to you."

I stared at it.

"Bring it back on your next appointment. I've known Jenny a long time. I'm sure you'll take good care of it, won't you?"

"Should I talk to a priest?"

"You're talking to one."

"You're a priest?"

"Not a priest, a pastor. I was Reverend Miller before I became Dr. Miller."

"But you're not a pastor any more, are you?"

"I left the ministry when I became a psychologist."

"Jenny never told me."

"I don't readily volunteer that. Don't want anyone thinking I have a grudge against the church."

"So, you really have no religious authority whatsoever."

"No, but I can tell you what a priest will tell you."

"What's that?"

"Believe in God. Believe in Jesus. And no harm will come to you. Can you do that?"

"I don't know."

He put out his cigarette in the ashtray. Residual smoke crept up to the ceiling. "Good luck."

"So, are you going to tell me how it went?" Jenny asked.

"Dr. Miller let me borrow this." I pulled out the crucifix from the cedar box and placed it on the kitchen table in front of her. "It belonged to a 13th-century Spanish count, El Conde De Consuegra."

"Is it really from the 13th century?"

I looked at her without flinching, trying to get past that fake-inquisitive look of hers.

"Why are you looking at me like that?" she asked.

I continued the staring contest, saying absolutely nothing.

She started giggling like a school girl. "El Conde De *what*?"

"De Consuegra."

"I guess he changed the name," she admitted. "That sounds so much better than the name he was using. When did you find out the story was fake?"

"When he said I could borrow it. Come on, you don't really think I'd fall for anyone giving me such a valuable sacred object if it were real, do you? Especially after just meeting me. It's not a baseball card, you know. Why did you do this to me?"

"It's worked before. We went over a few case studies in class where the subjects actually changed their behavior because they believed in the power of that object."

"Did he ever tell them the truth?"

"That the object was really from the religious store? Never! That's what got him in trouble with administration."

I heaved a deep sigh. "I guess we're back where we started."

"Not exactly," she said. "If you really believe in this magical religious nonsense, then it shouldn't matter if the cross is really from the 13th century or not."

She was right. I tried to walk it off by retreating upstairs and turned on the news for the weather report, part of our nightly ritual. In my T-shirt and shorts, I waited for her to come to bed.

She came in with a glass of water in her hand and put on her slip as she got ready for bed.

"My father was forty-two when he died," I said.

"Your father must have been a lovely man, but he isn't you."

"The day he died, they wheeled his bed out of the room. We walked with him to the elevator. There was no room for us. Mom and I were walking away—Dad looked directly at me from his bed and waved me over. The orderly propped him up, and I got really close. 'Don't be afraid,' he said. His eyes were a dark yellow color."

"Liver dysfunction. I'm sorry you had to see that at such a young age."

"I don't think he was in any pain though." I moved closer to her. "They have cutting-edge sedatives. I hope they pump me full of pain killers when it's my turn so I won't feel a thing."

"What a horrible thought," said Jenny. "Go to sleep."

I turned the TV off. The room was dark again.

Jenny took only a few minutes to doze off, though I must have been up for hours, tossing and turning, not just because of her loud, occasional snoring, but because I knew it was time to face my fears. That's what I kept telling myself.

The cross lay on the night stand by the bed.

The faint light from the window showed colorless objects in front of the bed—the dresser, the armoire. I tried to make out the blurred items on the mirror when the black figure moved through the doorway and stopped in front of the bed.

It stood, looking my way.

In one motion, I found myself standing and staring back in silence.

The figure's cowl made it impossible to know what he looked like.

I took one step back and picked up the wooden cross on the night stand. I moved toward him and got within a few inches, but he turned to the door and walked out of the bedroom.

"Jenny!" I shouted.

She didn't move.

I caught the back of him as he walked down the stairs to the kitchen. I followed behind at a distance, the cross still in my hand. Through the doorway, I saw he was facing the window. I felt for the light switch by the door and flicked it on.

This wasn't happening.

He was still there.

I walked towards him in full light, touched the cowl with the tips of my fingers, and then in a blind fit of odd nerve, pulled down the hood revealing a face angry at me, a skull, the same skull I had seen when I was a child, only now he was real.

I leaped back, flipped a few chairs over, and slammed my head against the edge of the table as my back hit the wall and the floor.

I scrambled to find the cross. It was still in my hand. I held it out in front of me, startling him for a few seconds—but only a few. He wrenched it from me and crushed it with his hand, throwing the broken pieces to the side and coming closer.

I jumped to my feet and ran to a corner of the kitchen. He was blocking the doorway, so there was nowhere I could go but to the back of the room. Then, he was gone.

I didn't move. Any movement might have prompted him to come back, so I remained still.

I tried to breathe again, and there was movement next to me.

I turned to see a man sitting at the edge of the table; I recognized him immediately, but couldn't decide whether he was really there: my father.

I couldn't understand what he said exactly, but I knew he wanted me to sit next to him. He didn't look at me but stared out in a trance. "Dad," I said.

I received no response.

I said it again and placed my hand over his. It was like touching a rock—no life in it. He turned his hand and grabbed me so I couldn't pull away.

This wasn't my father.

A skeleton held me and began to pull me. I screamed. Out of a corner of my eye, I saw Jenny walk in the kitchen. "Jenny!" I called.

She didn't flinch; she walked casually from the doorway to the fridge.

"Jenny, please help me!" I cried.

She didn't turn but kept filling her glass with water from the ice dispenser. When her glass was full, she walked out, but paused and turned my way. "You're being silly," she said.

Everything went dark.

It took me a few seconds to get my bearings. I was sitting up in bed, looking out the window at the night sky, and Jenny was shaking me.

"Hey," she said, "you were dreaming again."

"Yes, I was dreaming." I got up and stood by the side of the bed, anxious to push back at who or what, I wasn't sure. "It was a dream," I said again.

The wind shook the trees outside, banged the gutters, brushed against the window.

"It's starting to get ugly out there," Jenny said. "We're gonna get snow."

"Later," I told her. "The weather man said it'll come later, not now."

"What's the matter?" Jenny sensed the edge in my voice and flicked on the lamp by her night stand.

She blinded me temporarily. "Please turn that off."

"You don't want it on?"

"We still have a few hours before daybreak, and I'm going back."

"Going back to sleep?"

"Yes," I said. "Round two." I dug my head firmly on the pillow and wrapped myself up in the blanket.

Now that the pretense of reality was gone, I found myself on top of a mountain. The wind was blowing fiercely, pushing me closer to the edge. Things were moving fast. No long discourse. No debate.

I pushed back, though not at the wind—at the two hands that were doing the pushing.

I looked behind at the bottomless abyss before I tumbled off the edge, but I didn't fall for long. Suddenly, I was fighting to stay afloat adrift the waves of a vast and angry ocean. The rain fell hard as I struggled to stay above water.

"Is this the best you can do?" I screamed.

Something pulled my feet and I went under.

The water was murky. I could barely make out the dark figure that was coming my way, showing me its giant mouth and sharp teeth, getting ready to rip me apart.

I shut my eyes, trying hard to think of a different place.

I was in a quiet meadow where the grass seemed to go on forever. I walked and walked.

"Where are you?" I shouted. "Take your best shot. I'm not going anywhere. Show yourself."

He appeared within a few feet from me, but without movement, a flat silhouette, an idea that had taken on too much weight. I watched as he stared back, motionless.

Without any hesitation, I grabbed his head, gripped it like an NBA player palming a basketball in midair. He squirmed; I squeezed harder and crushed that bony head of his to a fine dust. The cowl swooped to the ground.

He was gone.

I screamed again with no clue as to what I was saying. Flashing images came fast: a cauldron filled with soup boiling inside me, a copper spoon crushing black cells. Images mixed with other images, saying so much that I was at a loss for words. I screamed until my face was hot, my throat burned, my arms trembled. My screaming blurred it all, and I kept screaming until my body took a jolt.

"Esteban. Wake up!" Jenny shook me.

I sighed heavily and tried to settle back down. It took me a minute. I stared at the ceiling fan.

I was awake.

The next time we met Dr. Singh in his office, he revealed the results of the bone marrow test. The disease had not spread. Subsequent visits offered the same results.

"The medicine worked," he said after the chemo phase had run its course. "There are nubs in your stomach. You may have them the rest of your life, but they will most likely remain dormant. You're going to be fine."

I got up from the exam table and buttoned my shirt. "Doctor," I said in a semi-serious tone. "Did I mention I found the secret to immortality?"

He looked at Jenny, who looked at me, pursing her lips to show me she was trying hard to restrain herself.

About the Author

Pablo Patiño is a self-employed entrepreneur who lives in Long Island, New York, with his wife and four crazy daughters. This is his debut story.

The Cold Gets In

Mary Thorson

Milwaukee, 1952

The morning after the Schulz murders, Betsy and her father sat in the back of St. Hedwig's so they could leave right after communion. Before they left for church, her father had been looking over the paper. He asked her, in his low mumbling so she needed to come closer to hear, don't you know him? He kept a dirty finger on the paper, right underneath the headline: *Family Members Murdered; Teen Son Missing*. Betsy felt a wave of dread travel the length of her body, almost pulsating, and she tried to grab the page.

"I'm not done, yet," he said, pulling it closer to his face.

She leaned against the kitchen counter and waited for him. Then, he folded up the paper, set it down, and went to the front hall to get ready. She read it as fast as she could before he came in, saying they had to go. The words only registered as flashes as her father walked back into the kitchen: *Katherine, 38, found in the kitchen. Robert, 11, found underneath the bed. Kathleen, 6, found in the closet. John, 16, missing.*

"It's time, now," Betsy's father said.

They ducked into the back pew like intruders, and Betsy's face became uncomfortably warm. When it came time for communion, they marched slowly up the aisle. She pressed the wafer to the roof of her mouth with her tongue and held it there. You're not supposed to chew Christ, her father told her once, so she would let it melt and become like a plastic coating. They were almost to their front door by the time it was gone. Going to church wasn't something they had done until after Betsy's mother died the year before, so Betsy wasn't all that familiar with the routine, but she knew sneaking out like this was disrespectful. She could feel the whole church watching her leave.

The next day at school, Linda Lepinski was waiting by their shared gym locker to tell Betsy they had found John Schulz. She put a hand on Betsy's arm, as if what she had said was meant to be consoling. Betsy stood still with her dress in her hand, wanting desperately to bury her face in it. The echoes of conversation that had been bouncing around the locker room became quieter. The other girls were closing their lockers slowly, in order to hear.

"He's been arrested," she said, like an apology.

They caught John in Missouri after he stopped at a diner for breakfast. He had seen a family in the car ahead of him with two small children in the back seat, which he later told police had given him "a hard time." As Linda continued, Betsy wondered if, at any point between the family in the car and the coffee at the diner, maybe he had stopped at a phone booth. He knew her number by heart. He had told her so. She remembered when she first told it to him. She watched him write it down the length of his arm.

"Did you know?" Linda asked.

"Know what?" Betsy whispered.

"I mean." Linda squirmed. "Did he say anything?"

She hadn't asked this question quietly enough. Betsy felt like her skin had been set on fire. The corners of her eyes started to sting from an effort not to blink. Linda's hand was back on her arm, and when she tried to rub it reassuringly, Betsy jerked herself away. She just missed hitting her hand against her locker—though she braced for the metallic pop, anyway.

When John first asked Betsy out, he wanted her to watch the sunset with him on the beach. She had to work at the theater that night, but she wanted him to ask. She couldn't tell if the hairs on his upper lip were for lack of trying or lack of growth. She thought she might be able to count them all, and the end result would be somewhere under fifty.

"Not really," she said.

"Why not?" John took a step back.

"I don't really have the time to wait for Earth to flip its rotation." She waited for a second. She wanted him to get the joke.

"Lake Michigan is east," she said.

"Your parents don't let you go down there or something?"

"No. Not that. Lake Michigan is east and the sun sets in the west. You can't watch the sunset from the lake."

"Sure you can, I've done it plenty," John said.

"From Lake Michigan?"

"Sure," John said.

"Then you must be some kind of Greek god, like Apollo."

"Who?"

"Apollo, god of the sun," Betsy said.

"Well, do you want to or not?"

"Do you even know my name?" Betsy asked.

"Do you know mine?"

"Yeah—Apollo, I just told you. Everyone knows who you are."

And they did. John Schulz had transferred over to Riverside in the beginning of the year. He had been expelled from his old school, and everyone knew that, too. But, for what, the rumors ran wild. Someone said he sent a kid to the hospital with a broken back after he threw him down the stairs. Someone else said that he punched one of his teachers after they had held him in detention. Someone said he brought a knife to school. Someone said it was a gun. Someone said he had tried to burn the school down. Betsy was too afraid to ask.

A few days after he asked her out, Betsy was walking with her father up the steps of St. Hedwig's when John appeared behind them. He tried to talk to her father, who hadn't even noticed he was there.

"I go to school with your daughter over at Riverside," John was saying with his hand out, slipping in front of them.

"Okay," her father said, not taking his hands out of his pockets.

"Daddy, this is John Schulz."

"He said so."

"Well, anyway, I was wondering if I might take your daughter out sometime, sir?"

"Mass is starting, Betsy." Her father walked ahead, keeping his head down while he got in the door as it was closing behind someone.

Betsy pulled at her hair nervously while John tried to gather himself.

"Hard man, I guess," John said.

"Not hard, I don't think. I guess—well, it's difficult to explain."

"Doesn't like me much; easy to tell that."

Betsy touched John's arm, and he took a step down to be closer to her.

"No, he's just not interested…in anything. He doesn't really care one way or another about anything."

"So he wouldn't care if I called you sometime?"

At the lake, Betsy moved her hand along the rock in order to reach his. The sun was going down on their backs, and Betsy had to squint when she looked at him. His breath came out frozen, and he was trying not to shake with cold as the wind burned up their faces. The beach was all white. The icecaps had trapped the waves, and she could only hear the echo of them moving underneath.

"This was stupid. I shouldn't have brought you here. You must think I'm some kind of idiot. A real jerk."

"Actually, did you know that it's warmer by the lake than anywhere else?"

"You're smart, huh?" He was annoyed, and she didn't know what he wanted, but she wanted to know.

"Not really."

"Don't lie. I'm sure you get straight As. Perfect student and all that."

"I don't. I promise." Betsy was lying.

He knew it somehow. He rolled his eyes and started looking off in different directions, like he had to get somewhere else.

"I don't know how to drive a car." She almost shouted it. Despite the cold, her face flushed, and her armpits started to dampen.

"What?" Aloof, as if he hadn't heard her just fine.

"I don't know how to drive. My dad's never taken me out. I'm sixteen. I should be driving like everyone else, but I've never even gone down an alley."

"How come he doesn't take you?"

"I don't know. He's never asked, so I don't ask."

"I'm a good driver, you know," he sniffed, the snot running from his nose. "I might show you some things."

"Really?"

"Sure. I guess."

"That'd be great. It's embarrassing, really."

"My dad sometimes lets me take out the car, but when he's out it's just my mom, and she yells and screams at me like a real bitch."

She had never heard anyone describe a mother like this. Betsy thought of how hard it was for her mother to breathe, at the end.

"But, anyway, I don't care. I just take it whenever I want it."

"You get in trouble?"

He shrugged. "Yeah—but who cares, you know? It doesn't matter."

And she knew it didn't.

He took her out for driving lessons, but Betsy never got out of the passenger seat. She didn't think he would ever let her move over, but she really didn't mind. The two of them sat on the bench seat of Arno Schulz's Kaiser Deluxe. John twisted around the radio knob, but the car wasn't on yet, so all it did was make a clicking sound.

"I asked my dad if I could take his, even though it's new. Look here." He gripped the knob of the gear shift, and Betsy kept her hands tucked between her thighs.

"It's manual," he said. "Lots harder for girls. My mom made him get her an automatic, even though manual's more fun. My dad says that's when you're really driving."

John was smiling, and Betsy felt like she was spying on him.

"Put your hand on top of mine." Without asking, John reached for her. His bare knuckles swept the inside of her thigh, his dry skin scraping against her nylons. Betsy held that feeling in the breath inside her mouth. He placed her hand on top of his so her fingers fit between his. They both looked at their hands and waited for the other one to do something.

"Try shifting up to first," John said softly.

She pushed the gear forward, but it wouldn't budge. Her hand slid hard against his.

"It won't go," she said.

"Shoot, sorry. I forgot—I forgot to press the clutch down. Sorry." John laughed and stomped his foot on the pedal. "This is how my dad taught me. He had me sit up next to him in front, even if my mom was in the car—well, sometimes. He let me shift while he was driving starting when I was eight years old."

"My dad never lets me do anything at all. You're lucky," she said.

"Yeah, right." John rolled his eyes. "Watch this." With his foot still on the clutch, he slipped the gear into neutral. Betsy felt the muscles and tendons get tighter underneath her limp fingers. Little blue veins had appeared in between his knuckles. She hadn't noticed that the car was moving until after she felt his eyes on her, waiting for her to react. So she did. She squealed a little, and from the look on his face that seemed to be what he wanted.

The Friday night before the murders, John's hand was sweaty when he put it on top of her thigh. Betsy could feel the dampness through the tiny holes in her nylons. He had cut the engine right when Johnny Ray was belting that his girl should go on and cry. When it was suddenly silence, the air in the car seemed muffled, as if someone who had been screaming was stopped. John's pinky was moving against the hem of her black woolen skirt like it had an itch. Betsy studied his little nail; it was short but had a crooked edge because he had chewed it. Betsy had noticed those little white specks on his nails, like her father's, but she never saw them on her own.

John had crept underneath now, and his fingertips started to press on the inside of her thigh. She hated it. In church, when she would sit herself down on the hard pew, Betsy would watch the fat of her thighs spread out to either side and meet flush in the middle. They would sweat no matter how cold the church was. They were sweating now, and it was cold.

John wasn't looking at her. He was watching his hand. His nose began to run and he sniffed. Betsy wanted to give him the tissue she had in her pocket, but she didn't want to move—afraid that she would scare him off. His dry lips were slightly parted, and Betsy could see his breath falling out of his mouth. She opened her own mouth, hoping she would suck in some of his air.

"It's okay," he said, but she didn't believe him.

She put her hand on his, which was now completely hiding under her skirt, and she spread her thighs apart—almost able to hear the tear between them.

She hadn't said no. Not exactly. She had told him "maybe later."

He showed up at the theater hours after the killings. From the ticket booth, she could see him crossing the street while two of his friends waited by his mother's car, not the good one. John had started jogging across Farwell Avenue, but once he saw Betsy watching him, he slowed down to a strut. He didn't speed up when a car turned onto the street, and its headlights lit him up. In that unforgiving yellow light, Betsy could see how pale he was. She thought that he seemed angry and on edge by the way he was coming. It was almost like he was barreling toward her, though he was going so determinedly slow.

"Hi, there," she said to him.

As if he hadn't expected her to be there, he cocked his head and flashed something close to a smile. He leaned against the window and kept his hands in his pockets.

"Hi, yourself," he said, pointing his chin in Betsy's direction.

"You here to see a movie?" she asked.

The only thing they had showing was some cartoon picture that she knew John wouldn't be caught dead seeing.

"No, I don't think so. What are you doing tonight?"

Betsy screwed up her face. She could see how ugly it looked in her reflection in the glass so she quickly straightened it out and smiled at him.

"What do you mean?" she asked.

"Just asking you a question. What—are—you—doing?"

He sounded it out for her, slowly and mean. Betsy tightened up her eyebrows and stared at him. He shrugged up into his coat a little more and didn't look at her straight.

"I'm working. You see I'm in here, right?"

"Alright. I meant later, okay?"

"Sure," she said.

"So? What about later?"

"I don't know. It'll be midnight when I get off."

"And what?" he asked.

"My dad'll be waiting for me to come home."

"You lie. Your dad is probably dead asleep right now. He won't even hear you come in."

"I don't know. I don't think so. Not tonight. Why not tomorrow?"

"Please, tonight, Bets? Okay?"

His hands were out of his pockets and gripping the tiled counter that wrapped around the little room she was in. He was breathing hard, as if he were gasping for air, as if his shoulders had just become incredibly heavy, and they were weighing down his lungs. His eyes were wide open. The amount of white showing was unnerving. They were watering, but he wouldn't blink; even if he wanted to, he was willing himself not to, Betsy was sure of it. He was frozen there.

"Maybe later, then," she said.

"Yeah?" He smiled, and something inside him seemed to shift and let go. Like he might cry. It was the saddest looking smile Betsy had ever seen.

"Yeah, maybe," she said.

"Okay, then. I'll come back later—midnight. We're going to the game, but that'll get out earlier."

"Fine."

John pressed his palm against the glass and held it there. That pathetic smile was still on his face. Betsy knew she should respond in some sweet way that might alleviate him, but she didn't. One of his friends reached into the car and honked the horn. John took his hand off the glass as if it had burnt him. He walked back to the car and then drove off.

Later, she waited for him. For a few minutes, she watched her boss lock up the main office and turn off the lights in the lobby. She was on an uncomfortable wooden bench, keeping an eye out for a car that might pull up outside and park underneath the marquee. The lights were still running. Betsy had always thought of the moving light as one living thing that jumped from lightbulb to lightbulb, like a ghost possessing the glass one moment and then leaving it empty the next. Having burned everything up, it would just move on. Her boss came over and asked if she needed a ride. She told him that she didn't; she was waiting for somebody who'd be there soon. It was a quarter past midnight, and she knew that John wasn't coming back.

"Well, I have to turn out the lights. Are you sure you don't need a ride?"

"I'm sure."

He stared at her for a second then turned them off. They faded orange, like burning embers. It would have been better if she had just left with John when he came, she thought.

Later, John told the police he had a good time at the game, mostly—until the end. The screams bothered him, but he stayed until it was over.

After that Monday at school, she sat silent at the kitchen table. Her father was eating, and she could hear his jaw popping every time he chewed. Her mother would talk over it during dinner, because she hated the sound, telling long stories about nothing just to get to the end of the meal. Betsy was expecting the thing to become completely unhinged one day, and she knew that would be her problem. When he was done, he rubbed his face with his big hand and sighed.

"That boy was bad," her father said, finally.

Betsy's cheeks flushed red.

"I knew that when I met him. You can tell about that kind of evil."

"You didn't know," came from her scorched throat.

"Maybe not all people can tell, but sharp ones can." Her father tapped his forehead.

"And you tell me now, then?"

"Not my business," he said.

"Not your business—" she swept her hand in front of herself, accidentally knocking the coffee pot to the floor.

Betsy watched it shatter and spill out over the black and red tiles. He didn't even react to the sound. He kept his eyes lazily open and fixed on her. Betsy pushed back her chair so it scraped against the floor, and she grabbed the rag from the oven. She got on her hands and knees and started to clean the mess, but the harder she wiped, the more it spread, with coffee grounds like rocks scratching the tile.

"Yeah, with some people, you can just know it," he said.

She kept wiping until the mess was all around them.

She dreamt about John that night. Except, when she dreamt, she wasn't herself—she was him. She asked his mother for the car. She went upstairs. She got the shotgun. She asked, again for the car. She called his mother by her first name, "Kathy," because that's what John had done. She pulled the trigger and felt the recoil push into her shoulder while she watched Mrs. Schulz collapse on the kitchen floor. She stalked through the house after John's brother and sister. She paused over the girl because he had done that. When she woke up, she still felt trapped there in his skin—but not in his skin. In her own.

The day they brought John back from Missouri, hundreds of people were at the train station, but Betsy didn't see anyone there that she knew. A lot of reporters stood around, talking to each other, smiling and laughing. She felt as though someone was walking over her grave. She wanted to get closer, but the crowd was too thick. Too many elbows ready to jab out to protect vantage points. Betsy didn't have a chance. She stood shorter than the majority of the crowd. Her height was a thing John had liked. It was a joke that John liked to play, him being so tall and her so short; he'd prop his arm up on top of her head and rest it there, saying, "You're just right, Bets." The air was thin down where she was in the crowd, so Betsy stood up on her toes and took a deep breath. A flash went off. Someone shouted his name. Then it was like a lightning storm. She heard it, over and over again. His name. "Why'd you do it, John?" All those strangers asking, "Why'd you do it, John? Why'd you kill your mom, John? Why'd you kill the kids?"

She couldn't see him behind all those people, but the general direction of the crowd began to shift, and she knew where he was. He was like a magnet. Betsy was pulled with the crowd. She wanted to be facing him dead on if she could get a look at him. The flashes didn't stop, and she thought she could see the top of his head, the lights bouncing off his straight black hair shining with grease. Then, there was a gap in the crowd, and she could see him. Pale, but making a strange face—the sort of smile you have when you're not supposed to have one at all. She couldn't quite tell, but she thought maybe he could see her. She had the sudden urge to stick her hand up and wave at him. She opened her mouth to yell for him, but then his face changed. He looked like a wounded animal, trying to hide when cornered. He turned and dipped his head and the crowd moved toward the doors. Outside, she could see the police car waiting with its lights already on. The flashes kept going and were hitting the windows, making it hard for her to see it when John fit all of his awkward limbs in the back. Suddenly everyone scattered. There was a giant noise that gradually got quieter as they fled the station. In a matter of seconds, she was almost alone in the room. The ticket takers stood wide-eyed at their stations.

A stuttering boarding announcement came over the loud speaker, and finally, she started toward the doors. When she stepped outside, the wind hit her with a breathtaking force. She hunched her shoulders up to her ears and started walking toward the Wisconsin Ave. bus. It was a barren darkness, the kind of night that makes the world empty and sharp. When she reached the bus, the driver wasn't in it. The keys were gone, and there was a sign hanging over the steering wheel: BATHROOM BREAK, BACK IN 10.

She stood in the aisle, looking over the rows of empty seats. Finally, she walked to the back and sat in the dark. The light from the street lamps glowed outside, but didn't make it in. The wind rocked the bus, slipping in through the door and loose windowpanes. Betsy unbuttoned her coat and pulled her knees into her chest, then buttoned it back up over them. She bowed her head and breathed into the inside of her jacket. She thought about the warmth inside his dad's car. "You see? It's like this," he would say.

XOXOX XOXOX XOXOX X

About the Author

Mary Thorson is from Milwaukee, WI. She got her undergraduate degree in Creative Writing at the University of Wisconsin-Milwaukee, and is finishing up her MFA at Pacific University's low-residency program in Oregon. She has been previously published in *Chrome Baby* and was nominated for a Pushcart Prize for her short story, "The Hive Broke on a Sunday."

Do the Faceless Remember?

Megan Neumann

They were in study hall when Haley held out her phone and whispered, "Take a look at this."

Not thinking much about it, Vera picked up the phone and watched. The video was creepy, sure, but Vera knew it had to be fake.

The grainy video showed some dirty hospital room. A girl with long black hair and a soiled hospital gown sat on a bed, her back facing the camera; whoever held the camera moved around the girl to show her face in profile, and something about her was strange. Her lips didn't protrude enough. Her nostrils were nonexistent. When the camera moved again, Vera saw the girl's face had no features.

In place of eyes were two slight dents. As Vera watched, the girl's nose flattened, shrinking to a hill of flesh. Her mouth was still there, but just barely. The girl tried to open it, but strings of flesh like web zigzagged between the top and lower lips and seemed to be pulling together, forcing the girl's mouth shut. No sound came from the phone, but Vera imagined the girl was screaming.

"That's dumb," Vera said, trying to sound casual even though she was creeped out. Haley had been on a creeping people out kick lately, but Vera wouldn't give Haley the satisfaction of acting afraid. "It's so fake," Vera went on. "I'm not even scared."

Haley smirked, still holding her phone in front of Vera's face.

"It looked legit to me," Sadie said quietly. She sat behind them, her head down, not making eye contact with either of them. Sadie never made eye contact with anyone.

Haley turned and gave Sadie a cold look. Haley was always giving Sadie that look, and Vera never understood why Sadie didn't stand up to Haley, or at least stop hanging out with her.

"It's just special effects and makeup," Vera said.

"No, it's not," Haley said. She locked her phone and tossed it into her bag. They were supposed to be doing their homework, but they never did. Instead, they'd spend the hour on Instagram or Twitter, looking at other people's photos, at other people's statuses and lives. Haley loved trolling the girls at school, the girls who had snubbed her in the past. Vera had gotten sick of Haley doing this. Just the day before, the two of them had gotten into a fight. But Haley must have gotten over it since she was talking to Vera now.

"It's a disease," Haley said, a smile creeping onto her face. "I found some forums talking about it. There are bunch of other videos like this. People with their faces disappearing. It's spreading, but no one's talking about it on the news because the government wants to keep it quiet. People would panic, you know?"

Vera scoffed and rolled her eyes. "That sounds made up. Did you just make that up? Or are you just a sucker for dumb stories?"

Anger spread across Haley's face. She turned bright red and the smile faded, her lips forming a hard line.

Thankfully, the bell rang, and Vera stood to leave. She was tired of Haley's love affair with creepy videos and being a weirdo in general. Sadie was the only one who tolerated her lately. If it wasn't a video, Haley would find some other prank to scare them, but Vera was too old for that now.

When they were younger, ten or eleven, Haley was the tough one, the one who would stick up for the three. But with her toughness came a meanness, a meanness sometimes directed at Sadie and Vera. She liked to boss them around, make them feel like they needed her. If they ever stood up to her, she'd pull a prank. Or tell them some bizarre story that they'd dumbly fall for. Once Vera thought aliens had replaced her parents. As proof, her mom had to describe in detail how Vera had peed her pants in the fourth grade and had come home crying wearing soiled jeans.

That was a long time ago. They were seventeen now—seniors— and Vera realized a few years ago she was just as smart as Haley; she didn't need Haley telling her what to do. Vera wanted to stop being friends, but they had been a trio for a long time. Leaving all their history behind was hard to do. Harder than Vera wanted to admit.

They didn't have many classes together anymore. Vera had moved to all AP; Haley and Sadie hadn't. They did have study hall together, and there they'd take up their old ways. Haley would go online and make fun of the people, the girls who were mean to them. She'd create fake accounts to post cruel things. At first Vera thought it was funny, but it grew repetitive and tiring.

Vera was glad the semester was almost over. Next semester they'd have no classes together.

"You think you're so much smarter than us!" Haley yelled when Vera made it to the door. "I'll prove you wrong. You'll believe me soon."

Vera let the door slam behind her, proud of herself for not giving into Haley.

Hours later, though, when she was home, she felt foolish. Haley always made her feel that way, as if Haley's bad behavior was Vera's fault, and Vera's reactions were somehow just Vera being insensitive. She picked up her phone and texted Haley. "Sorry about today. Maybe the video is real. I want to believe."

A few seconds passed. Then Vera received a text from Haley. "Good. Look at this." Another text appeared with a long URL made up of an IP address followed by lots of random numbers and letters: https://133.22.553.2/slie2n22/iwjrlw/bytHePickwppsk/22n5i&soi. Feeling dumb for doing it, Vera clicked the link. She wondered how Haley always got her to do dumb things, things she would regret later.

The page opened onto another video.

Her phone's screen filled and became dark. She couldn't make out anything in the video. She heard a sound, but she couldn't tell what the sound was. Only that it was a soft, dull sound which unsettled her, though she wasn't sure why. She turned up the volume and brightness on her phone. She thought she could make out some shapes. Yes, she could definitely see a pile of something in the center of the screen, something moving slowly, pulsing. She stared at it for a few seconds more until she realized she could make out the shapes of hands, feet, and other body parts. The pulsing thing in the center of the screen was a pile of naked bodies. The sound in the video was the writhing of the bodies in the pile. Had Haley sent her a video of an unenthusiastic orgy? She pinched the screen and zoomed in. The heads had no faces.

Vera dropped her phone and covered her ears. She didn't want to hear the bodies moving. The video would end soon, or so she thought, and then it would be safe to look at her phone again. But the video seemed to be on a loop or be several minutes long.

Another text message popped up, and Vera was relieved to reach down to her phone and click on the message. Anything to stop the video from looping.

"Did you see it?" a message from Haley said.

Her hands shaking, Vera typed, "WTF? That's sick. It's obviously fake. But still sick. I don't want to see these stupid hoax videos anymore. You're sick to want to watch them. I wish I hadn't texted you."

She sent the message and turned off her phone. She shouldn't have sent the first message to Haley anyway. Haley liked making people uncomfortable, making them squirm. She would never change, and Vera knew that.

Haley came around to Vera's lunch table the next day. She set her tray down, leaned in, and said, "It's sick, yes, but it's true. Just because you don't like something doesn't make it fake. Most real things are horrible. You're miss genius history girl; you should know that."

Behind her, Sadie wandered up to the table. She looked ill. Vera wondered if she, too, had seen the pile of faceless, writhing bodies and hadn't slept the night before.

"If it's true," Vera whispered, "then why haven't I heard about it on the news."

"Who cares about the news? Everything we need to know about it is already online. You've got to see this other video."

Haley passed her phone beneath the table.

"I don't want to see another video!" Vera yelled.

"This one is different. It'll change what you think."

Vera stared down at the video on Haley's phone, knowing she really shouldn't look. But curiosity got the better of her.

The same hospital as before appeared on the screen, the walls grimy with reddish brown stains. Some doctor in a dingy lab coat held up an x-ray. He was speaking, but once again the video had no audio. The X-ray he held up showed a person's head or at least the silhouette of the head. There was nothing in it, though—no cavity for the brain, no sockets for eyes, no teeth.

"That's what happens to them," Haley said, leaning in so she could whisper into Vera's ear. "That's what they look like on the inside, but they keep moving. They're still alive even without their faces, even without a brain. They can't breathe, but still they live."

Vera shook her head. "This looks even faker than the other one."

Haley slammed her phone down on the table. The video of the X-ray played again. Haley jerked her head at Sadie. "Even this idiot knows something weird is happening. Believe me or don't believe me, I don't care. You used to be smart, you know? You used to know what was good for you. Come on, idiot." Haley stood and left Vera's table, dragging Sadie with her.

Sadie stared back at the video, her face frozen with terror. Vera didn't get it. She and Sadie had seen scarier things in movies. Haley had played worse pranks on them. Why was Sadie so scared?

The next day there were posters all over the school—blurry screenshots of the videos Haley had shown Vera with the words: IT'S REAL. IT'S HAPPENING EVERYWHERE. SEE FOR YOURSELF. Beneath the images was a QR code, most likely linking people to one of the videos Vera had seen before.

She started to pull them down as she passed them, but there were too many. She saw other kids pulling the posters down and laughing. Did they know it was Haley who had put them up? Just as Vera wondered this, she saw Haley coming around a corner, carrying a stack of the printouts. Everyone saw her with them. Some people gaped at her; others just laughed. As soon as Vera saw Haley, she turned and avoided her for the rest of the day.

Sadie leaned against her dented Toyota with her head down.

"You know you don't have to hang out with her anymore," Vera said.

"I know," she mumbled, "but we're friends."

"Did she make you help her with those posters?"

Sadie shrugged.

"Why is she so obsessed with this?"

"She says she's scared for you. She doesn't want you to end up like them."

"Why would I end up like them? And there is no *them*, by the way," Vera said.

Sadie shrugged again and got into her Corolla.

When Sadie didn't show up to school the next day, Vera went to Sadie's house in the evening and knocked on the door. No one answered, but she saw Sadie's car parked out front. She turned the knob on the front door and found it was unlocked. Inside, she called out, "Sadie!" but no one answered. She knew it was no use calling for Sadie's mom who always seemed to be away, either working or with a boyfriend.

"Sadie!" she called again, walking down the narrow hallway leading to the three bedrooms. The house smelled musty and like cigarette smoke. Sadie's mother smoked in the house and rarely opened a window. Vera pushed open the door to Sadie's bedroom and found it empty aside from Sadie's bed and dresser and piles of dirty clothes. The other two bedrooms were empty too.

Vera walked to the kitchen, where a sliding glass door led out to a neglected backyard. She stood, listening to the noises of the house. The appliances hummed; a fluorescent bulb above her buzzed. And there was another sound. She heard something behind a door she had always assumed led to the garage. She pressed her ear against it and listened; a thudding came from the other side. Vera opened the door and found a staircase leading down to a basement she had no idea existed.

The sound grew louder with the door open. "Sadie?" There was no answer, just the sound from below. It was like the thudding of a fist on a hard surface.

Vera walked down the stairs to the dark basement. The thudding became louder. She groped for a light switch along the wall but found nothing. She walked to what she thought would be the middle of the basement and paused. The sound was so loud now, so close. Vera took her phone from her purse and held it before her, touching the screen so it would provide some light.

The light came on and she gasped, dropping her phone. What she saw was impossible. In that instant, she thought she saw the form of a person walking into the wall in front of her. The person had Sadie's hair, Sadie's clothes.

Vera fell to her knees and splayed her fingers wide, searching the floor for her phone. She found it and turned on the flashlight, holding it outward toward the form.

Sadie stood with her back to Vera. "Sadie?"

Sadie slammed into the wall, stumbled backward, and slammed into the wall again.

Vera grabbed Sadie's shoulder. She started to turn her friend around and then paused; she feared what she might see if she turned Sadie's body completely. She swallowed and held her breath, knowing there was no way she could leave Sadie's basement without seeing the truth.

Vera jerked Sadie's shoulder to one side and spun her friend's body. She saw Sadie's smooth, featureless face. It didn't even have a mouth with webbed flesh.

Vera backed away, not believing this was real, thinking she was in a dream and would wake soon.

When she reached the top of the stairs, she turned and ran to Haley's house. Haley was the only person who would know what to do. Haley would be able to fix this. She could stop the prank because that's all it was, right? A prank. And Haley would end it.

Haley opened the door and sighed when she saw Vera's face.

"It happened to her, didn't it? You saw her, didn't you?"

Haley looked up and down the street, as though afraid someone would see the two together. She pulled Vera into her house. They sneaked past Haley's parents, who sat on the living room couch watching TV, oblivious to their daughter and Vera. They went to Haley's bedroom, and Haley shut the door quietly.

"Okay, listen," Haley said. "I told her not to look at it, but you know Sadie, she's dumb. She couldn't stop herself. Maybe she didn't think it was real, maybe it was just her curiosity."

"What are you talking about?"

Haley groaned and threw up her hands as if exasperated by Vera's questions already. "You know how I can't stand all the other girls in school, and I love posting crap on Facebook or harassing them on Twitter, right? Because they're bitches and they deserve it."

Vera nodded.

"Well, one day I decided it wasn't enough to harass them. They needed to pay."

Vera shook her head. She truly was exasperated by Haley's nonsense. "I'm not following you."

"Just shut up for a second, okay? God. This is why I showed it to you. Because you're becoming a real bitch like everyone else."

Vera started to protest, but Haley held up a hand.

"I found this site, okay? A site for revenge. And that site linked to another site and that site had instructions on how it worked with a link to another site. And that site linked to the videos. And those videos contained a virus. Not a computer virus, a real *human* virus. Only it's not spread through regular germs, okay? It's something in the images on the computer screen. Now I know this sounds crazy. I didn't believe it either at first. In fact, I wasn't even sure this was going to work, but I thought 'Hey, why not give it a shot?' So this virus, it's something embedded in the images. When you see it, when your brain interprets it, it starts to take effect. You turn into one of those things. A person without a face, without a brain. And then you're contagious. But only through videos. Each video I showed you had the disease in it." Haley took a breath and smiled.

Vera let out a quick laugh. This was all part of the hoax. Sadie wasn't really a faceless person stuck in her basement. This was a trick she and Haley were playing for some sick reason.

"This is ridiculous. This is a joke, right?" Vera sat on her bed and put her head in her hands.

"I wish it was. It would be a great joke, right?"

"But you watched the video, too," Vera said, panicking because a part of her started to believe this was real.

"Did I?" Haley asked, her voice becoming high and cutesy. "Did you ever see me watching anything?"

Vera tried to remember all the times Haley had shown her the video. It had always been Haley shoving the video in front of Vera's face.

"You put up all the posters," Vera said slowly. "How many people at school have watched it now?"

"Initially, I just wanted it to be a few of the girls I've always hated."

"You mean girls like me?" Vera asked.

Haley smirked. "You were supposed to be our best friend. Then you started to act like you were better than us. You're not better than us—I mean me, since Sadie's gone now. But everyone always treated us like we were trash. So I thought, what the heck, why not infect the whole school? So who knows how many people have it now? Maybe the whole town!" Haley burst out laughing, and then paused. She gave Vera a thoughtful look. "You shouldn't click on every link someone sends you. Even if you think they're your friends."

Vera's heart started pounding quickly; her stomach churned. She thought she would vomit or faint. Could any of this be real?

She rushed out of Haley's room and out of the house, not pausing to say goodnight to Haley's parents. In the distance, she heard Haley laughing in her room.

She couldn't go home. She was too worked up, too disturbed. She needed to put an end to this. Haley's house wasn't too far from the school. She'd go there and take down the posters. As she walked, she reassured herself that this *was* a prank. She'd see Sadie the next day, perfectly normal, with a face and everything. She would take down the posters and everything would be back to normal.

Vera entered the school through the front door and found the hallways completely lit, as though school was still in session. The parking lot was full of cars, too. She remembered there was a debate team match in the auditorium that night. That was fine. She'd pull down the posters while everyone watched the debate.

She started down the hall. From the posters, hundreds of the sick, featureless faces looked down at her. She tugged on each of them and ripped them in half. She passed by the auditorium and paused. That's where the debate should've been. She should've heard talking coming from there, but the whole school was silent. She paused at the auditorium door and slowly pushed it open.

The auditorium was dark. She couldn't see much of the audience. She could, however, see the two students on the well-lit stage. Behind them, a large projection screen provided a close up of the debate, so that even in the back of the auditorium Vera could clearly see the two people on stage and their smooth, eyeless faces.

Vera screamed and covered her mouth. No one turned to look at her. She stepped into the audience and saw that they, too, were faceless. They were either sitting or walking aimlessly around the auditorium, bumping into each other or into things. One faceless person came ambling up to Vera and touched her face. Vera let out another scream but felt it die prematurely.

Her throat had closed; she couldn't breathe.

She backed out of the auditorium, running down the hall and out into the dark parking lot.

In her panic, Vera wondered if the faceless remembered their lives before. Could they have thoughts when there was nothing inside their heads? She hoped they didn't. It would be horrible to remember and do nothing with those memories.

As she felt her lips sticking together, her nostrils closing, her eyelids growing heavy, she saw her friendship with Haley, the two growing apart until they were strangers. She remembered the fear when she first saw the video. She remembered doubting any of it could be real. These images replayed over and over.

Even though her eyes had vanished, she could see her past clearly.

)O)O)C)O)O)C)O)O)C)C

About the Author

Megan Neumann is a speculative fiction writer living in Little Rock, Arkansas. Her stories have appeared in *Crossed Genres, Daily Science Fiction*, and *Luna Station Quarterly*. She is a member of the Central Arkansas Speculative Fiction Writers' Group and is particularly appreciative of their loving support and scathing critiques.

SUICIDE IN REVERSE
(AFTER MATT RASMUSSEN)

Bri Faythe

At three o'clock in the morning two days ago, they found my body on the shore of the lake I spent my last birthday swimming in. Still in my alcohol-stained lingerie, water spilled from the corner of my mouth and pooled in the leaves stuck to my cheek. My red lipstick was replaced by the blue shade that death leaves behind. The police arrive in groups and wear somber faces. They know in their guts that this was not an accident.

Beautiful things do not fall quietly. The plastic pill bottle is still floating when my body starts to sink. The bubbles are peaceful; the snap of a tree branch followed by the crack of a human limb is not. I tethered myself to a branch below a bird's nest when I did not think the pills alone would bring me home. The rope refused to hold. Drunken fingers cannot tie eloquent knots; they only know how to find their way into another person's mouth. Several pills fall into the water below the tree I cling to. I toss the rest to the back of my throat straight from the bottle. My hands shake too fiercely to pick them up one by one. I notice I've been crying for quite some time.

My mother woke up at three this morning to the sound of the sink full of dishes tipping over. My dress was pulled down to just below my waistline. Dried alcohol left a trail from the corner of my mouth to my sternum and my makeup was smeared across the face of the boy standing next to me. My mother asks me to stay home with her tonight.

XOXOX XOXOX XOXOX X

About the Author

Bri Faythe is a college student living in Tampa, Florida, where she spent the majority of her childhood writing stories past her bedtime. A retail worker by day and concert-goer and slam poet by night, Bri primarily writes and performs spoken word poetry but is trying to expand her reach. This is her debut fiction piece.

THE LEAF PEOPLE

Heather Sullivan

J ack opened the window shade and stared at Ashley's trees—the real ones—the ones that stalked his thoughts and urged him to excel. Their brittle winter skeletons were heavy now with buds: pitiful cocoons clinging to pitiful twigs, leaves waiting for Nature's permission to bloom. The neighbors' virtual trees remained full and green despite the seasons, reminding Jack that he could not yet afford such a landscape. *Soon*, he thought. *Soon*.

He was startled by the *thunk thunk thunk* of Ashley's prescriptions landing in the drop-off chute. Annoyingly located below their bedroom window, it was easy access for both parties involved: the delivery van, as this chute was close to the street, and Ashley, as her side of the bed was at arm's length from the convenient metal handle. All she had to do was fling her wrist from beneath the sheets, pull, and reach into the dark cave that bestowed these weekly goods. This time, Jack noticed, she did it without looking: head on pillow, eyes closed, her fingers—like greedy tendrils searching for rich soil—burrowed until they clutched the bottles. Then they retracted, dropping their gifts on Ashley's stomach.

Jack knew that these movements had become ritual, just like her hand slapping the snooze button on that relic she insisted upon keeping. Every morning the alarm clock wailed like a tortured bird, and even though Jack had installed the silent *Gentle Nudge* program into their bed's hard drive months prior, Ashley still refused to use it. She refused to use a lot of things. Mainly his expert advice on psychological disorders.

"Jack, I am not a hypochondriac," she'd said. "Nor am I pretending to be in pain due to some deep-rooted emotional issue. My limbs *really* ache and my muscles *really* burn. My doctor is almost certain I have fibromyalgia."

"Which, might I remind you, was once considered a disorder of the mind."

"That's *exactly* my point. *Now* they know better. *Now* it's a *real* disease with *real* physical symptoms, so save your jargon and help me rub this cream into my back."

Then she'd lie there dousing herself with anti-itch lotions and muscle-tension relievers, swallowing pills, and squeezing drops of wart-remover randomly on skin that, to Jack, appeared fine— beautiful actually, for his wife had perfect skin. It was her mind that was flawed. Her mind was a deep, cracked cavern into which Jack no longer delved.

Months ago, when Ashley's "symptoms" had begun to surface, Jack had tried to help. Once, as he had stared at her imaginary warts, he could almost envision them growing more rings, expanding in size, and pulsing, just as she'd described, so he had confirmed the warts' existence as an experiment. Perhaps, this approach would lend insight into both his wife's condition and his profession at large. When Jack "saw" the warts and "felt" the knife tips threatening to push through her toes, Ashley had bloomed on their bed, her legs and arms opening up to him. "Just be careful, so my skin doesn't scratch you. It's hard and scaly all over," she had whispered. But she had been marble-smooth.

Another time, Jack had tried to convince Ashley that there was nothing physically wrong with her, that her imagination was causing these strange "growths," the sore joints, and the knots climbing her spine.

"But you *said* you saw them. You *said* you felt the lumps."

"Metaphorically," Jack had replied, "I did. I'm trying to figure out what's wrong, Ash. I'm trying to look at this from different angles."

"Don't even try to mess with my head like you do with your clients. You act like you understand, but you really don't listen. To me or to them."

"*You're* the one who doesn't understand, Ashley! I'm the doctor here. I know what I'm doing. I'm working my tail off and you just don't appreciate it!"

She had turned her back to him—rolling to deliberately hog the blankets—and shut off the light. "You're not *my* doctor."

Despite Jack's continued attempts, Ashley had closed up about her sickness ever since—a morning glory shriveling in darkness. Now, as he watched his wife slathering her body parts with ointment, Jack felt the urge to leave the room.

Jack sat down at his desk. The monitor made its familiar hiss.

"Number 865299 requests access," he said into the computer's face.

"Granted," she replied.

"Report waiting room status."

"Full at six. Five emergencies. One code 1307 has been confirmed. Number 535."

He killed himself? Jack's heart raced. "How did that happen? I thought he was finally coming around!" *Maybe I should've eased up a bit on the breakdown process, but he seemed like he was handling it well.*

"Presently, no further details are available," her voice said.

Maybe he wasn't truly interested in recovery. Maybe he was a lost cause.

Lost long before I met him.

"Reschedule my regular eight o'clock. I'd better take the first emergency now."

"Number 9879 is ready," she reported.

"Really?"

Number 9879 had been tough—the kind of client who required a slower, subtler uprooting. Some needed just a few jabs at their tender spots to get them moving, and by inflating these inadequacies, Jack was merely speeding up the necessary cycle. Before they could be helped, psychiatric patients needed to plummet downward until they crashed against the rocks of hell. Only then could they covet something brighter. Only then could they envision the glittery path back to mental health. And Jack was their guide: a lighthouse illuminating the darkest corners of their minds before leading them to safety.

This technique, though taxing, was also beneficial for Jack. Once they hit the bottom, clients requested frequent emergency meetings. Due to intensity and inconvenience, these sessions were triple the price of regular appointments. The rescheduling and the strain would pay off, Jack told himself. This is how he could best serve his growing list of clients. And this is how he'd earn admittance into Shrink Rap's elite Psychiatrist's Guild, as affiliates must maintain a steady increase in revenue, coupled with a rise in emergency cases—this demonstrated one's commitment to the patients in distress. Once his membership was conferred, Jack would enjoy higher pay and the even higher respect of his colleagues. He was finally getting closer: his ratings were up and his file was nearly immaculate.

"Doc? You there?" Voice 9879 startled him.

"Of course I am," Jack said. "I know you've reached the low point. But at least now you can start climbing back up."

"Actually, Doc, that's not it. I feel great. I'm out of the slump and I couldn't wait to tell you what I've discovered. I've been keeping a journal, and I've finally figured out where my negative thought patterns stem from. If I can change them, maybe I won't…"

"I'm sorry 9879, but it sounds to me like you're at the start of another manic attack. Eventually you will swing back into a state of depression. The cycle will continue unless you start taking your medication. It's the only way to regulate the chemical imbalance in your brain. I really don't think self-analysis is the best way to move forward from here."

"But it helps, Doc. Just listen for a minute. Let me explain what I…"

"You really don't need to explain. I understand completely."

"But how can you understand when I haven't told you about my…"

"Because I've worked with many bipolar patients. Just trust me on this, okay?"

"All right. Well, I guess that's it then."

"Why didn't you let the poor guy talk?" Ashley was standing in the doorway, scowling. "It seemed like he wanted to share something important with you. And you kept cutting him off. You know, you could be a little more sympathetic toward his needs. You used to be good at…"

"Ashley, please stop butting in. I'm getting tired of this constant badgering. You don't understand my client's condition. Sympathy will have an adverse effect in this situation. It will only prolong and validate his denial."

"I'm just trying to point out that maybe you should recognize…"

"I am perfectly capable of recognizing the warning signs. Now I've got a bunch of emergencies lined up, so why don't you run off to school and let me do my job. It's about that time."

Rubbing her neck, Ashley left. No matter how sick she seemed, she always made it to work. "I can't let those kids down."

Relieved by her departure, Jack met with his next client in peaceful solitude.

The *bleep bleep bleep* of the kitchen door's keypad, followed by the *click click click* of Ashley's heels, signaled her return that afternoon.

She was trimming flower stems, shaking their green tips into the garbage disposal when Jack walked into the room. He watched as she filled a vase with water, arranged the bouquet, and set it on the table.

"What are you doing, Ash? What's all this?"

"I felt like bringing some color into the place."

"If you want color, why don't you set up the virtual bloom display like I showed you? They're much brighter than those."

"I *grew* them," she answered, waving her hand at the pale pink buds while walking toward the sink.

She pulled a head of lettuce from a plastic bag on the counter.

He sighed, noticing the other bags on the floor. "Did you go shopping?"

"Yes."

"We have the list programmed. There's no reason to waste your time in the store."

"Apparently that's what everyone thinks. But sometimes, I miss it. I miss saying excuse me when I bump carts with someone. Today, I even missed the lines. It was weird, Jack. The place was almost deserted."

"What's weird about that?"

Ashley chopped the lettuce into strips. "Things were different before. Like that time you locked the keys in the car when it was pouring out. Remember, the bags got all soggy, and the apples fell through and started rolling around the parking lot? And, we chased them and…"

"Thank God for Auto Voice Command. We waited over thirty minutes for that Triple A guy to show."

"It figures," she said.

"What figures?"

"It just figures."

She began dicing a tomato, her wrist flicking quickly.

"I'm going to fool around with the machine for a bit," he said, noticing her ears were a strange, iridescent pink—not her regular I'm-pissed-at-you-pink. Perhaps it was the fluorescent light above the sink casting this odd hue.

Later that night, Jack created an optical lightning storm in their bedroom, complete with sound effects.

"Must you always compete?" Ashley motioned toward the window.

"With those measly bolts?" He shook his head at the frail flashes of light in the sky outside.

Jack was mid-session when she came home from work the next afternoon. He heard her book bag thud to the floor, her shoes clicking their way toward the bathroom, and then a loud, disturbing crash.

"Please hold," he said to 699, "I'll be back in just a sec." Lunging from his chair, Jack dashed into the kitchen.

The table was overturned; the vase had shattered. The flowers' pastel heads rested in puddles on the tile, their leaves reaching out like arms from a sea of splintered glass. In the midst of it all, sprawled on the floor, was Ashley. Rubbing a handful of petals on her cheek, her eyes wet and wide, she looked up at him.

"Everything just went black, but this feels good." She moved the petals up to her forehead and held them there. "Cool and soft like a washcloth."

She's lost it.

She stood suddenly, glass falling from her head and clothes like rain. Her arm dropped to her side. Petals stuck to her forehead and cheeks.

"I don't know why I bother anymore. They don't need me. They need a warm body to monitor the room's safety," she exclaimed, pacing.

"Ash, what are you talking about?"

"Today," she sobbed, "today one of my students raised his hand, and it surprised me since it hardly ever happens. And do you know what he said?"

"What?"

"He said, 'My teacher's broken.' At first, I didn't know what he meant, but then I went over to his cubicle and," she paused, exhaling in fast, raspy breaths, "his *screen* was blank. Those kids don't even know how to write."

"*That's* what this melodrama is about? I've been telling you to get an online classroom for years. It's more productive, more financially rewarding, and they're all on computers anyway, so what's the difference? You've got to start accepting the reality of your profession, Ashley."

"But handwriting is becoming a lost art form, and it's sad. Actually, what's worse is no one *talks*. The students don't even talk to *each other,* and I wish I could do something about it. I just don't get it."

"If you taught online, you could force group discussion in a student chat room. You could make it a requirement. Plus, you'd have a lot more professional freedom overall."

"But conversation shouldn't have to be *forced*. It should occur naturally."

Tears slid over the petals on Ashley's cheeks; she looked like some freakish 1960s flower child who'd been following The Grateful Dead for far, far too long.

"Well you're right. You just don't get it," Jack said. "I'm going back to work. I have a client waiting."

"I'm sure you'll give him great advice like you do with all the others. It's really upsetting the way you…"

"That's enough," he screamed.

Furious, Jack left the kitchen.

A few weeks later, it happened.

"Jack, it's Chip. I'd like to set up a meeting to discuss your promising future with Shrink Rap Enterprises. I am impressed with what I see here. Your Guild initiation grows nearer every hour. And it is possible that by the time we meet, your induction will be at hand."

Jack felt the adrenaline rush into his ears; his heart pounded in his head. Exhaling a long-awaited breath, he trembled with its sweet release as his boss's voice continued:

"Dinner, perhaps? This week? It would be really convenient if we could do it at your place. We're in the middle of remodeling. Michaela says she'd love to come along since Ashley will be there. I hope it's okay. I'll listen for your reply."

Jack panicked. *I've got to get her behavior in check. She's got to stop critiquing my therapy methods. Just keep her mouth shut. She should be praising my hard work in front of Chip! I wish I could send her away for a few hours, but they're expecting to see her. Besides, where would she go?*

"Hello, Chip. Dinner sounds great. Of course my place is fine. How about Friday at seven? I'm really looking forward to it. Oh, and, yes, do bring Michaela. Ashley would love to see her."

On Friday Jack woke to the machine's frantic bleats.

Rolling over, he noticed pink fluff on Ashley's vacant pillow, and he'd shuddered at the recollection of the previous evening. Once in bed, she'd begun plucking petals from the vase on her nightstand, sticking them all over her face. "They make my head feel better," she'd said. Then, twisting fitfully in the sheets, she'd scratched her hands and feet until Jack said, "Ashley, please! Either leave, or cut it out. I need to get some sleep. Remember? My *boss* is coming tomorrow and I have to be chipper. In fact, so do you."

Quietly, she'd left the room.

Jack brushed the foliage aside; for an instant, one piece fluttered in the air like a moth encircling an invisible bulb.

Stretching, he walked into the office and lifted the shade. The world was bathed in mist and the sun floated in a grayish haze. Ashley's trees had finally sprouted leaves; only a few twigs were still adorned with pale green buds.

When he sat down in front of the screen, a voice said: "Attention, Doc, the world is trapped in a globe. I am drowning in plastic snow. One more flake, and I'm back to Mother Earth, breathing her moist soil. One more flake, and I'll escape to her cool womb, for this tomb is fake. Number 9879."

Jack responded, "I liked your last one better. This one's a bit sappy, don't you think? But hey, I'm no poet. How's the lithium adjustment working out? Let me know if you still have the shakes; I'll up the Inderol. We'll chat more at your appointment tomorrow night. Until then, Doc."

Trudging into the kitchen, craving caffeine, Jack nearly tripped when he saw Ashley lying naked on the counter. Her arms were stretched toward the window and both palms, fingers spread, were pressed against the glass. Her eyes were open; a smile curled the corners of her lips. A fine blue power flecked her body's canvas and, as Jack stepped closer, he saw water beads escaping from the pool of her bellybutton, freed by the cadence of her breathing.

"What on Earth?" he exclaimed. "What on Earth are you doing?"

Her head turned languidly toward him.

"I'm mimicking that tree over there." She pointed. "I really feel a connection with it. Like we're kindred spirits or soulmates. It's like we understand each other."

This is ridiculous. "Shouldn't you be getting ready for work?"

"You know, that guy's poem was really beautiful. Tragic, too. Don't you think?"

"*What* guy?"

"The one I heard talking just a few minutes ago. He sounded pretty desperate. Maybe you should've…"

"You've got to stop this nonsense immediately! Chip and Michaela will be here tonight, and it is absolutely *crucial* that you hold it together. You're not a counselor. You're my wife! How about showing a little support?"

"I think I finally got the bug out of my system." She moved her arms from side to side. "My body doesn't hurt when I do this. It's like I can feel the wind."

"Ashley." Jack needed a different approach: redirection. He took a deep breath. "Hey, why don't you get down from there and help me get the place ready? Maybe you could toss your flowers and put out the cyber roses. They're wilted anyway. Besides, we want to make a good impression. Having too much organic stuff around might imply that we're against technology."

"I need air." She sprung from the counter and headed for the door.

"Jesus, put some clothes on!" Jack said. "We have neighbors!"

"We do?" she replied. "I hadn't noticed."

She's out of control! She's going to destroy my career!

He scurried to put on his shoes, grabbed a bathrobe, and stepped outside.

Sunlight blasted into his face; agonizing rays scorched his eyes, leaving black blazing orbs in their place. By the time Jack regained his sight, Ashley had buried her feet, like two roots, in the patch of earth along the driveway. She stood with arms outstretched, head tilted back, her breasts, blue-speckled like robins' eggs.

"Ashley, come back in the house!" He tried to drape his robe around her.

She shook it off.

"Please. Just come inside and try to get some sleep."

"I'm not tired."

"You can't stay out here like this."

She wiggled her fingers and smiled. "I like it out here."

Jack walked back into the house.

Italian Dinner Number Three arrived promptly at delivery time. The table was set. The virtual bouquet was majestic—an array of exotic flowers shimmering in a three-foot vase. Each petal was perfectly shaped, each leaf, its own dazzling shade of green. Jack had considered using it as a centerpiece; but, deciding it might be a distraction and unwilling to shrink it down, he set it up in the living room. To enhance the effect, Jack projected the image against a mirror. Both the reflection and the real thing would meet his boss head-on when he entered the front door. Ashley had showered and looked presentable, though her hair was still sopping wet when Jack beeped in their guests. An eight-legged metal creature wearing a glowing neon collar followed them.

"What's that?" Ashley jumped back.

"A dat," Chip replied, "a digitally automated tarantula. Michaela here just *had* to have one because *both* Zoë *and* Sheila upgraded. We skipped the daddy long legs altogether."

"He's such great company. Fred, come over here and meet our friends."

The metal spider creaked on hinged legs across the floor and sat on Jack's shoe.

"I think he likes you," Michaela said.

"Machines don't have feelings," Ashley said.

"Well it seems like this little guy does." Jack laughed nervously. *She'd better watch it.* "Hey, let's eat while the food's still hot."

Around the table, the couples gathered. All of the dishes were passed except a small covered bowl that sat beside Ashley's plate. Jack watched in horror as she topped her spaghetti with the fine blue powder inside.

"What's that?" Michaela asked. "Some new vitamin supplement?"

"Miracle Gro," she replied.

"Oh?" Michaela laughed. "You're a riot, Ashley. An absolute hoot."

Jack and Chip laughed, too.

"So Michaela." Jack tried to distract her eyes from Ashley's plate. "Did you happen to notice my new blooms?"

"Of course I did. As soon as we walked in. They're *gorgeous*."

"It took me a while to get the stems just right. But it was worth the effort."

"It seems like you've been applying the same winning attitude to your job." Chip doused his pasta in tomato sauce. "Let's just get right down to it, Jack. I've been watching your numbers, and I commend you for surpassing your quota."

"Thank you." Jack felt himself blushing; he twirled his fork around noodles.

"Likewise, I am pleased with your taking on so many emergency cases. That is what Shrink Rap likes to see. I did notice that unfortunate code 1307, but I'm sure you did the best you could."

"Yes," Jack said. "I did. And I still feel terrible about it."

"Well on the bright side, you have had a *tremendous* increase in revenue. It's the best we've seen in months." Chip sipped his drink.

"Really?" Jack looked at Ashley, who was frantically spooning blue dust into her mouth, chasing it with gulps of water. *She's mad. Absolutely insane, best to not call further attention to this embarrassing display.*

At least it's keeping her quiet.

"So, tell me, what *is* your magic approach?" Chip's eyes were on him.

"It's really just common sense."

"Enlighten me," the boss said. "I'm all ears."

"Well, I can't describe it without going into specifics. And that would breach confidentiality."

"You're so damned ethical. I like that. It's a rarity these days."

"I'll say." Ashley said through blue lips.

"We're lucky to have people like your husband in this world," Chip said. "The field of psychiatry is booming, and we need troopers like Jack who welcome the challenging cases."

"But doesn't that tell you something? I mean, if it's booming, maybe there's a reason. Maybe people in general just aren't happy. But why? Why is that? I think the counselors need to spend a little more time listening to their clients' concerns."

Oh, please stop. Say no more. You're going to blow it. You're going to wreck my life. Jack was sweating. His ears were burning and the fork slid from his hand.

"If clients weren't pleased with our services, they wouldn't keep coming back now, would they? It's not about time. It's about helping as many people as we possibly can. And that we certainly do."

"But don't you think they should interact in person? It might give the patients a chance to open up. Plus, the counselors would see their facial expressions, their gestures. I mean isn't body language crucial to understanding human behavior?"

"I wouldn't call it crucial. And it's really not practical in the business sense," Chip said. His cheeks were red.

Say something Michaela! Stop eating and help me. Help. Me. Shut. Her. Up.

"Well I…" Ashley choked on her words and started shaking. She coughed until a blue wad flew from her mouth. All ten fingers were stretched out before her. Suddenly, green sprouts poked through the surface of her palms and grew upwards. One by one, her fingernails bloomed into dark green leaves. They shot out and opened up like bats spreading their wings. For a moment, their beauty—the texture like wet sea glass, veins merging like vacant streets, beads of dew glistening under dim lamplight—captivated Jack. Then, he stared in disbelief as Ashley's hands grew brown and scaly, her fingers stiffening. Pink flowers sprang from her ears. She sat smiling, her skin radiant, almost glowing.

Michaela clapped. "That was quite a show. Amazing! I've never seen anything like it."

For an encore, Ashley pulled the leaves from her fingers with her teeth and spit them onto her plate. Instantly, Jack noticed, her hands were the same again, except for a slight yellowish tint.

"Man, that was incredible," Chip exclaimed, picking up a leaf. "It even *feels* real. Sorry Jack, but I think she has you beat in the VR bloom department. What kind of holosculpture body software are you using? It must have something to do with that blue stuff."

"It's a secret," Ashley replied.

Jack faked a grin.

"I thought you were just a teacher," Michaela said.

"You need to showcase that talent somewhere," Chip said. "It's absolutely breathtaking!"

"Would anyone care for some tiramisu?" Jack asked.

"Actually, we should probably get little Fred off to bed," Michaela said, motioning to the sleeping metal spider curled up in the corner.

"Before we go, I'd like to say congratulations, partner. You should be proud." Chip shook Jack's hand.

"Of her? I sure am." *That sneak*, he thought.

"It's official," Chip said. "You're in the Guild."

"Are you serious?"

"Your membership was confirmed this afternoon. Enjoy the prestige it brings, you've certainly earned it."

"How about that, honey?" Jack beamed.

After good-byes were exchanged, Chip and Michaela, with the tarantula cradled in her arms, left.

Ashley sat still, staring at her plate.

"What are you *really* doing at that school?"

Silence was her only reply.

Early Saturday morning, the Guild's anthem played through the walls, luring Jack from cozy slumber to his desk.

"Report on emergency couch status."

"Full at twelve," she said. "No. Wait. Eleven seats now occupied. One vacancy."

"Report on departure code."

"1307. Number 9879," she said.

"What does that mean?" Ashley's voice startled him. She was sitting in a chair in the corner of the dark office.

"That 9879 decided to off himself. Sometimes they just slip through the cracks."

"He was a *person*, Jack. You can't dismiss him like that!"

"He was one of a thousand weaklings."

"That poem he sent yesterday was his cry for help. It was so obvious. How could you *not* see that? I tried to tell you, but *no* you wouldn't listen," she cried.

"And next you'll accuse me of *killing* him. He killed himself. By choice. So don't even *try* to blame me. Go water your trees with those tears."

Ashley stood and left the office as Jack returned his attention to the screen.

Hours later, she had not returned. When he went into the kitchen for a snack, Jack's bare feet stuck to the tiles. Blue dust and flower petals covered the floor. *She's a mess. An absolute disaster.*

Passing the window, he peeked outside. At last, Ashley's trees had finished blooming: every bud had opened and canopies of leaves shaded the yard. Sunlight streamed through branches, creating shadows that gracefully swayed on the ground. Everything swirled in green.

Well it's about time they got on with spring, Jack thought. Yet, in the distance, something snagged his wandering gaze: a pink blur— some flowering shrub, a weeping cherry, perhaps, but an eyesore all the same—stood out from the otherwise-pleasant monochromatic scene. The tree hadn't been there before, or maybe it had. Maybe now it was just more noticeable in contrast to the emerald hues. Then all at once, Jack knew for sure: he had found the culprit, the nuisance, the maker of those dreadful petals Ashley trailed all over the place. He raced back into the office.

"Number 865299 requests immediate landscaping services," he said into the computer's face.

"Granted," she replied.

I've got to stop her from planting any more of those damned things. If I had the funds now, I'd have them all removed…but it won't be long.

Within forty-seven minutes, the pesky tree was gone.

Humming the Guild's anthem, Jack felt an odd sense of freedom as he took on his next client.

)O)O)K)O)O)K)O)O)K)K

About the Author

Heather Sullivan is a founding member of Ocean State Poets, a nonprofit whose mission is to give voice to Rhode Islanders by conducting workshops and readings across the state. Her chapbook, *These Onyx Hours*, was published by Finishing Line Press in 2014. She is the editor of two poetry collections, *Butterfly Wings* and *Poems on Branches*, published by Salve Regina University, featuring the works of 75 individuals. She presently serves on the editorial board for *Crosswinds Poetry Journal.* In 2007, she was appointed Assistant Creative Director of The Writers' Circle, Inc., where she worked for three years. In 2007, she was a panel judge for Barnes and Noble's state-wide Maya Angelou High School Poetry Contest. She holds a master's degree in English and won first place in *Writers' Digest*'s 1999 Competition in memoir. Her work has appeared in *Tiferet: A Journal of Spiritual Literature; Balancing the Tides; Where Beach Meets Ocean; The Providence Journal; Newport Life Magazine*; and *The Origami Poems Project*, among others. Her essay "Compassion" aired on Rhode Island National Public Radio's *This I Believe* series, and she has appeared on several local television programs. She lives in Portsmouth, Rhode Island with her daughter, Page Sonnet, and can be reached at www.poetheathersullivan.com.

LETTING IN THE CAT

Kaitlyn Downing

January 16ᵗʰ—

I can't remember how the first inkling crawled its way into my thoughts. Perhaps the frequency with which her name came up in conversation lately was what began it; it may have been earlier— maybe when his best friend Pete and she broke up, or earlier still, when they all rented that house together. I can't say. I only know that, like a cat scratching at the backdoor screen to get in, the idea presented itself to me today that maybe they are more than friends, or that one or both has romantic feelings for the other.

Still, as we sat tonight in that nearly empty restaurant deciding what to order, I felt that feline inkling begin to scratch at the door of my intuition. Mark was prattling on about where Aimee and he had gone the other night, and how much fun she is to be with, and how close friends they are, blah blah blah...I tried not to feel jealous because, of course, he loves me. Who else could he talk about his mother's alcohol problem with? Who else would he sob his heart out to when she screamed *Your father isn't your real father,* hold him like a small child and rub his back, saying *It's not true, you look just like him. She only said it to hurt you*? He asked me to marry him one starry night on the park swings: *When we're done with college, I'd be honored if you'd be my wife.* And I never questioned his feelings, because I was his first, and you never forget your first, but I could not help thinking, *How did this happen? How did he grow so close to her without my knowing, without some warning?*

There is that nagging scratching at my mind again...am I over-reacting?

February 2nd—

I cannot stand hearing her name anymore: *Aimee, Aimee, Aimee,* she's all he talks about, it seems. I do not know what to do, or if there's anything I can and should do, but I cannot help feeling as though I'm losing my boyfriend to this girl.

He denies that he's secretly attracted to her, insists that they're only friends, but the amount of time they spend together is growing, and I can't seem to explain it. True, they're housemates, but is it normal to want to spend more time with a friend than your girlfriend, whom you profess to love?

I can't say I hate her; in fact, if things were different, I may have even considered her a friend, if one can be friends with someone she doesn't respect. She's pretty, I guess: shoulder-length brown hair, brown eyes, thin (in all fairness, thinner than I am). However, her nose is too big with a bump in the middle (she's French), she has no chest (which makes me wonder if Mark could find her attractive, considering how he loves mine), and anyway, her life is going nowhere. Since high school graduation, she's been working as an attendant at the Center for the Developmentally Disabled with no plans for college or improvement. She also has this free-love Bohemian crap going, and that is where it becomes impossible to trust or respect her. She will sleep with anyone. Mark tells me how she was fucking her ex-boyfriend while she was supposed to be with Pete, about all the boys she parades in and out of her bedroom, no matter who she's supposedly dating at the time. That makes me nervous; if she'll cheat on the guys she dates, what would stop her from seducing Mark? Not that it would matter if he didn't return the interest, but who's to say he doesn't? He certainly talks about her enough!

But why would she act so nice to me? Why try to win my friendship? If she thinks it will make me less suspicious, she's really stupid. Maybe they are just friends, and she is just trying to put my mind at ease.

I sense an intimacy between them that can only be achieved through shared sexual experience—that easy way of being next to someone, close and some places touching, but totally unselfconscious and comfortable. It's as if they've touched it all before in a much more intimate way, so the little ones aren't even noticeable anymore.

Maybe he's been cheating all along, but I was too trusting to notice. What if it's like John and Andrea, and everyone already knows. Gods, what a horrible thought! Mark wouldn't humiliate me like that, would he? I can feel that scratching again, that cat clawing on the screen, that awful sound inside my head, so loud, so insistent. It spurs me onward, propelling me to know the truth. Maybe they really are friends. I have to believe that they are, or I'll go crazy, but at the same time, I have to know for sure.

February 11th—

I called Mark to see what we were doing tonight, and he's already made plans with Aimee! This is supposed to be *our* night; we always go out on Saturday nights, and it's been that way since we first started dating more than three years ago. And now he's with Aimee?

Alright, in all fairness, he didn't actually say he was with her, but it has to be her. Pete won't speak to him ever since he started hanging around with her; apparently, he thinks she's been sleeping with Mark since before they split up, which I just found out. I don't know if that's true or not, but Pete definitely thinks so, or he wouldn't have broken up a lifelong friendship over it. Anyway, John's out with Andrea, and Mike is working (for once), so who else could it be? I called Andrea's mother to see if Andrea knew where he was, and I called his cousin Jimmy, but he said he didn't know, and that's everyone he knows.

He must be fucking her! Why else would Pete hate his guts? I ran into Pete this afternoon, and he told me how they were getting too close back in December, how she would always hang all over Mark, how she and Pete were always fighting about it. Pete thinks I'm an idiot for believing his bullshit story; he thinks what Mark is doing to me is unforgivable, that everyone thinks so. He said this guy Paul saw them out last week and they looked pretty intimate.

I can't believe Mark would hurt me like this! I give him everything, both in and out of bed. Why would he want someone else, and most especially, why her? He knows her history; can't he see that she'll fuck anything that moves? That she doesn't care about anyone but herself? Is some fling with a cheap slut worth more than three years of love to him? I'll bet he thinks I'll never find out. Isn't that what all men think when they screw around, that the girl they "love" will never find out, so it's okay; they're justified? This is a small town; there're only so many places he can hide. Someone is bound to catch them, and that someone might as well be me before the whole world knows.

2:12 a.m.—

I'm so pissed! I couldn't find him; I looked everywhere: the IA, the Great American Pub, Sully's, Cappie's, Maximillian's, Friends, Griswold's, 3's, the Pelham, every bar I could think of where he might be (or at least I checked the parking lots of these establishments—his car was nowhere to be seen, and she can't afford a car).

As I drove up and down the streets, the grey tabby cat from the screen door beside me was in the passenger seat, meowing out the window. It seemed as if it was following me at first, which I know sounds weird, but how else does one explain seeing the same cat on every street? First I saw it at the stop sign in front of the IA while I was looking for his car. It sat unmoving by the front door, as if saying, "Check in here. He's in here." I almost parked and went in, then I thought that might be going too far.

Then, when I turned the corner, there was the cat again, sneaking around the tires of a parked car, and just looking at me with those glowing night-time eyes. I decided to drive across town and check 3's. As I pulled into the parking lot, the cat was loping along the sidewalk in front of the bar. It was the same at Maximillan's and Cappies, and at Sully's, he leaped onto the hood of the car and pawed at my windshield.

I probably should have gone home, but I was compelled to find Mark. I kept hoping I'd catch him with Aimee, maybe catch him kissing her on a darkened street or touching her in the starlight and she pressed up against him, feeling his hardness against her stomach, maybe touching what she has no right to touch because he's *mine*!

I was finally parked in front of Mark's house, so I could wait for them to come home. The cat perched on the front step and casually licked its paw, grooming behind his ears and his face as though everything was fine, and my boyfriend wasn't out with the town slut until all hours of the night. I don't know how long I waited, but they played "Wonderful Tonight," and I cried and cried, thinking how we had danced one summer night. We had just gotten out of the car, left the door open so we could hear the radio, and slow-danced right there in the rain.

When I had dried my eyes, the cat had disappeared.

February 15th—

Yesterday was Valentine's day. Mark and I went out to dinner, and for the first time in a long time, I didn't think about Aimee. He was sweet and affectionate and didn't bring up her name once. It was like it used to be between us; he wished he had ordered what I had, as usual, but was too independent to order it simply because I did, and as usual, I teased him about it. He picked off my plate, knowing that it drove me nuts, but having fun trying to avoid my stabbing fork. We laughed so much, it was as if nothing had happened, and I wanted so much to believe that nothing had. I just don't know. I want my Mark back, the Mark I fell in love with, the Mark who would never hurt me for all the world.

I just want things to be as they were.

March 10th—

Outside the IA tonight, it occurred to me that what I was doing was not rational, that normal people did not follow people, or look in their windows with binoculars, or drive around all night looking for a light blue Honda with TE-229 on the license plate. Normal people's hands would not have been shaking at the prospect of finding him with her, maybe naked, entwined, silhouetted against the candlelight or worse, writhing in frantic carnality on a floor of dirty clothes, devouring each other with vampiric greed. In my mind, I could see him sucking her nipples like he sucks mine: rough, needy, insistent. He putting his soul into his kisses and her taking them like casual notes that you read once and throw away.

Normal people would not scream with rage at being denied this, at finding nothing. A normal person would be thankful to find nothing. But I cannot be happy. I know he's cheating with that deep, core-of-your-being knowledge that can't be explained yet can't be denied. I cannot eat, and the cat stalks my sleep, sending me dreams of Mark and Aimee that tear through the prey of my mind like a lion taking down antelope. The cat follows me everywhere like smoke to the nearest non-smoker—reminding me of my ever-present need to discover the truth.

We can't go out anymore because I picture him with her; when he kisses me, I think "Is this how you kiss her?" I look at him with scorn and say, "Wouldn't you rather be with Aimee?" And so we fight.

We've been fighting too much these last few weeks.

"When you act like this, I would," he spits.

The cat peeks from behind bushes, scampers across the street as we pass, huddles in wait between car tires.

"Go fuck her then. I know that's what you want. Do you think I can't see that you want her? You don't love me. If you did, there wouldn't be enough room for anyone else!"

The cat darts into the hedge, and I am crying through my anger.

"We've been through this already," he says, his face hard, his blue eyes unyielding. I can't believe how handsome he is when he's angry, and suddenly, I want him. "I'm getting sick and tired of trying to convince you that it's not like that." He is turning the car around, and I know he is taking me home. Panic sears through me, and my mind screams; I feel him leaving me, his love, his warmth, leaving me, pulling away. I'm losing him. I can't lose him! He's everything! He's mine and no one else's!

"I'm sorry," I plead, trying to fix the damage, knowing it to be irreparable. "It's just that you spend so much time with her. You don't understand how it makes me feel!" I know I'm whining, and I hate myself for being so weak, so pathetic. How could he love someone so pitiful? No wonder he was in love with her; she was independent and strong. She didn't need him like I need him. "I just love you so much."

"Then why can't you trust me?"

"I do trust you. It's her I can't trust."

"No, it's me you don't trust; admit it. You're so jealous, you can't see beyond it!" He was turning down my street.

The cat was sitting on my mother's car, curled up in satisfaction.

"How can I trust you when you've admitted you're curious about other girls? You've asked to see other people—how many times? How many times have we broken up because of your curiosity, and how many times have you returned, all apologetic and full of 'I love you's? You do everything you can to make me insecure. Would you trust me if the situation were reversed?" I was trying not to yell, because it's what the cat wanted, but my voice kept getting louder the more frustrated and indignant I became.

"What's wrong with you? I couldn't help the way I felt, and you knew that. I thought we were past that. Lately, all you do is bring her up, like you're obsessed with her or something. I've told you we're just friends. That's it. We're friends, Jess. Besides, she has a boyfriend."

"And if she didn't have a boyfriend, you'd fuck her? Not that that makes any difference to her. She's cheated before. Why not with you?" I was so angry, my whole body pounded with the heat of it. I wanted to slap him and fuck him at the same time.

"I'm not dealing with you tonight," he sighed, a drawn-out tired sigh. "Just go home."

"Can't you see that she only wants you because she can't have you?" I hissed. "You're the Flavor of the Month, Mark."

"Get out of the car, Jessica."

"Fuck you, Mark," I said, slamming the door so hard my hand vibrated, tears coursing down my face.

The little grey cat sidled up to me, rubbing against my jeans and purring. Despite my reservations, I reached down and stroked its head, letting my hand slide down his back and up his tail. He purred louder, and I scratched behind his ears, thinking that at least *he* understood. He danced a little circle around my legs and lifted his front paws to my knee.

"You hungry, little guy?" I asked, as he followed me up my back stairs. My dog was at the door as I opened it, and she must have scared the cat away, because when I looked back, he was gone. Someone probably owned him anyway.

March 11th—

10:23 a.m.—I tried to call Mark today. Aimee—that fucking bitch—said he wasn't home, but I know she's lying. All she does is lie.

12:30 p.m.—I called him again. She says he won't be home all day. Why won't he talk to me?

7 p.m.—I tried to call him four times. I refuse to talk to *her,* so Rachel answers the phone now. "Honestly Jessica, he's not home." What the fuck!

11:33 p.m.—He's obviously not talking to me on purpose. Part of me wants to go over there and make him talk to me, and another part wants to forget it. Doesn't he realize this only makes him look guiltier?

I wonder if they aren't giving him the messages. Rachel is Aimee's little toady anyway; she probably wouldn't tell him if Aimee asked her not to. Maybe I should just see if his car's there.

1:11 a.m.—His car was there, parked right behind a red Volkswagen. The cat and I watched the house for an hour—slouched down so as not to be seen—with him curled contentedly on the seat. He purred every time I pet him, loving the attention. I couldn't see anything, so I drove the Ocean Drive. That always makes me feel better, watching the moonlight glint off the wet rocks and hearing the hush of peace in the waves.

March 13th—

Mark's light was on. It glowed like cat's eyes through the second-floor window.

It was by that light that I would hurt him.

Every single thing that he's ever drawn me, written me, given me is in a brown box. The pastel nude he drew of me for art class, all the love notes, the gold Claddagh ring he gave me for Christmas last year—when I saw the little velvet box I had hoped; my heart had stopped beating and jumped to my throat: *could it be? Mark and I forever?* But no...just gold, no diamond. Still, I had worn it every day—The Grateful Dead T-shirt he brought me back from an Anaheim show, his picture (for once, out of its beloved frame) which didn't look much like him now; he was so much more handsome, in the box. All our memories and tangible objects of love are there, in the box.

They made me sick to look at now. Knowing them to be tainted, like our relationship, stained like red wine on a white carpet; I wanted them banished forever from my sight. I had wanted to destroy them, burn them and leave the ashes for him to find, but I couldn't do it. Neither would I suffer to see them in my room every day. They were relics of an outdated religion in which its worshippers had stopped believing and now held no sacredness, no sense of the holy.

I slim-jimmed his car door—easier for its manual lock, a trick I picked up from an ex-boyfriend who teetered on the edge of the law—and, as I placed the box carefully on the driver's seat, the cat climbed in the box and nested there, round like a fur muff.

"Out," I said, gently lifting him up. He was so soft, downy, and warm.

Mark couldn't miss it, so he would be confronted with all the memories of every thing he had ever done or said.

He'd remember sitting on the green wooden bench in the park where we'd picnicked and he'd asked me to marry him the beach in St. Petersburg splashing in the golden water, making sure to shuffle our feet...sitting on the rocks of that little pebble beach around the Ocean Drive comforting crying trying not to be scared until we knew what the test said...us parked in Colt State Park talking in phony redneck accents making up the lines as we went along drinking vodka...we were in the car making love while driving down Indian Avenue at two in the morning listening to Led Zeppelin...for a brief second we were fighting throwing unfinished drinks mind-erasers in O'Brian's Pub but I left that behind and we watched the moon atop the lone boulder at First Beach glorying in togetherness... we were in China Town in Boston in the run-down adult movie theater...we were washing my Chow Chow...sledding at Fort Adams with Rusty and Shaena before she ran away...exchanging drunken vows of forever on asphalt tennis courts under the stars...swinging on the children's playground jumping off...holding hands in the Chau Dynasty so intent upon each other that we weren't really there either and it was only us and no one else in the world...skinny-dipping by the light of the half-moon the chill breeze made bumps upon our skin but it was so warm...watching movies all curled up on my bed juice on the bedtable...we went to Buzzard's Bay so he could draw and I could write and there were fishing boats and the sun set on the docks and the houses glowed purple and red and after we had gone to dinner even though he was wearing army shorts and I my father's old boxers that my mother had never had the heart to throw away and now we were breaking up but no I wouldn't think about that no this was the bad times and I wouldn't think about the bad times I'll think about the good times like before...there were so many good times.

*March 14*ᵗʰ—

He left the box on my porch this morning.

He wasn't home when I got to his place. I knew because the cat had made me call his work for his schedule, pretending to be his mother. He wouldn't be home until six-thirty. That gave me two and a half hours to sneak in and find something incriminating. Aimee and Rachel were both at work. Aimee worked for that group home and did three days on, two days off rotation. Rachel was a waitress, and I watched her leave for work half an hour ago. I waited just in case she had forgotten something. It was a common mistake in the movies, and it wouldn't be mine.

I parked my car in the library parking lot at the top of Brewer Street and walked down. I was lucky in two ways: his room had a separate entrance, and that entrance was located around the side of the house in an almost dark alleyway. In a movie, it would look convenient, but it also happens to be the way it is.

That good fortune ended when I found the door locked. Mark was not one to lock doors. The cat appeared at my feet, making figure-eights around my legs and purring. I reached down to stroke its silky back. The thought occurred to me that maybe he had locked it deliberately to keep me out. That made me laugh. As if I weren't more resourceful than that!

After checking the front door, I crept back to the open window (leave it to Nanook of the North to keep a window open in March!)

and tried to force the screen up. The cat suggested cutting through the screen, and I thought it was a marvelous idea. My car key sliced neatly into the metal mesh, and I edged it along the bottom and up the side, then up the other side so I could pull myself through. Did James Bond know the key trick, I wondered? Thank you, kitty.

I squeezed and shimmied my body through the jagged hole I had created, trying not to cut myself on the metal tips. I felt a prong tear my jeans and thought it a small price to pay for proof. No warrant, no permission. I didn't need permission to know the truth; it was my inalienable right to search for information that directly pertained to me. The cat jumped through effortlessly.

I wished I could be a cat.

The drawers came first: I poked, prodded, pawed through clothes, receipts for silly things like CDs, jeans, car parts, and shampoo. Top drawer, second, third, fourth, and finally, the larger bottom drawer.

My hand froze upon stacks of folded notebook paper. Shaking, my palms unreasonably sweaty (funny how this could scare me the way breaking into his apartment had not), I drew out the first and opened it: *If you were a simple shepherd, and I your country lass...,* "Sonnet I"...my poetry to him.

All my poetry. He had saved it all. Despite all the bitch's machinations, he still loved me! I could win him back! Somehow, I would make that stain go away, and things would be the same again.

There wasn't much else to look through, really. Just the bureau, his desk where he created all his beautiful artwork, under the bed, and the closet. All turned up nothing. I was about to leave when my eyes landed on a piece of paper poking from the glass jar on the desk that held his paintbrushes, Exacto knife, and charcoal pencils. I grasped it and unfolded the ivory paper slowly.

Dear Mark,
Last night was wild. Exactly what we'd both been waiting for. March 13th is a date to remember. Can we do it again?
Love,
Aimee

Yesterday? *Yesterday* was the first time they had sex? But it couldn't be! Not yesterday! Surely it had been going on before...she wrote *yesterday*?

The day I left the box.

My mind spun, and the cat meowed at the cut-open window. *Proof...*

Should I confront him? I had to talk to him; I had to know. I decided to wait until he came home.

12:12 a.m.—Of course I can't sleep. I don't remember coming here. Everything just keeps playing over and over in my head like a horror movie, when the girl is running from the killer, and even though he's only walking, he seems to be closing in.

"How dare you go through my stuff?"

But no, that was later. First I heard the footsteps thunking up the wooden steps, stopping at his door. From my spot on the bed, I watched the handle turn and the door open and the look of wary surprise on his face at finding me there. And I, sick cold dead inside, the note clutched in my trembling clammy hands, could not even say hello.

"What are you doing here?"

His eyes alighted to all the openings.

"Now that's a fine greeting." Was that my voice? It dripped out like last week's coffee, gloppy and stale.

"How did you get in here?" His eyes met mine and traveled to the gaping screen. "You *cut* my screen?"

"I had to." Yes, that was my voice, too. So calm. The rest of me floated along the void where pain is excluded. Part of my mind spasmed with seizures of panic that seemed to have direct links to my clutching hands.

"Why?" His look of utter incomprehensibility began to chisel through my wall of deadness.

"I had to know." I looked at the moist, crumpled note in my hand and felt tears leak across my cheeks, making uneven tracks to the sides of my nose. I was not attractive when I cried; my face scrunched up and got red. I was not a Demi Moore crier.

His eyes darkened to indigo when he saw what it was that I held onto so tightly. "How dare you go through my stuff?"

"Aren't you even going to bother to explain?"

"Do you really want an explanation? Do you?" His face grew mean as he spat the words at me. The cat arched his back and hissed at him, but he was too involved to care. "It's true. We had sex last night. I was drunk and damned upset after you left that box in my car. And I started to think 'Fuck it. If she's going to accuse me of sleeping with her no matter what I say, then I might as well have the fun of doing it.' So I did. You know, the irony of it—it wasn't even good." He laughed bitterly. "You left that box to hurt me, and it worked. I fucked Aimee to hurt you. And it worked." By now, his voice was soft, and there were tears in his eyes. "And I'm sorry."

I tried desperately to calm the cat down, petting and smoothing its raised fur with both hands, but it spit and hissed from its spot on the bed. The calm spot in my mind grew and became an even larger island in a turgid lake. Mark seemed to fade into the distant fog, and there was only myself and the cat, and we sat silently on that island and watched the lake grow more and more turbulent. Maybe we should have been frightened, but we knew it wouldn't hurt us, that the winds blew around us and the noise swirled through the muffling fog, and we were content.

Somewhere, someone was crying, but it was all so far away.

Somehow the pain found its way onto our island. It seemed to hurt the cat as much as it did me, because he started crying again. Or was that me?

Out the window, I watched Mark drive away.

And then I knew. I would remove the stain of what she'd done. I would absorb the wine and make our white carpet pure again. I would cut out the stain. My island shrank until it was barely large enough to hold us, and the wind tugged at my hair, shrieking, the force of it pushing me closer, closer to those dark swirling waters. White foam ripped the surface, contrasting with the muddy red-brownness, and I felt myself losing balance and falling, falling...There was only the cat, the wine, and my hate...*eat, drink, and be merry for tomorrow you die, but why tomorrow when today is so stormy? Oh, parting is such sweet sorrow. Beware the Ides of March for he was not an honorable man but it is tomorrow, oh impudent strumpet...*

That sound! The door? The bitch is back.

Come here Fortunato, the Amontillado awaits. Must it be tomorrow creeps at this petty pace from day to day. Footsteps footsteps. Oh she's closer now. The stain. The cancer. My scalpel, a beautiful instrument so cold so almost heavy in my hand; the blade so sharp yet so dainty precise yet destructive—like nature, like woman—how deep it cuts for such a little blade. Her screams beautiful with the raging wind. Hold on, kitty, all is well. The wine on the carpet...so merlot... that stain will never come out. Look how fine the lines...pretty red drops like an abstract painting splattering thick across the canvas, her hands smearing like finger-paints ruining pretty red lines that's my painting. Hands off! Clawing clutching like my cat, my beautiful cat. Just one more line and the painting's done. Mark would love my artwork: pretty red lines, pretty red drops, drying slowly...*good night, flocks of demons; sing thee to thy rest...ah, but there's no rest for the wicked.* But oh, how kitty wants to come in. Why haven't I let him in before? I was painting. All is fine now, kitty. Now Mark and I are perfect. I got the stain out. I cut it out

Come in, kitty. This is where you live now. I will take care of you.

✕✕✕✕ ✕✕✕✕ ✕✕✕✕ ✕

About the Author

An Assistant Professor of English and former advisor of *Mobius* literary magazine at Pasco-Hernando State College in Florida, Kaitlyn Downing has an M.A.T. in English. As a semifinalist, her poem "Emer's Last Battle" appeared in the book *Tales from the Green Man* (2000). Her stories "Reaping Spring" and "Letting in the Cat" appeared in *Sinfully Twisted* (print) and in the early days of online at the now-defunct purpleverse.com (2006).

OVERDRAWN AT THE TIME BANK

Daniel Pearlman

1

On lunch break at Memorial Plaza, Jack Molino shook his head at the news projected onto his contacts that some poor slob had just won the second biggest Time prize in the thirty-year history of the Federal Time Bank Lottery. He took a bite of his crabster hero and frowned, knowing that another "winner" would soon be a loser as he sold off, for money, years and decades of the four and a half centuries—after taxes—of added Time he'd won.

Jack basked in his present moment, his Now—alone on a bench in the cool shade of century-and-a-half-old oak trees—sadly aware that today's Big Winner would then most likely lose his money in stupid schemes till he wound up less solvent than before he'd "won." He would emerge an even poorer slob—an unemployed pariah—forced to sell off bits and pieces of his own pre-winner lifespan just to get by, and die a premature death.

Jack thought he'd eluded all the gawkers and reporters. He'd put on crummy clothes and come down by service elevator from his office in One World Trade Center to avoid restaurants and eat lunch al fresco at two o'clock instead of noon. But the same panhandler who'd hit him up the week before now ambled toward him once again, as if he'd been purposely tracking him.

A softie Jack was not. Question was, should he try to get rid of that hapless soul by refusing another handout—or would the fellow just stalk him even more out of anger? With a shrug, Jack reached into his pants pocket for cash but could scare up only a measly few coins.

Approaching, the man ran his hand over his gray-stubbled chin. "Forgive me for disturbing you," he said. "I believe I was the recipient of a generous gesture of yours last week."

"I hope it afforded you a decent lunch," said Jack.

"Oh, it was enough for several. But more important, it afforded me a glimpse into your character—a personal confirmation of the judgment generally shared by most of the media, Mr. Molino."

"So you recognize me!" said Jack, his sandwich failing to reach his mouth. "You know, you could make a pretty penny alerting the press corps to my whereabouts. Probably a good idea, too, because right now I'm flat out of cash."

"Not a problem, Mr. Molino. Aren't they always saying that cash will soon disappear? I agree, even though the brotherhood of mendicants would lose the most by its passing."

"You don't talk like a mendicant," said Jack.

"I know," said the man. "It's a problem when your vocabulary doesn't match your status."

Jack now remembered from their past encounter that the man had a certain stilted way of speaking, but out of sheer politeness, he had decided not to ask him what he'd been in his former life, his life before the current depression the pols insisted was merely a recession.

"But how about accepting a few hours?" said Jack, tapping at the wide, transparent interband encircling his left wrist. Since the street value of an hour of Time was about a hundred bucks, the gift of a few hours could cover the expenses of a guy like this for a good couple of weeks. "Just give me your Federal Time Bank number. You do have some sort of Time Bank account, don't you? Most everyone has."

"I'm afraid I'm one of those rare birds who never got the implant."

"Really? Why not?"

"Because I don't intend to sell my Time merely to survive. Cutting short my lifespan to keep my belly full today just makes no sense to me. It's sort of like delayed suicide, isn't it? Anyway, thank you for the thought and—um, may I sit down?"

Jack nodded, and the man seated himself a respectful few feet to his right. "And besides, Mr. Molino, if I were you, I would under no circumstances tap into my—meaning *your*—Time account."

"Now *that* makes no sense! If I have one, why not use it?"

"Because it is a sure-fire way for our current coward of a President to loot it."

"And why would he do that, pray tell?"

"Because he's been using Time assaults to intimidate his political rivals."

"Political rivals? Since when am I in politics at all, Mr. …"

"Flynn."

"I am an economist, Mr. Flynn. I head the Time Bank's Risk Assessment Bureau."

"And you have a long-term position on the bank's board of directors, all of whom regard you as a thorn in their sides."

"I do nothing I know of to threaten them."

"That's just it, Mr. Molino. It's what you don't do that scares them."

Jack chuckled. "What I don't do? I don't drink, I don't dope, I don't chase skirts—been happily married to the same woman for almost fifty years—"

"Yes, Marietta, a brilliant political cartoonist."

"And illustrator of my children's books."

"And a further reason why you are deemed a threat to President Florian and those two other revolving-door presidents and their accompanying pack of lackeys, and your own fellow board members. They interpret her drawings as political satire and see your kiddie stories as allegorical attacks aimed at them."

"You are saying my wife is partly responsible for the way the administration regards me?"

"Partly, yes, Mr. Molino. And there's one other thing you *don't* do that worries the hell out of your fellow directors—and their White House enablers."

"And what may that be, Mr. Flynn?"

"You don't buy things you can't pay for in full."

"Like what, for example?"

"Like large blocks of Time. If you wanted, you, too, could buy them at ridiculously low margin—like your colleagues do, using other people's money, and profiting as their value goes up."

"Neither lenders nor buyers see any risks," said Jack. "Time stocks never drop in value because—well, Time never ends."

"I gather that what you mean," said Flynn, "is that the national Time tax ensures your bank's ongoing solvency far into the foreseeable future."

"It's certainly a safe investment," Jack agreed. "Now, if *everybody* had the right to buy Time stocks on margin—especially on the low margins available only to board members, our presidents, and the biggest supporters—there'd be fairness all around. But this clique is in control of so much Time that they've guaranteed themselves continued power for the next two hundred years!"

"Another four years would be menacing enough," said Flynn.

"Whoever they want to control," said Jack, "like the chairman of the Federal Reserve, for example—they let him buy gobs of Time on margins as low as five percent. It's goddamn criminal!"

"So what keeps *you* from temptation, Mr. Molino?"

"I do buy Time stocks, but never on margin, even though I'm privileged to do so. But you're asking why I always pay in full? It's a matter of principle. I'm not a saint, Flynn. I just can't get myself to imitate what strikes me as criminal behavior."

"Ah, principles! I haven't heard that word used for decades. But why buy all that extra time anyway, Mr. Molino?"

"You already know why the big boys do. To stay in power forever."

"And as for you?"

"Me? Two reasons, actually. First, I love these old oaks and want to stay around as long as they do…but more and more I have another reason."

"Which is?"

"Because even if it takes a hundred years, I want to stay on that board to provide them with a conscience—even if it's one they don't much listen to."

"Very commendable, Mr. Molino. But your lone refusal to buy Time stocks on margin—your exasperating honesty, in other words—is perceived as a threat to that gang of three in Washington. By owing nothing, you remain beyond their control."

"But I've never *openly* accused them of skullduggery."

"You don't have to. The people have inferred what you never explicitly say. They've had enough of being crushed by gangsters who've managed to pass on the presidency to each other over the last forty years and expect to continue at the same game at least for the next hundred."

"But as I said, Flynn, I have no political ambitions."

"It doesn't matter how you perceive yourself personally, Mr. Molino. Protest all you want; the people see you more and more as the only viable counterweight to the thieves in power who are responsible for this ongoing depression."

"I do my job in the Risk Bureau, that's all."

"Yes, even though your colleagues there run right over you."

Jack munched slowly on a bite of crabster that had lost its taste. "The worst thing is not all that low-margin buying," he said. "Worst is *how* our board of directors—with tacit government approval, of course—sucks up all that Time, already hoarding centuries of ordinary people's lives in only the past thirty years."

"You are referring to the Time tax?" said Flynn.

"The Time tax *scam*. People take it for granted. They've gotten so used to excessive taxes on everything else that they don't much notice a difference. They're used to taxes going up, so when the board of directors raises the Time tax, they don't even blink. Slowly but surely, the Federal Time Bank is stealing away people's *lives*."

"The poor wouldn't sell their precious Time if there weren't this depression, Mr. Molino."

Jack thought for a moment. "You're right, Mr. Flynn. It is in the *interest* of the board of directors to keep the people in poverty."

"You are an honest man, Mr. Molino. And that augurs ill for your health. I need to impress upon you that you are in danger. We've been watching your back, but that's getting more and more difficult."

"We? Who is we? And just who are *you*, Mr. Flynn? Without that scrubby beard, you might strike me as just a bit familiar."

Flynn fished a scrap of paper out of his pocket and handed it to Jack. "No time to get into all that right now. If you'd like to get in touch, here's my contact info. Ball's in your court, Mr. Molino."

Flynn looked warily around and slouched off through the evenly spaced and neatly trimmed ranks of oaks.

2

Jack got back to his office on the seventy-fifth floor of One World Trade Center in time to suit up and make a three o'clock emergency meeting of the board of directors.

The meeting had been called in reaction to the unexpected uproar over last week's decision to raise the tax on all Time transactions from two percent to a mere two and a quarter. At the long, shiny teak table, he sat as far away as he could from the dapper, athletic-looking, razor-mustached head of the board, Brit Kestro, who at age 117 was already living on who-knew-how-much borrowed (on the slimmest of margins) Time. Kestro had assured everyone that only a few chronic anti-government complainers would object, and that it was a necessary move to stabilize the deepening recession.

Kestro now repeated that old "necessary move" chestnut, focused in on the puzzled face of a newly-appointed board member, and condescended to explain it as he'd done to the clueless media all week.

"Could I have made it any clearer to those fumbling fools?" he said. "We, now, at the end of the twenty-second century, have come to accept that the 'gold standard' of all tradable commodities is Time. Time stocks have steadily risen in value, and they're in no danger of falling." He glanced sharply around the table. "If there were any doubt, why would all of you have taken advantage of the generously low-margin Time stock loans I long ago managed to secure—with presidential approval, of course—for all members of this board?"

"Not all," Jack mumbled, just loud enough for Kestro to respond with a quick, dismissive smirk.

"Now, as I tried to hammer into those lummox reporters' heads," continued Kestro, "the rise in value of Time stocks tends to offset the decline in most others—but because of the noticeable worsening economy, the Federal Time Bank needed to bolster its reserves, thus helping to restore confidence—"

"Excuse me, sir," Jack interrupted, "but how does slapping everyone with a further tax improve their economic well-being?"

"You're being irrelevant, Mr. Molino."

"I don't see how," said Jack. "We started with a basic Time tax on anyone *buying* someone else's Time. Without that, of course, there'd be no funding of a Time Bank. Then, about ten years ago, we slapped the tax on everyone *selling*—regardless of the fact that most people selling are *selling* because they're down and out."

"Everyone, rich or poor, pays the same *sales* taxes, Mr. Molino," Kestro countered.

"And now," said Jack, "on the slimmest of excuses—hiding our real motive, namely, sheer *greed*—to raise it another quarter percent will weigh more heavily on the poor guy than—"

"Mr. Molino, increasing the tax has had the support of every government economist."

"Hear, hear!" rumbled the voices of several directors.

"Hardly a surprise," snorted Jack.

"*Mister* Molino," said Kestro, fixing Jack with a laser-like stare, "we are in the business of stabilizing the market. We are *not* in the business of promoting economic well-being!"

Murmurs of approval rippled along the table. If a vote of confidence were necessary, Kestro would have had it hands down. The president of the board had made a *mot* that was sure to be included in the forthcoming minutes.

As the meeting droned on, Jack contributed no further comment.

3

That evening, Jack arrived home at their lovely old brownstone in Brooklyn. As he ascended the stairs to the second floor, he could already smell the dinner Marietta was preparing. She served up one of his favorites—roast chicken with leeks and asparagus—with the chicken coming from the actual bird, even though it was three times more expensive than the cell-grown molded variety.

"I can see you're disappointed," said Jack.

"What? For not winning the lottery? What would I do with another few centuries on my hands?"

"Divide them up with me," said Jack, who had not ever told her that he'd been buying extra Time over the many years of their marriage with the precise intention of dividing them up with her. "If you keep them all to yourself, you might wind up with a new spouse who'll expect you to change your entire culinary repertoire."

"Anyway," said Marietta, reaching out to the candle-flame with her failed lottery receipt and setting it on fire, "given the enormous prize, I did not spend much more than usual on a ticket this week. Only three hours."

"You gave up three hours of your life in pursuit of this damn will o' the wisp?" said Jack.

"I usually spend only a half-hour a week, but the prize was so big—"

"But every hour you fritter away on that lottery," Jack chided, "is an hour less of life *we* have to spend together."

He hadn't meant to hurt her, but he saw tears welling up in her eyes.

She got up and began clearing the dinner plates. "Women live longer than men," she said. "What would I do with all that extra time without you?"

Jack wanted to reproach her for using a grossly unfair appeal to sentiment, but just then the doorbell rang—*a blessing*, he thought, not wanting to get into a long and tearful to-and-fro just then. "I'll get it," he said, walking to the doorway in the living room. The video panel in the wall showed three men with close-shaved heads downstairs waiting to be let in. "Who are you, and what do you want?"

"We've been sent to deliver a message to you," said one of the dark-suited men, "from Somebody Very Important."

"Too important to deliver it himself?"

"Much too important."

A security scanner automatically screened them for weapons. They had none.

"Okay, come up."

They sat themselves down on the sofa, facing the pair of armchairs that were uneasily occupied by Jack and Marietta. They refused coffee or tea; they wanted to get right down to business. After speaking into a pen-like device, the man in the middle paused for several seconds, then nodded and looked back at Jack.

"Okay, Mr. Molino. A live hololine has been set up between you and the President."

"The president of what, sir?"

"The President of the United States. President Florian."

Marietta uttered a gasp, but Jack played it cool, just tightening his jaw, suddenly realizing that the media's relentless pursuit of him—as a moral counterweight to the tricksters who had been monopolizing the White House—had made him, too, into Somebody Very Important.

"You are authorized to speak with the President, sir. And remember that he too has a visual on you."

Suddenly, a life-sized figure popped out of the head of the "pen"— it was silvery haired, with thick white eyebrows and a ghostly pale complexion. The holobubble showed him seated behind a big desk before a couple of American flags.

"Good evening, Mr. Molino," he said.

"Evening to you, sir," said Jack.

"Let me cut to the chase. You've steadily refused to join a political coalition that wants you to head their ragtag party in opposition to my certain re-election come November. Is that so?"

"I prefer the private to the public sphere, yes."

"Private indeed! You work at a Federal agency—whose chair, as you know, was appointed by me."

"Yes, but my own election to the board was done by the majority vote of all our section heads, not by any member of your administration."

"That's a quibble, Mr. Molino."

"An important one, sir, since my appointment to the board is for a twenty-eight-year term, of which I've served only half so far. At the end of that term, I could run for another—that is, if I feel I have too much 'Time' on my hands to retire—point being that I remain immune from removal by the federal government. That, I think, leaves me in the private sphere."

"Who's talking about removing you?"

"The whole country is abuzz with talk about my being a 'thorn' in the side of the powers that be,'" said Jack.

"It's the thorns in leaders' sides, Mr. Molino, that keep them on the straight and narrow. So it may surprise you to know that I'm calling you to commend you, not to reproach you, for sticking to your principles."

"To commend me, you say?" Jack knitted his brows and cast an incredulous glance at a stunned-looking Marietta.

"More than to commend you. To reward you."

"And how do you mean to reward me, sir?"

"Mr. Molino, you were already a renowned economist before you joined the Federal Time Bank. But prior administrations have missed out on the opportunity to grant you long-overdue recognition. I, however, would like to offer you a cabinet post in my next administration. How would you like to be Secretary of Commerce?"

Jack sat momentarily speechless under Florian's benign smile. *Beware of gifts from Greeks*, he thought. "Mr. President…I'm honored, of course," he temporized, glancing at his ashen-faced wife, "but, you know, we really like living here in New York, and so…"

"Your income will double, and your retirement package will triple."

"You're incredibly generous, Mr. President. I'm overwhelmed. I'll need time to think it over."

"Gardner," said the President, "hand Mr. Molino the written offer I'd like him to read and sign." One of the three shave-heads laid a sheet of pixel-paper on the coffee table together with an e-pen for his signature. Jack scanned the sheet and could not repress a smile.

"You like it, I see," said Florian. "Then perhaps you won't need much time to 'think it over'?"

Jack passed the sheet over to Marietta.

"By the way…and while I'm waiting," said the President, "I must tell you that my family have been fans of your children's books for decades—especially as so wonderfully illustrated by your talented wife."

Jack's ungushing thank you was echoed by Marietta's equally subdued reply.

"I do have a question, though," said the President, "about your latest book, *The Giant Invader from Titan.* Certain politically-biased critics are reading it as political satire. I'm sure you don't intend it as such?"

"It's a children's book, Mr. President."

"Yes, but as to these critics, they focus on the way your shape-shifting Giant Invader is finally pinned down by those daredevil kids. They observe him for a while as he devastates the land, fending off attacks by assuming different forms, and then they figure out that the sequence of shapes he shifts into is always the same, and so they are prepared for the one they know they can tackle."

"Kids *love* the story," said Marietta.

"Oh, I'm sure of that," said Florian, "but what do you make of how these media folks read those predictable shape-shifts as analogous to the repeats in the U.S. presidency over the past few decades?"

"Highly imaginative," said Marietta.

"You can read whatever you like into almost anything," said Jack, shrugging his shoulders.

"So why won't you issue a denial of such politically-skewed comments?" said Florian, his pale face now glowing a bit pink.

"Because everyone has the *right* to read whatever they want into anything," Jack said, his voice firmer now than it was only moments before.

"Getting back to my offer, Mr. Molino—"

"Oh, as to that, Mr. President, I find it deeply offensive." Jack surprised *himself* at this sudden impulse of his to speak up.

"*Offensive?*" The President, startled, leaned forward over his desk, and his three minions on the sofa came rigidly to attention.

"What will all my friends say? Here I am not even running for office, and you already wish to co-opt me."

"*Co-opt* you?"

"You know, sir…on the principle that it is better to have your perceived opponents inside your tent pissing out, than outside pissing in."

"Now *I* am offended," said Florian. "But I am also quick to forgive. I give you five minutes to sign or not. After which my delegates will leave."

"Oh," said Jack, shaking his head, "I would need much more time than that, sir." And he handed pen and paper back to Gardner.

The holobubble burst, and the President's virtual litter-bearers immediately upped and left.

4

During the course of the next week, a raucous "Draft Molino" movement sprang up all over the country. The official opposition party, grown impotent against the Troika over the past forty years, joined voices with the party in power to attempt to stifle a populist groundswell that threatened them both. Those on the right and those on the left came out swinging against non-candidate Molino, their every slur increasing the people's support for a so-far headless Third Party.

The noisier things got, however, the more Jack withdrew into his turtle-like shell of intransigence.

At the office, he had become radioactive. With one exception—a supervisor named Manny—his staffers in Risk Assessment wouldn't dare stand near him any longer than they absolutely had to: to pass him a file, to show him some figures on a virtual screen. Manny had worked under Jack for close to ten years, was as loyal to him as a guard dog, and would discreetly pass on to Jack whatever hallway scuttlebutt he deemed worth repeating. It was rumored, Manny confided, that Jack's fellow board members were designing a petition to have Jack kicked out of his job on the grounds of incompetency.

But what worried Jack the most was the effect this populist tsunami was having on Marietta. She could go nowhere without being hounded. Their brownstone was under constant surveillance by next-to-invisible drones. Sleazy fictions were disseminated about the Molinos' aberrant sex-life.

And then, exactly eight days after the President's virtual visit, Marietta did the unusual thing of calling Jack at work. Her anxious face bubbled up above Jack's interbanded wrist. "Honey," she said, "I'm not feeling well. Today I opened up an envelope that someone slipped under our door yesterday. It looked like an advertisement. I ignored it till just now."

"What do you mean 'not feeling well'? What exactly is wrong?"

"I feel faint. Something's…wringing out my insides. I feel like I'm losing blood. And this message…please just come home right away, Jack. It's getting worse by the minute."

"I'm leaving this instant." He dashed out toward the elevators without a word of explanation.

During the half hour by autocab it took him to get home, she did not answer his repeated calls.

When she opened the door, she fell into his arms—literally *fell*. Her breathing was short and irregular. She felt sweaty and feverish. If it were a cold or the flu, she would have medicated herself and not bothered him.

"This is crazy. Read it," she said, thrusting a sheet of paper into his hands.

Jack read. The sender, according to the letterhead, was International Debt Liquidation, Inc. No address, no contact number, no hand-written signature were in evidence. And the content was an outrageous, preposterous *lie*.

"How is it possible that I owe some mysterious creditor seven million dollars, Jack?"

"It is *not* possible," said Jack, "and even if you did, why wouldn't they include information about who and how to pay? No, the point of this letter is to inform you of the preordained penalty—a punishment already set in motion."

"I have twenty-four hours to pay from time of receipt of notice. Failure to pay, it says, will trigger the 'automatic withdrawal of your Time, until 47 years, or as close to that sum as possible, is extracted from your lifespan, starting with the recall of any current Time loans outstanding.'"

"Who are these maniacs?" Jack was terrified. He stared at Marietta and seemed to see, moment by moment, the color slip from her face.

She looked up at him in horror. "I feel drained, Jack. I feel I'm being drained. Jack, I have no Time loans!"

Calling up a virtual screen, he set in motion a search for International Debt Liquidation, Inc. Nothing relevant popped up. "This company doesn't exist," he said. "It's clear what's happening. The point of punishing you is to get back at *me*."

"Jack," said Marietta, shivering, "you don't really think the President—that they would stoop to such low…"

"And he also knows I have the means to stop this attack, and he knows full well I'll use it."

Marietta winced at a sudden twinge of pain. "What are you talking about?"

Jack tapped his interband, called up a fan-shaped screen, and voice-inputted two account numbers and the phrase "Transfer 50."

"What was that all about, Jack? What the hell are we going to *do*?"

"I've just set in motion the restoration of every year, and then some, that the Time Bank's in process of draining out of you."

"How's that possible? Your own bank's turning against *me*?"

"A bunch of cowards are *using* the bank, attacking you to send *me* a clear warning."

"You *said* you were not into politics. Why don't they just…"

Jack noticed a change overcoming Marietta. The transfer was working. "How are you feeling now?"

Marietta pressed her hands over her heart. She took a deep, tremulous breath. "Yes, I think…my heart is not hammering so badly."

Jack shook his head. The immediate danger rapidly passing, it was now *his* turn to tremble. "That bastard will go to any length," he muttered, "absolutely any length."

"What did you just do? Those numbers. *Tell* me."

Jack had no other course but to confess. "I was saving it as a surprise for our fiftieth anniversary—only a year and a half away. All this time I've been investing all my royalties in…Time stocks."

Marietta's cheeks turned pink. "I had no idea you had accumulated *fifty years*, Jack!"

He reached out and clasped Marietta to his chest. "I'd stashed away exactly 127," he said. "All paid up. Expensive at full market price. No one could have taken them away—legitimately, I mean."

"They got 'round the 'legitimate' issue, didn't they?" said Marietta. "I'm sorry you had to lose so much—"

"Lose? Like hell!" Jack smiled. "I can see you're feeling better."

Marietta's eyes no longer looked so sunken. The pallor of only minutes before was fast retreating from her face. "What if this is more than punishment for the stand you took last week, Jack? What if this is to warn you that you'd better change your mind?"

"I'm not going to change my mind. I'm not going to be pressured by either side—my murderous opponents or my pain-in-the-ass supporters."

"You can't stay uncommitted, Jack. As long as you stay in no-man's-land, you're—we both—are big fat targets."

Jack paced the living room, nodding his head as if to say, *I know, I know.*

"Say something!" Marietta demanded. "I feel we are completely defenseless."

He stopped pacing and laid his hands on her shoulders. "Don't buy any more lottery tickets," he said. "That's how they got to you—through the Time lottery. Remember the first time you played the lottery? You had to get that painless little shot."

"I didn't think twice about it."

"Well, that painless little shot," said Jack, "sends a nano-robotic bug into your brain. I've got one too." He tapped his head. "Anyone who has ever had business with the Time Bank has got it, like it or not."

"How do you get rid of it, then?" Marietta raised her hands as if to pull at her hair.

Jack shook his head. "You can't. It becomes part of the brain. It's a complex organic structure called an endosymbiont."

"I would willingly undergo surgery to get it removed."

"No way," said Jack. "Its tendrils join two parts of the brain—the SCN, the little nucleus that synchronizes *Time*—all of the body's rhythms—with the pineal gland. The gland that regulates the endocrine system. Or something like that."

"You make it sound like a parasite."

"It is. It's a live transducer that sends coded pulse-patterns to your Time Bank account either to add or subtract blocks of Time. And the bank, of course, can do the same in reverse. You activated that little bug with the first lottery ticket you bought no matter how tiny a snippet of Time you paid for it."

"So you're telling me we're all a bunch of puppets dangling from strings attached to our brains?"

Jack nodded. *That fake bum Flynn knew what he was talking about,* he thought.

5

Without a clue as to what to do next, Jack found the slip that Flynn had given him and arranged to meet him for dinner the following evening in the Village. They sat in a booth at Slugs and Bugs and conferred over a large platter of steamed organic termites—the jumbo African variety that were the tastiest.

"You know me," said Jack, "but all I know about you is who you are not."

"First off, my name is not Flynn. It's Sammy Avenda."

"The name is familiar," said Jack.

"I'm glad I'm not often recognized," said Avenda. "I am the whistle-blower who punctured the Mars colonization bubble some twenty years ago."

"And caused the crash that launched a monster recession?"

"Yes, but if you wind back a bit, I am also the astronaut that the corporate execs wanted to leave stranded on Mars—as by contract they could. Remember? They claimed that saving me would bankrupt them. But their real reason for abandoning me was not to have a surviving witness to the failure of their colonization scheme."

"I remember now. A competing company that had lost the construction bid went out very expensively to rescue you—and you came back with evidence of the equipment failures—something about the self-assembling 3-D printers…that doomed the whole project."

"Yes," said Avenda, "the printers were designed to use Martian soil to build habitat. But few got to print anything because they mostly failed to self-assemble."

"I had no sympathy for all those corporations that went belly-up," said Jack, forking a large white cylindrical body into his mouth. "They brought it upon themselves. Greed."

"They paid the piper," said Avenda. "Low-margin buying cost them ten times what they'd invested—and they got wiped out."

"That made you a very unpopular fellow, Avenda."

"And that's why *you've* become so notorious yourself, Molino. But you're a Cassandra. You're warning of a Time bubble *about* to burst. I simply brought back news of a fart accompli."

They both laughed—then grew serious.

"So what brings you into *my* orbit?" asked Jack.

"Apart from my opposition to Things As They Are? It ought to be obvious to you that the Mars debacle killed the main reason for the creation of a Federal Time Bank."

Jack lowered his head and sighed. "Congress will someday *have* to restore funding for a multi-century colonization voyage to the stars."

"Fat chance," said Avenda. "I would have been one of the lucky few provided with a three- or four-hundred-year round trip."

"Right now, it's the pols and the bureaucrats—our stay-at-home astronauts—who are grabbing up all that Time," said Jack.

"And if they get rid of *you*, Molino—before you get too big to be easily disposed of—they remove the only foreseeable obstacle to absolute power, the power over Time."

"All this while," said Jack, "I've tried to steer clear of moral issues. I've tried to stay technical—warning my colleagues about the dangers of buying up Time stocks on very low margins. They refuse to see Time stocks as subject to ordinary market fluctuations. So as to their ever-gaining absolute power over Time…what if the bank goes under?"

"What if?" echoed Avenda.

"Listen," said Jack, "when I bring up the theoretical possibility of a collapse, my colleagues' standard reply is: 'That could only happen if Time were to come to an end.'"

"Wouldn't it be a good thing if the bank did go under and drown the rats who've hijacked it, Molino?"

"Why throw out the baby with the rats?" said Jack. "When I came on board, one of the vaunted purposes of the bank was to act as a kind of safety net—providing at least some temporary respite to people totally screwed by circumstances."

"Become President, Molino, and you'll find a way to make that institution serve the people!"

"I don't even look like a presidential contender," said Jack. "I'm round at the waist, gray at the top—"

"I didn't want to get involved in politics either," said Avenda, "but now, as you can guess, I am the shadow-dwelling liaison between you and millions who see their only hope in you."

"You're running one hell of a risk, Avenda."

"And what about you? How many more attacks on Marietta can you handle before you'll reconsider?"

Jack's hand shook so much that two fat termites slipped off his fork and rolled out onto the floor as if alive.

6

Within a few days of the emergency meeting of the board, Chairman Kestro's cocky remark—"we are not in the business of promoting economic well-being"—got leaked to the media and further raised the hackles of an entire suffering nation. Jack was already used to the silent disdain of his colleagues, but now he endured waves of beady-eyed hostility: the board had taken it on faith that he was the source of the leak—and that his purpose was to strengthen the Draft Molino movement.

Jack did not think that anyone at the bank knew of the crisis that Marietta had gone through. But he was soon proven wrong. Not everyone's hostility stayed silent. While still shaken by the attack on Marietta, he happened to be leaving his office one day when he all but bumped into Kestro. Ordinarily, Kestro would barely toss him a nod. This time he affected a cheery grin and said, "Say hello for me to your *wife*, Jack!"

So not only did Kestro *know*, Jack deduced, but he was Florian's instrument for carrying out the attack. Manny reinforced these suspicions when he told Jack that Kestro had recently had a spate of mysterious holocalls from the White House.

The pressure on him to run for office was reaching fever pitch, and the encounter with Kestro had nearly pushed him over the edge. But Jack's distaste for politics prevailed, and a better plan now struck him as well worth a try. *Why not deflect attention from himself by supporting Avenda as a candidate?* he thought. *Ex-astronaut and fearless whistle-blower Avenda!* Tall and lean and craggy-looking, the popular-hero type, he would fit the bill perfectly. People would forget that Avenda's courage had had an unfortunate consequence—an earlier recession that some still thought responsible for the *current* far deeper meltdown owned and designed by the self-recycling Troika.

Avenda would have no need to skulk in the shadows anymore. Public acclaim would provide him with impenetrable protective armor. Jack devoted several nights to roughing out a plausible campaign, then decided to call his new friend and arrange to meet him again.

Over the next two nights, Jack called several times but failed to get a reply. Next day, however, while immersed in work at the office, he received an interband call marked "urgent." It was from Marietta. A sinking feeling came over him.

"*Again?*" he said to the downcast face that hovered above his wrist.

"No, not at all! *I'm* fine. But check out the local news, Jack. Do it *now*."

Jack switched to the Manhattan channel. A dronecast zoomed in on a scene that included a gaggle of police and an ambulance. "Though carrying no ID," said the on-scene reporter, "a quick gene-test has revealed the identity of the victim as Samuel Avenda. Avenda was sole survivor of the last expedition to Mars, the whistle-blower both praised and reviled for puncturing the so-called 'Mars Bubble' and exposing the insolvency of some of our biggest banks."

The lens zoomed in on the body of Avenda as medics transferred him to a stretcher. Jack zoomed in even further and saw the bloody, smashed-in skull. The distorted facial features were barely recognizable.

Jack felt a wave of nausea.

"As of this moment," the reporter continued, "we've not been provided with any clue as to who might have committed this heinous assault, nor with what deadly weapon. As to motive, there are many who lost fortunes because of Avenda. But that was a long time ago."

Jack switched back to Marietta.

"You dare not get involved," she cautioned. "If you're thinking of organizing a protest or making funeral arrangements or even sending flowers—"

"They did this to send a message to *me*," said Jack, "to persuade me to reconsider their offer."

"You won't...will you?" said Marietta.

Jack's heart thumped wildly and his throat contracted. "They're pretty insistent, aren't they?" he finally choked out in reply.

The public wasted no time in assigning blame for the murder to thugs in the pay of the White House. Diligent reporting had quickly discovered that over the years, on several public sites, Avenda had severely criticized government economic policy. Outcry from the media now pressured Congress to set in motion a thorough investigation of the crime. As Jack well knew, with an election just over a year away, Florian did not need an issue like that to mar his expensively self-constructed image as the sole wizard who, given *another* second term, could set the country back on its feet.

With the public clamoring more noisily than ever for Molino to step up to the plate, Jack was not surprised to get a visit, within days of Avenda's murder, from a White House gofer asking him to meet with the President—not by telepresence, but *in person*—at FBI headquarters, located conveniently for Jack in the same tower where he worked. "Don't imagine," said the gofer, "that the President came up from Washington just to see *you*. But being here anyway—"

"I know," said Jack, "he thought he'd squeeze me into his crowded schedule."

"You got that right."

Jack thought it best to agree.

On the day before his meeting with the President, he upset his already distraught wife with a statement of his latest notion:

"I think it might be possible to defeat them by joining them," he coolly declared as Marietta refilled his coffee cup.

She avoided his gaze. "So *that's* what's going through your mind?"

"By joining them, I mean like a monkey wrench joined to a cogwheel."

"You're deluding yourself." She stood up and started to leave the room.

"Wait," said Jack. "Listen to my plan."

7

He was ushered into a small office where President Florian, ensconced behind a desk, greeted him effusively and invited him to take a seat. In person, Florian looked physically smaller than the image of him projected by the media.

"Let's not waste any time," he began. "The Draft Molino movement may be getting louder, but the stubborn refusals of Molino himself are causing defections among the organizers."

"Yes," said Jack, "I understand that some ex-astronaut named Avenda has defected—has in fact become very defective."

"A has-been. Would have done the movement no good," said the President.

It took a powerful effort for Jack to keep from exploding. "Politics is not my strong point, Mr. President."

"Maybe not, but even so, I still see you playing a positive role on the national scene during the next four years of my tenure." Florian leaned forward with a smile so artificially broad that Jack thought it would crack his parchment-dry cheeks.

"Mr. President, let's be candid," said Jack. "First of all, the pollsters are far from certain you'll be re-elected."

"Those polls are all biased," said Florian, his rubber band lips snapping back into a down-curving slit.

"Maybe so, but I have a suggestion about a role for me to play that will pretty much guarantee your re-election."

"Really now!" Florian's eyes twinkled with skeptical amusement. "I can understand your willingness to step aside from politics, so what makes you think now of getting even more involved—and on the 'wrong' side, so to speak?"

"Mr. President," said Jack, "if I can be said to have an agenda, it is to do what I can to relieve people's misery, and if I see that goal as achievable only by joining forces with you, then that puts us both on the 'right' side."

"You amaze me, Molino! What could you possibly do to support me when everything you stand for *opposes* me?" Suspicion radiated from the President's deep-set eye sockets.

"You can announce a moratorium on the Time tax. Not only that, you can initiate a *giveaway* program of Time stocks to the nation's most needy—those who've practically traded themselves into an early grave. And I will publicly and gratefully accept the charge of putting such a program into effect."

"Hold on, Molino. You will state publicly that you have agreed to implement a charitable program conceived and created—by executive order—by *me*?"

"And, in that manner, we both get what we want," said Jack.

"Is that so? What do you calculate is in it for me?"

"Most of the votes that would otherwise go to me. In short, re-election by a landslide."

Florian leaned back, rubbed his chin, and stared out blankly into space.

"You would provide millions of people with temporary relief," Jack pursued.

"Forget millions!" snapped Florian. "A few thousand, okay. But we'll let them think it's millions."

"I'm sure we'll find some reasonable compromise," said Jack. "Whatever, it'll be enough to do the trick. And then, as to what happens *after* the election is entirely up to you. But I would suggest some reasonable, affordable continuation of the program—headed by me, to maintain its credibility."

"It's true," Florian said pensively, "during all my years of tenure I probably have not focused enough on charitable endeavors. Throwing out crumbs to a few hundred bums…not a bad idea, Molino."

"I doubt, however," said Jack with a deep sigh, "that anything of the sort is going to meet with Chairman Kestro's approval. Besides, he harbors a completely irrational—I would say pathological—detestation of me."

"Kestro. Hm. He could have retired ages ago," said Florian.

"I guess some people just like to cling to power," murmured Jack, shaking his head.

"Yes, that's so," mulled Florian, missing Jack's irony. "But why should I give a damn about his approval?"

"I believe," said Jack, "that by law the Federal Time Bank operates independently of government oversight."

"We'll see about that," said the President. "Meanwhile, Molino, go ahead and write up our proposal for the Florian Time Relief Program. Between you and me, though, we'll call it Crumbs for Bums."

8

It took a week for the nation to get over the shock. The only defender of the oppressed had betrayed the desperate millions by teaming up with the oppressor. But despite disappointment, hope still lingered. The people were reluctant to give up faith in Molino the man—no matter where he stood along the political spectrum. And Jack had wasted no time implementing "Florian's" program.

First Jack suspended the Time tax. Then he issued Time credits to a first group of thousands of unfortunates, people who had sold almost all their lives away to afford just the basic necessities. Their faces and voices, replete with gratitude, began to dominate the media. And the polls began showing an upward shift in the President's approval ratings.

Exhilarated at the initial success of the program, Florian spurred Jack on to speed it up.

"It'll be more than a few thousand, though," Jack warned.

"You keep count on your end," said Florian. "I'll be counting the polls."

Jack accelerated the program as much as he dared, always looking over his shoulder. His aim was to balance the President's lust for rising approval ratings against the growing suspicion of his fellow board members that the unprecedented giveaway was showing signs of recklessness.

But as far as Jack was concerned, there was no recklessness involved at all. With less and less restraint, he was deliberately and determinedly returning to the people the days and months and years of life stolen from them, pocketed by an institution, the Federal Time Bank, that he had slowly come to realize had no moral legitimacy at all. If his colleagues had any suspicion, thought Jack, of the true motives that drove him, they'd have done all they could to keep him from giving away even as much as one hour!

From the beginning, Jack's fellow board members could not contain their resentment, anger, and righteous indignation at the power conferred on him to run his little charity right under their noses but exempt from their control. Chairman Kestro, in memo after memo, for the first time in his long career, dared openly oppose the President, the very man to whom he owed his appointment as head of the board in the first place. Whereas his memoranda were models of legalistic jabber, he could be heard down every corridor spewing invectives and vowing revenge.

Kestro's legal maneuvering began to grow teeth. He managed to dig up a few weighty clauses scattered among the bank's foundational documents that threatened to halt all the good works in progress.

Not that either Kestro or his cronies could see "progress" in a rate of depletion of Time stocks now about equal to their earlier rate of accretion.

Week after week, the negative numbers—positive from Jack's point of view—were flashed in Jack's face. "Don't worry," Jack responded, hoping to allay his colleagues' distrust. "There's a method to my madness."

A method there was. But Kestro and his crew perceived only the madness, and they finally managed to bind up the program in tangles of bureaucratic tape, blocking Jack at almost every turn. The media saw and loved the madness—and the public clamored for more. Jack now faced a growing barrage of criticism for slowing the flow of the giveaway, for backing away from what the people claimed they'd been promised and demanded as their right.

Burgeoning dissatisfaction was taking a toll on Florian's ratings as well. The President was not happy and began to accuse Jack of faint-heartedness, cowardice, and subversion.

Crushed between hammer and anvil, fearful that his game would soon be exposed, Jack sat alone in his office one afternoon composing his letter of resignation to President Florian. Marietta had sadly agreed with him. He had best err on the side of caution. He had pushed the program as far as he could. If left up to him, he would push it much farther. Did either side suspect how far he'd wanted to push it?

Heavy of heart, Jack had at last raised his finger to hit SEND when Manny—now executive assistant to the Florian Time Relief Program—rushed into his office, wide-eyed and panting.

"What is it?" asked Jack.

"Chairman Kestro," gasped Manny. "He's just now upped and died!"

Jack sank back in his office chair and gazed in disbelief at his overjoyed assistant.

"People saw him shuffling around, cursing and fuming, for at least a half hour before…before he dropped."

"What was he saying? Vowing to have me up on charges? Boasting about defeating me and the traitors who set me up?"

"I'm told," said Manny, "he was ranting and raving against President Florian. He was heard saying repeatedly, 'After all the favors I did him, that bastard.'"

"Won't matter. They'll blame me anyway," said Jack.

They hurried down to join a stream of bewildered employees who were all asking each other what had happened. On arrival at a crowded scene just outside Kestro's office, he managed to catch a glimpse of blue-suited medical responders, along with building security, carrying a stretcher toward the elevator bay.

However much Jack detested what Kestro had stood for, however much he had loathed his monumental abuse of power, he suddenly found that he no longer felt ill will toward the man. All his pent-up rancor had suddenly drained away.

When all the excitement had died down and a dazed work-force had returned to their stations, Mrs. Bremante, the deceased's secretary—and elderly lady who never showed emotion and even now shed not one tear—called a meeting of all the available directors.

Jack's arrival cast a pall over the boardroom. The air became thick with hostility. The few steps it took him to reach his chair felt like wading through a vat of molasses.

"All I know," said the secretary, "is that poor Mr. Kestro was presented today, suddenly, with an enormous bill from a creditor he did not recognize. He was given only one hour to pay up! The document is now in the hands of the building police."

An all-too-familiar scenario! thought Jack. A line from Shakespeare sprang to mind: "Hoist with his own petard."

The room filled with mutterings. "One hour? That's absurd!"

"But it's perfectly legal," said Ms. Bremante. "If you take a gamble and you buy on margin, and your stock goes down, not up, your broker—who's put up the cash to cover the full amount of your purchase—has every right to issue a margin call—and demand immediate repayment. He doesn't even have to alert you. He can instantly grab as much of your collateral as needed to cover what he's loaned you."

"That's absolutely heartless!"

"They should be charged with murder!"

"It's just business," said the secretary, shrugging her narrow shoulders. "Evidently, in poor Mr. Kestro's case, he was so far out on a limb that he did not have enough to cover his creditors' losses. Not even with his last drop of Time."

At least for the moment, Jack had ceased being the center of attention, but he could sense that the moment wouldn't last very long.

"But his assets," a board member noted, "—and he was heavily into Time stocks, like the rest of us—did *not* go down in value."

"So on what grounds could anyone have legitimately issued such a call?" shouted another, visibly trembling. "Does anyone see the market collapsing? Of course you don't. In fact, it's been stable, better than stable, for years."

"Are you blind?" said another. "The market has been wincing at the extravagance of our ongoing 'Time Relief' program. We're hiding the real stock-depletion figures, but if our friends out in the real world were ever to find out—"

"And if someone has already found out?"

"Don't be ridiculous! Kestro would not be the only one to pay."

"So why such a narrowly *targeted* margin call?"

"The conclusion I draw," said still another board member, "is that someone in a position of power *forced* this margin call—precisely in order to destroy Chairman Kestro!"

"And who, may I ask," said one of the directors who had up till now stayed broodingly silent, "who among us is always in the habit of reminding us of the *dangers* of buying up Time stocks at the margin rates we're entitled to—contractually entitled to, I might add?"

"And maybe it's about time you listened," said Jack.

All eyes—menacing, accusing—turned toward him. He felt under pressure to defend himself, but he was not going to be intimidated.

"And isn't this tragedy most conveniently timed?" said someone else. "It looks like the Florian Charity Show can now proceed unhindered—till we all drop off a cliff!"

"Despite what some of you may be thinking," said Jack, "I have nothing personally to gain from all this. The Time Relief Program is benefitting the people, and the people—for the first time—have begun to see *us* in a favorable light."

"Mr. Molino," said one of the Board members, "our deceased chairman evidently had a deal—an arrangement, I should say—with the President to let you proceed with this political gimmick of a relief program, at least until even *he* couldn't stand the hypocrisy of it all. But we—all of us here in this room—are *not* obliged to allow this phony giveaway program to continue."

"Hear, hear!" a chorus of voices croaked.

"We regret the President's illegal interference in the internal affairs of this bank," another board member piped up, "and the one thing we can do to eliminate it, Molino, is to remove you from this board on the grounds of 'conduct unbefitting' your position."

Another round of "Hear, hears" broke out.

"Are you sure your motive for removing me," Jack retorted, "isn't simply to continue unhindered in your game of sucking the marrow out of people's bones, raising their Time taxes, fattening your portfolios?"

"This is getting us nowhere," snapped the previous speaker. "I move we vote on expelling Molino now!"

There was a knock at the door.

"Come in!" said Ms. Bremante.

A balding clerk entered the room and gazed uneasily at the array of solemn faces. "It is ur-urgently requested," he stumbled, "that you activate the boardroom holostage, to the District of Columbia channel. That's all I'm permitted to say." He clumsily bowed out of the room.

"Whoever pushed him in here had one helluva nerve," someone growled.

"Are we tuning in or not?" said another.

And a third someone, clapping twice, activated the holostage, a theatrically large, dark recess set in one of the long sides of the room.

The D.C. channel popped to life. The scene showed the President, in real time, addressing a select group of reporters. He was in the midst of a eulogy, praising the wisdom, the prudence, the dedication of a man who had served his country well for decades:

"Not only a true patriot," the chalk-faced President perorated, "but a dear personal friend, Chairman Kestro shall be sorely missed. But he has left the business of the Time Bank in very capable hands. As you all know, as President it is my duty to appoint a new chair, whenever that becomes necessary, and I have chosen for that grave responsibility a man you all know and admire, a man whose sole concern is the welfare of the people. Just minutes ago, I sent word of his appointment to the office of Jack Molino, director of the Time Bank's Risk Assessment Bureau. Confident of his acceptance, I can announce my decision without any waste of *time*—ha ha—and thereby balance the bad news with some good. Any questions?"

Someone clapped twice and the stage went dark. Jack sat back in shock and witnessed the gloom that descended upon the faces of everyone in the room. No congratulations. No wish-you-wells.

The only acknowledgment? A stretch of funereal silence.

9

The news of Jack's elevation to chairman did not sit well with Marietta. To calm their shattered nerves, she served them both a generous shot of scotch. They sat on the sofa next to each other, and after clicking tumblers, she reached out and laid her hand gently on his. "You had best resign, Jack," she advised. "You're nothing but a pawn in a deadly game. You don't think your colleagues are going to sit by and let Florian, using you, take over control of the Bank, do you?"

"Pawns sometimes turn out to win games," said Jack, savoring a meditative sip of his drink.

"What is that supposed to mean?"

"I'll quit when I finish what I started."

"Finish what?"

Jack twirled his drink, around and around, and gazed up at the ceiling. "What would happen if there were *no* Time Bank at all, Marietta?"

"Well…that's an odd question."

"What would happen?"

"I guess," she said, "people would be free to buy and sell their time without a percentage being siphoned off to fatten a bureaucracy so powerful that…"

"That it acts like a second government?" said Jack.

"That's one way of putting it."

"And what else would happen?"

"You'd be out of a job."

"Hell, I'd be able to write full-time!"

10

Jack had little time left to make sure that there'd be little Time left.

He knew, upon entering his office the day after Kestro's murder, that the game had to be played out within a matter of hours. He called up a virtual keyboard and tapped away assiduously for nearly ten minutes. "Manny, what would you do if you suddenly found out you were the proud owner of ten solid years of Time stocks?"

"Are you kidding?" said Manny, his eyes narrowing with suspicion. "I'd either use them to live that much longer, or else, being young, cash some in, buy me a two-cabin hydrojet and cruise the world's oceans for a year."

"Well, you're in luck—and without even winning the lottery."

"How's that?" said Manny.

"I've just paid out a bonus to every employee of the Time Bank below the rank of department head. I've transferred a ten-year block to each and every one of you."

"That's crazy!" Manny croaked. "Even if you *are* chairman of the board—"

"By sometime this afternoon, my friend, I'll have returned to the remaining twenty million Americans all the Time taxes they've ever paid, with interest. You didn't think I'd leave *you* guys out in the cold, did you?"

"Jack…" Manny moved his lips for a while but nothing came out. Finally, "Jack, you can't do this without breaking the bank. There won't be any Time stock left!"

"That's precisely the idea. Haven't you noticed how President Florian just loves this giveaway program? As his chances for re-election look better and better, he doesn't give a crap how I do what I do, so long as I do more of the same. Why else do you think he killed Kestro?"

"But it's all bound to backfire," said Manny.

"All good things—as well as bad—come to an end," said Jack.

"As soon as he sniffs what you're up to—"

"I'll be next? You're right," said Jack. "Tell me, how long do you think it'll take before the other board members catch on?"

"Couple of hours maybe. They don't usually follow the in-house figures real-time. But now, with you at the helm…"

"That's why I need to work fast," said Jack. "Do me a favor, Manny. Wander around. Keep your eyes and ears open. I'm particularly concerned with what the big boys might be doing—or planning, or whatever."

Jack worked straight through the lunch hour.

When Manny came back, his facial muscles were twitching.

"You don't look well," said Jack. "Something you ate?"

"Word is out," said Manny. "The halls are buzzing. No one seems to know exactly what's up, but everyone's expecting Armageddon."

"I'm glad for the confusion. It gives me just a little more time to—"

"Jack, sure there's confusion, but that doesn't mean the members of the board don't know *exactly* what's up. They met for lunch."

"Without inviting me? A sign of disrespect, I'd say."

"I ran into a friend of mine, one of the security guards. He had something very peculiar to tell me. He said that Ms. Bremante had just requisitioned some lethal-grade sting-guns from Supplies."

"They wouldn't freaking dare," said Jack.

"You have to get the hell out of here. Like now," Manny urged.

"I need just a little more—"

Suddenly Jack's interband signaled he had an emergency call. He wouldn't have answered, except that it might be Marietta using an unfamiliar number. He tapped the band and up ballooned the pallid face of the President.

"Whatever you think you're doing, Molino, stop this instant. Your colleagues tell me you're pissing out Time stocks as if there's no tomorrow."

"They're right, Mr. President. There *is* no tomorrow," said Jack.

"Then this is all…deliberate?" said Florian, his pallor now even more ghostly.

"No one thought it could happen, Mr. President, but this is *The End of Time*."

"Molino, you are criminally insane. Your colleagues are right. To prevent you from causing irreversible damage, I am forced to end *your* time…Molino, I regret having to forward you this bill—from creditors whose identity I am not allowed to reveal—but if you can't put together sufficient assets to pay within exactly one hour—"

Jack ended the call. He was not interested in opening the file containing any so-called bill. "Manny," he said, "an hour may give us just enough time to beat him. Don't look so glum. Punch up a contact file of every broker on the Exchange."

It took Manny only a few minutes to cobble together the list and wisk it over to Jack, who typed a Time stamped message that had been brewing in his mind for days:

From: Office of J. Molino, Board Chairman /Federal Time Bank.

To: All Brokers, Traders, and Managerial Personnel on the Exchange.

Subject: Emergency Announcement: Collapse of Federal Time Bank

The board of directors, headed by Chairman Molino, regrets to announce that due to unforeseen and catastrophic circumstances—these will be explained in a later communication—the Time Bank no longer can meet its capitalization requirements.

The bank has returned all accumulated tax receipts, with interest, amounting to 85 percent of its Time stock holdings, to the general public. At this moment the remainder, too, is devolving to the needy from whom it was extracted. Totally insolvent, we are going out of business. I rely on you to act responsibly to prevent any possible panic.

After Jack read it to Manny—who listened in utter amazement—
he hit SEND. "Now, Manny, let's have a leisurely look at what ensues
on Wall Street."

"Jack." Manny's voice failed, and bubbles of saliva formed at
the corners of his mouth. "We have no time for leisurely looks
at anything. Florian is out to kill you. You've got to gather up all
remaining Time stocks *now* and neutralize that phony bill, which is
sure to be so damn big—"

"Stop panicking, Manny. If things work out as I hope—"

"Forget about hope, will you? If Florian doesn't get you, those
boardroom bastards will."

"Take a look at the board, Manny. The stock market board. That's
where all the action is."

"Jack, how can you cold-bloodedly sit there and do *nothing*?"

"I did do something, Manny. Look! I set in motion the panic that
I asked them all to prevent."

"Great, just great!" said Manny. "And what the hell good does
that do *you*?"

"It's all a matter of timing, my friend. It all depends on who
manages to do who first. Are you noticing the nose-dive in the price
of Time Bank stock?"

"And so?"

"Creditors all over the planet are desperately making margin calls
without much concern about sending out warnings to debtors."

"Jack, will you come to your senses? The President has sworn to
kill you—in less than an hour!"

Jack's interband vibrated in emergency mode. This time it was
Ms. Bremante.

"Yes, Ms. Bremante?"

"Mr. Molino," she shrieked, "something terrible is happening."

"And what is that?" said Jack.

"I've just received calls from the secretaries of two members of our
board of directors: Mr. Wilde and Mr. Spenda. The two gentlemen
appear to have been stricken by some sudden, incapacitating illness.
They have collapsed and—and here I'm getting a call on my other
line, from the secretary of Director Delgado."

"I'll get right back to you, Ms. Bremante. I'm getting another urgent call myself."

"What the hell's going on?" shouted Manny.

"Shh," said Jack, placing his finger over his lips. He tapped his wrist to receive the new call. It was the President again. Florian's ghostly face and disheveled mop of white hair ballooned out above Jack's wrist.

"Stop it!" demanded Florian. "Tell them to give me…a little more time. My assets are spread out over…" The President's eyes suddenly opened wide. One of them turned completely white. All Jack saw after that, before losing contact, was a burly arm looping around Florian's slumping shoulders.

Manny stood speechless, staring at the empty air above Jack's wrist.

"I wonder how the rest of the Troika is doing," Jack said.

"What are you going to do now?" asked Manny.

Jack pondered for a moment. "I'm not going into politics. That you can count on."

)O)O)( )O)O)( )O)O)( )(

About the Author

Daniel Pearlman (1936-2013) was a speculative/fantastic fiction writer whose work is infused with dry humor and satire. He received his Ph.D. in Comparative Literature at Columbia University, then traveled across Italy with Ezra Pound, becoming a scholar of Pound's work. His book *The Barb of Time: On the Unity of Ezra Pound's Cantos* was published in 1969 by Oxford University Press and made him a prominent figure on the academic scene. As a professor at the University of Rhode Island for 25 years, he trained and inspired countless writers. His published collections include *The Final Dream & Other Fictions* (1995), *The Best-Known Man in the World & Other Misfits* (2001), and *A Giant in the House & Other Excesses* (2011); his novels—*Black Flames* (1997) and *Memini* (2003)—are about the Spanish Civil War and a future ruled by amnesiacs, respectively. "Overdrawn at the Time Bank" also taps into Pearlman's love for political satire and fantastical/alternative worlds, and is an unpolished first draft that he'd completed just two months before he passed away. We are proud to feature it here through special arrangement with his widow and *Read Short Fiction*, and are grateful to his mentorees, who provided insight to ensure that any editing done for publication stayed true to Dan's voice.

ABOUT KRISTI PETERSEN SCHOONOVER
Guest Editor

Kristi Petersen Schoonover's short fiction has been featured in *The Adirondack Review, Barbaric Yawp, The Illuminata, Carpe Articulum Literary Review, Afternoon, The Haunted Traveler, I Like Monkeys, New Witch Magazine, MudRock: Stories & Tales, Toasted Cheese*, and many, many others; by far, however, her favorite short pieces are those she wrote specifically for anthologies as diverse as *Unnatural Tales of the Jackalope, Canopic Jars: Tales of Mummies and Mummification, From the Corner of Your Eye: Cryptids*, and *Bugs*.

Skeletons in the Swimmin' Hole: Tales from Haunted Disney World (Admit One Literary Theme Park Press, 2010), her collection of ghost stories set in Disney Parks, has been called "spooky alchemy at its finest" by Famous Monsters of Filmland's Peter Schwotzer; her Pushcart-nominated novel *Bad Apple* (Vagabondage Press Books, 2012) was noted "deeply disturbing in the best way possible" by SciFi Saturday Night.

She served as co-editor for *Read Short Fiction* and was the recipient of Norman Mailer Writers Colony Winter 2010, 2011, and 2012 Residencies. She holds a BA in Creative Writing and Literature from Burlington College and an MFA in Creative Writing from Goddard College; prior to all of that, she was a student at the University of Rhode Island, where up until 2014 she was a member of the Pearlman Writers Group.

She serves as co-host for *Dark Discussions*, a horror film podcast.

She lives in the Connecticut woods with her housemate, Charles, her husband, Nathan, and three cats, and she still frequently goes to bed with the lights on. Visit her at www.kristipetersenschoonover.com.

See how it all began.

Download your FREE copy of Vol. 1 today,
wherever ebooks are sold!

AUTHORS WANTED FOR

INK STAINS
ANTHOLOGIES

We are looking for unique dark fiction submissions for upcoming editions of *Ink Stains Anthology* from Dark Alley Press.

Submissions are now open for pieces 3,000-20,0000 words for all works that fit under the Dark Alley Press banner, including those in the following categories:

- Dark fiction (including lit fic)
- Gothic fiction
- Supernatural/paranormal fiction
- Horror
- Steampunk
- Black Comedy
- Fantasy

Authors of acquired pieces for *Ink Stains Anthology* will receive a flat fee payment upon publication. For more information, check out our website.

www.inkstainsanthology.com